FAMILY PLOT

ANOTHER JOHN PICKETT MYSTERY

FAMILY PLOT

SHERI COBB SOUTH

FIVE STAR
A part of Gale, Cengage Learning

GALE
CENGAGE Learning·

Farmington Hills, Mich • San Francisco • New York • Waterville, Maine
Meriden, Conn • Mason, Ohio • Chicago

LIBRARY OF CONGRESS CATALOGING-IN-PUBLICATION DATA

South, Sheri Cobb.
  Family plot : another John Pickett mystery / Sheri Cobb South. — First edition.
    pages ; cm
    ISBN 978-1-4328-2963-6 (hardcover) — ISBN 1-4328-2963-7 (hardcover)
    ISBN 978-1-4328-2971-1 (ebook) — ISBN 1-4328-2971-8 (ebook)
    1. Police—England—London—Fiction. 2. Aristocracy (Social class)—Fiction. 3. Widows—Fiction. I. Title.
PS3569.O755F36 2014
813'.54—dc23   2014025064

First Edition. First Printing: November 2014
Find us on Facebook– https://www.facebook.com/FiveStarCengage
Visit our website– http://www.gale.cengage.com/fivestar/
Contact Five Star™ Publishing at FiveStar@cengage.com

Printed in the United States of America
1 2 3 4 5 6 7 18 17 16 15 14

To the talented ladies of the Weekly Writers' Workshop:
Cindy, Cheryl, Phyllis, Shelley, and Mary Jo,
and to Beth Taylor, proofreader extraordinaire.
Thank you for welcoming this Alabama transplant
and making her feel right at home.

AUTHOR'S NOTE

Among the questions I am asked about this series, most (aside from the obvious ones about if, when, and how John Pickett and Lady Fieldhurst will ever get together) concern the character of Pickett's magistrate, Mr. Colquhoun. How, readers want to know, is his name pronounced, and why did I choose to give a character a name so difficult to read? According to *Debrett's Correct Form,* the name is pronounced "Ca-HOON." I chose it because Patrick Colquhoun was a real person who served as a magistrate in London from 1792 to 1818. I confess to fudging my history a bit; my sources place him at the Queen Square Office in Westminster, but I can find no evidence that he ever served in that capacity at the Bow Street Office. Certain aspects of his life, however, dovetail so nicely with that of John Pickett that I hope the reader will forgive me for taking a bit of artistic license.

PROLOGUE:
IN WHICH IS PRESENTED AN INTERESTING PROPOSAL

The opening night performance was over. The final lines had been uttered, the final curtain rung down, the final bows taken. Celebrated Shakespearean actress Elizabeth Church, clad in the flowing white gown she'd worn for Ophelia's mad scene, could still hear the crowd's applause as she navigated the narrow backstage corridor, dodging stagehands and scenery with the ease of long practice. With any luck, the audience's appreciation would be enthusiastic enough to maintain a lengthy run, staving off the day when she must succumb to the least objectionable of her admirers in order to keep a roof over her head and food in her belly. An actress's career lasted only as long as her beauty, and as her thirty-third year drew nearer, she could sometimes feel Father Time's cold hand upon her shoulder.

She pushed open the door of her dressing room and saw Tilly, the theatre's maid of all work, waiting inside to help her undress. Closing the door behind her, she turned her back and allowed the little maid to undo the laces and slip the gown over her head.

"Oh, ma'am," Tilly breathed as she hung Ophelia's costume in the clothespress, lovingly caressing the folds of cheap satin. "You were beautiful tonight, just beautiful. No wonder all the gentlemen love you." Her gaze, more awe-struck than envious, encompassed the half-dozen bouquets of roses scattered about the small room.

"Hardly 'all,' Tilly," said Mrs. Church. ("Mrs." being a

courtesy title awarded to all actresses of her standing, as there was not, nor had there ever been, a Mr. Church.) She shrugged her arms into the sleeves of her dressing gown and tied it about her trim waist.

"Enough that you could take your pick, anyways," Tilly insisted, pouring water from a pitcher into a basin on the dressing table. "Isn't there one that you could favor? That earl, maybe? He's a handsome one."

"Indeed he is, and I daresay he would worship me madly for at least a month." Mrs. Church seated herself at the dressing table and bestowed a pitying smile upon the stage-struck maid. How to explain the concerns of three-and-thirty to a buxom lass not yet out of her teens? She turned to the mirror and picked up a cloth, preparing to wash off the heavy theatrical makeup necessary for turning a grown woman into Shakespeare's virginal heroine. She plunged the cloth into the basin and grimaced. "Cold. Tilly, would you—?"

"Aye, ma'am, I'll be back in a trice with hot water." Suiting the word to the deed, Tilly snatched up the pitcher she'd just emptied and hurried from the room.

Mrs. Church had to smile at the little maid's eagerness. Although Tilly had never said as much, she suspected the maid harbored a secret ambition to someday tread the boards herself. She only hoped that, should the opportunity ever present itself, Tilly would not be too disappointed to discover that the reality fell far short of her rosy imaginings.

To her surprise, the doorknob rattled and in the mirror's reflection she saw the door swing open. How in the world, she wondered, had Tilly obtained hot water so quickly? "Back so soon?" she asked. "That was—"

She broke off and stood up abruptly, knocking the chair over in her haste. The door was now fully open, and the figure framed in the doorway was not Tilly, but a tall, willowy gentleman whose form-fitting pantaloons, watered silk waistcoat, and cutaway coat were clearly the work of one of London's premier tailors.

"What are you doing here?" she demanded, instinctively clutching her dressing gown closed at the neck.

He advanced a few paces into the room and closed the door behind him. "Never fear, I have no improper designs upon your person—exquisite though it is," he added, flicking a connoisseur's gaze over her *déshabillé*. "In fact, I wish to discuss a rôle which I thought you might find of interest."

Whatever she had expected, it was not that. "A rôle?"

"Picture this, if you will." He righted the chair she had knocked over, then settled one hip on the corner of the dressing table and made a frame of his hands in an approximation of a scene on the stage. "A picturesque old house on the Scottish coast, where lives a man, old and ill, his last wish only to see the daughter he cast off some fifteen years ago—a daughter, moreover, who bore a striking resemblance to your own fair self."

"I see." Her lips tightened. "You wish me to deceive this man by posing as his long-lost daughter."

" 'Deceive' is such a harsh word," he protested. Seeing her eyebrows rise, he added, "Surely it would be an act of compassion to give this poor old man some comfort in his final days."

"And how much compassion did he show his daughter?"

"Very little, it is true—a circumstance he has come to regret deeply. But a deathbed reconciliation between father and daughter—" He gave a soulful sigh. "—It has a certain Lear-like quality, does it not?"

"Surely he must see through such a subterfuge," she observed. "No loving father would fail to know his own child, or to recognize an imposter."

"Ah, but he has not seen her in fifteen long years," he

reminded her. "Besides which, the mind has a way of seeing what it wants to see."

Her mouth twisted in a wry smile. "Or failing to see what it does not wish to acknowledge."

"You would not set out for Scotland at once. You would be well prepared for your rôle in the interim."

"And my recompense?"

"Five thousand pounds sterling."

Five thousand pounds. The difference between a comfortable, even luxurious, retirement and a never-ending procession of lovers, wealthy and generous at first, but less so as her beauty began to fade—a dreary sequence that would no doubt end in poverty, prostitution, and disease. It was the specter that haunted all women of her profession, whether they admitted it or not. She drew her chair closer to him and sat down.

"Tell me more."

CHAPTER 1
IN WHICH AN ACQUAINTANCE IS RENEWED

Julia, Lady Fieldhurst, slightly scandalous widow of the recently deceased Viscount Fieldhurst, sat in the family box high above the stage of the Theatre Royal in Drury Lane, watching the thespians' performance of *Hamlet* with mixed emotions. At first she had been gratified (to say nothing of surprised) when the current viscount and the dowager viscountess, mother of her late husband, had arranged this excursion. The Fieldhursts were sticklers for propriety, all the more so for having weathered a recent scandal, and it had, after all, been a scant six months since her husband's untimely demise.

"A ball or anything of that sort would naturally be out of the question," her husband's cousin, the new Lord Fieldhurst, had added hastily when proposing the outing. "But a dramatic work, suitably sober and uplifting in nature, must surely be unobjectionable."

"Needless to say," interposed the dowager viscountess, with the fixed intention of saying it anyway, "we will not stay for the farce that follows Shakespeare's tragedy, and we will instruct the footman not to admit visitors to our box. Any display of frivolity would be most inappropriate, given the circumstances."

Lady Fieldhurst had wondered at the time why, if they were determined to rob the experience of any pleasure, the Fieldhursts bothered to go out at all. Now, however, as Hamlet declaimed onstage against his mother's hasty remarriage, she wondered if the evening's entertainment were intended as less of a social event than a word of warning. Although she had been cleared of any wrongdoing in her husband's death, his family was still quick to take offense at any perceived slight to the late Lord Fieldhurst's memory. Still, she wondered how even they might think that, having been unexpectedly released from one unhappy marriage, she would be eager to rush headlong into another.

In fact, she was more than a little surprised at their willingness to make such a public appearance as the box in Drury Lane while still in mourning. Then again, she had had occasion to learn over the years that the dowager's notions of propriety, so rigid regarding the behavior of others, were surprisingly elastic where her own wishes were concerned.

She glanced to her left, where the new Lord Fieldhurst sat with his chin sunk into his cravat, snoring gently. Beyond him, the Dowager Lady Fieldhurst scowled down at the stage, no doubt looking for something to criticize. Not for the first time, the younger Lady Fieldhurst wondered at her own inertia. Why should she linger in London, especially in October? The only members of the *beau monde* still in residence were members of Parliament and their families, obliged to remain in the Metropolis for the autumn session. It was not as if she had nowhere else to go; whatever else might be said of her husband, he had at least spared her the indignity of being dependent upon his family's charity. Her widow's jointure left her comfortably settled, and might even stretch to a modest holiday in Bath or Tunbridge Wells. Yet with the exception of one ill-fated house party in Yorkshire, she had remained in London to face down the scandal surrounding her husband's death. She knew she would always be welcome in her parents' home in Somersetshire, but in some aspects even the Fieldhursts' domineering ways were preferable to the sweet tyranny of a doting father who insisted on treating his twenty-six-year-old daughter as if she were still in the schoolroom.

Her gaze drifted down to the pit, where those of the lower orders paid two shillings for the privilege of sitting shoulder to shoulder on backless benches throughout the performance. Occasionally her attention was caught by the pale oval of a face as one of the theatre patrons below, a female wearing a hideous purple bonnet, glanced up at her with an expression of mingled envy and resentment. Lady Fieldhurst sighed. She supposed it must seem unfair to the masses below to have the prosperity of the privileged classes on display every time they raised their eyes.

Still, she wondered if they knew how fortunate they were in having the freedom to live their own lives without regard for the expectations of others. The female in the purple bonnet, for instance, she thought as she pleated the folds of her black satin gown with black-gloved fingers. How lovely it must be to go out in public wearing whatever one wished, without fear of others whispering behind their fans how shocking it was that Lady Fieldhurst had put off her blacks so soon, and after her husband had died in *such* a way!

As Hamlet ordered Ophelia to a nunnery on the stage, Lady Fieldhurst played a little game with herself, selecting patrons from the pit at random and weaving life histories for them. The fat man enjoying the performance so boisterously had clearly had too much to drink, and was now postponing the moment when the curtain would fall and he would have to return home to his wife. The dour man in black sitting behind him was obviously collecting material for a scathing sermon on Sunday. The younger man, the one seated between the fat man and the ugly purple bonnet—

He turned his head slightly, and she stiffened. Was it?—could it be?—yes, she was almost certain. She placed her black-gloved hand on the balustrade and leaned forward for a better look. He glanced up toward her box, a young man with curling brown hair tied back in an old-fashioned queue and a slightly crooked nose, and she was sure. Turning slightly on her chair, she gestured to the footman positioned just outside the box.

He appeared at her elbow in an instant. "Yes, my lady?"

She glanced toward her husband's relations, the sleeping viscount and the distracted dowager. Lady Fieldhurst lifted her chin, her mind made up. "I wish you to deliver a message."

"She's up there, you know." Lucy, seated in the pit, jerked her sharp chin toward the rows of boxes overhead, where the wealthy and privileged assembled to observe the actors and each other.

John Pickett looked up, the Prince of Denmark and his troubles forgotten. "Who? Where?"

"You know who I'm talking about," Lucy said, adding a disdainful sniff for effect. The dyed ostrich plumes adorning her purple bonnet seemed to wag their feathery heads in disapproval. "That viscountess of yours."

"She's not mine." Pickett couldn't quite keep the wistful note out of his voice, and mentally cursed himself for a fool. True, he had saved her from the gallows when it appeared she would be convicted of murdering her husband. They had even kissed once, but that had been purely a matter of expedience: he was investigating a possible murder, and they'd had to have *some* reason for skulking about in the middle of the night, long after everyone else in the house had gone to bed. He'd never flattered himself by supposing it had left her with a burning desire to repeat the experience. But he hadn't seen her at all since July, and that had been more than three months ago—three months, one week, and four—*stop it,* he told himself firmly, fixing his attention on the stage. He had no doubt she had already forgotten the incident; he would be wise to do the same. He wouldn't look up at the row of boxes overhead—he wouldn't crane his neck for a glimpse of her—he wouldn't—

He looked up when someone tapped him on the shoulder. A liveried footman stood there, his head and shoulders blocking Pickett's view of the boxes above.

"Begging your pardon," the man said, "but the Viscountess Fieldhurst requests that you join her in her box." He gestured toward the boxes over his shoulder. "If you will follow me?"

"What, me?" Pickett half-rose from his seat, then froze as the implications became clear. "Here? Now?"

"Down in front!" shouted a voice from a few rows back.

"Aye, siddown!" a few more joined in.

Pickett, caught on the horns of a dilemma, paid them no heed, but addressed himself to the waiting footman. "I—I can't—I'm not properly dressed—"

"Very good, sir. Shall I convey your regrets to the lady?"

"Yes, please." Then, as the footman began to move away, "No! Wait!"

"Don't mind me," Lucy muttered, pointedly turning her back on Pickett. "After all, I'm nobody!"

Pickett, stumbling over the legs of the fat man seated at the end of the row, cast an apologetic glance in her direction. "I'm sorry, Lucy. I'll be back directly."

"Aye, I'll just bet you will," she grumbled.

Pickett followed the footman up the aisle to the lobby and thence up three flights of stairs to the uppermost tier of boxes. It seemed to Pickett that the higher they climbed, the thicker grew the carpet beneath his feet and the more elaborate the gilt and plaster ornamentation adorning the walls and ceiling. With each step he became more painfully aware of the shabbiness of his black tailcoat and stockinette breeches—the best he owned, to be sure, but glaringly out of place in these rarified heights. At the top of the stairs, the footman led Pickett down a curving corridor lined at intervals with paneled doors. He paused at last before one of these, then flung it open.

"Mr. Pickett, my lady," he announced, and stepped back to allow Pickett entrance.

There she sat, the candlelight gleaming off her pale hair in radiant contrast to the stark black satin of her gown. She looked up as he entered the box, then smiled and held out her hand. In that moment, Pickett forgot all about his plebeian attire; his attention was all for the beautiful woman before him.

"My lady," he said, bowing awkwardly as he took her proffered hand with the air of one receiving a precious gift.

"It was good of you to come in answer to my summons," said her ladyship, making no great effort to retrieve her hand. "I hope I was not interrupting."

"No, no, not at all," he assured her hastily, dismissing poor Lucy out of hand. "It was kind of you to send for me."

"It is always a pleasure to see you, Mr. Pickett. I trust you are well?"

"Quite—quite well, thank you. And yourself?" Privately he thought there was something of sadness about her eyes. He hoped her husband's relations were not making her life a misery, as he knew they had done in the past.

"Yes, I am very well, thank you."

Having exhausted their supply of platitudes, they both lapsed into silence. Pickett released her hand with some reluctance, unable to think of any excuse for retaining it.

He gestured toward the stage below. "What—what do you think of Mrs. Church as Ophelia?" he asked, filling a silence rapidly approaching the point of awkwardness.

"Her performance seems very affecting, although of course it must suffer in comparison to that of the great Mrs. Siddons. Did you ever see her perform?"

He shook his head. "I never had the pleasure."

"It was one of her last appearances before leaving Drury Lane. She was rather too old for the rôle—already well into her forties, I believe. One might think she would have appeared ridiculous, and yet somehow she did not."

"Do you come often to the theatre, then?" Pickett asked, trying not to sound too eager. As his residence consisted of two hired rooms over a chandler's shop further down Drury Lane, the theatre was a convenient and inexpensive form of amusement; now, with the possibility of seeing her ladyship here on a regular basis, its charms increased exponentially.

"I did, either here or at Covent Garden, but this is my first visit since—" Her swift downward glance took in her black-gloved hands and her black skirts. "Since last spring. And you, Mr. Pickett? Do you come here often?"

He nodded. "I live not far from here."

"Do you indeed?" She could not have sounded more interested if he had just confided that he owned the theatre in which she sat. "Where, pray tell?"

He was immediately sorry to have introduced a subject on which he would hardly appear to advantage. "Just two rooms above a chandler's shop further down the lane, not the sort of place you would care to visit." He shrugged. "But the theatre makes a welcome change from Bow Street. One sees so much of the worst of human nature there."

"And yet you provide a valuable service, as I have cause to know." She gestured toward the empty chair on her right. "But I must not keep you standing all evening! Will you not sit down and watch the last act with me?"

Oh, how he wanted to accept! But besides Lucy glaring up at him from the pit, there were the Dowager Lady Fieldhurst and the current viscount, both fully awake and alive to his unwelcome presence among them, and both making their feelings known with disdainful expressions that spoke volumes without saying a word.

"'Thank you, my lady, but I—I really must go," he stammered, backing his way toward the door. "I left a friend in the pit— she'll be wondering what's happened to me—"

"The young woman in the ugly—in the purple bonnet," said Lady Fieldhurst, her eyes widening in dawning comprehension. "I beg your pardon. I didn't realize you had a—a female companion."

"No, Lucy is just a friend—still, I'd better—pleasure seeing you again—if you'll excuse—"

Still stammering incoherently, he ducked out of the luxurious box and retraced his steps back down to the pit where he belonged.

"I vow, I was never so embarrassed in all my life." Confronting her errant daughter-in-law over a rosewood tea table, the Dowager Lady Fieldhurst set her teacup onto its saucer with a firm *clink* as if to emphasize her point.

The younger Lady Fieldhurst had known she would not escape last night's indiscretion unscathed, and had not been at all surprised when her mother-in-law was announced at the unconscionably early hour of one o'clock in the afternoon. Now, thus called upon the carpet, she gripped the delicately curved handle of her Sèvres teacup until her knuckles turned white.

"And after we'd had the footman decline admittance to the Duke of Westover not twenty minutes earlier!" the dowager continued, shaking her head in apparent bewilderment. "What excuse we might offer His Grace for slighting him in such a way, I can't imagine."

Julia regarded the carpet with downcast eyes, presenting (at least outwardly) the picture of filial obedience. "If the Duke's good opinion is so easily lost, I wonder at your desire to further his acquaintance."

"The family has been the subject of enough scandal over the past six months that we can scarcely afford to offend anyone, let alone a person of His Grace's stature within Society. Really, Julia, what can you have been thinking? We had agreed not to entertain visitors in our box."

Although she remembered the dowager instructing the footman to deny them to any visitors, Julia could not recall having been consulted on this issue at all. Nor would it have presented a problem, even if she had; she'd had no intention of entertaining anyone in her box, much less inviting anyone to call there, until she had recognized John Pickett in the pit below.

"I owe Mr. Pickett a great debt," she said, keeping her voice steady with an effort. "Surely there can be no objection to my acknowledging him when I see him in public."

Except, of course, that she had done a great deal more than that. He had not noticed her presence at the theatre, and wouldn't have, had she not summoned him from his seat in the pit. Much as it galled her to admit it, she very much feared that Mother Fieldhurst had the right of it. The poor man had clearly been embarrassed, and once the initial greetings had been exchanged, neither one of them could think of much to say to the other. The camaraderie they had enjoyed during those weeks in Yorkshire was now at an end; without a dead body to throw them together, it seemed a Bow Street Runner and a widowed viscountess could find very little common ground. She had already expressed her appreciation to him for his part in exonerating her of any wrongdoing in her husband's death; it was past time to let the acquaintance drop. Surely nothing could be gained by continuing to harp upon the matter.

"George and I fear that Bow Street fellow may presume upon your acquaintance and attempt to exploit the connection." The dowager helped herself to a second seed cake. "We believe it might be wise for you to leave London for a time, at least long enough for the *ton* to forget last night's indiscretion. By the time you return to the theatre at Drury Lane, Mr. Plunkett will have ceased to look for you there."

"His name is 'Pickett,' not 'Plunkett,' Mother Fieldhurst, and it was I who sought him out, not the other way 'round."

"All the more reason for you to leave the Metropolis," the dowager replied, unperturbed. "Now, George's sons, as you may know, have had a difficult time of it since poor Frederick's death. George thought it might be pleasant for them to enjoy a brief holiday in Scotland before the start of the Michaelmas term, with you as their chaperone. I confess, I think it a very good plan."

"George's sons are having a difficult time because it turns out that their father was never legally married to their mother," Julia pointed out with some asperity. "If anyone is to leave London, perhaps it should be George."

The dowager fixed her daughter-in-law with a gimlet eye. "Surely I need not point out to you that the rules are different for men. And George is not just any man, but the seventh Viscount Fieldhurst. A title, as you must know, covers a multitude of sins."

"How very fortunate for him, for he has certainly committed a multitude of them," Julia muttered, sipping her tea. She had never liked Caroline Bertram, but that lady had not deserved such shabby treatment from the man she had believed to be her husband. As for the three boys born of the irregular union, Julia did not know them well, and could only hope they would prove to be more agreeable than the rest of the family.

Yet however much she might resent her husband's mother and heir for taking charge of her future, she was forced to the galling conclusion that they were right: she needed to escape London at least for a little while, in order to give her thoughts some more suitable direction than a lanky young man with curling brown hair tied back in a queue, and a female in a hideous purple bonnet for whom she had inexplicably conceived an acute dislike.

CHAPTER 2

IN WHICH LADY FIELDHURST IS EXILED
TO SCOTLAND FOR HER SINS

Over the course of her six-year marriage, Lady Fieldhurst had had many occasions to regret her childless state. The trip to the Fieldhurst estate at Inverbrook was not one of them. George had sent his own carriage to fetch his three sons from their mother's house in Bath, so by the time Lady Fieldhurst and her charges left London the boys had already been three days on the road and were heartily sick of each other's company.

It did not take long for Julia to enter wholeheartedly into their sentiments. Edward, a strapping lad of eight, was inclined to whine and pout at any suggestion that he might allow one of his brothers a turn at sitting next to the window. Julia could form no opinion of Robert, the bespectacled middle child, for he passed the entire journey with his nose stuck in a book, returning only monosyllabic answers to any question put to him. As for Harold, at eighteen the eldest of George's children, he sported a swollen eye that had undoubtedly been black and blue a few days earlier, but was now faded to green and yellow. This contrasted jarringly with his choice of travelling costume, which suggested an incipient dandyism, but the expression in his undamaged eye was so filled with smoldering resentment that she dared not inquire as to the cause of his injury. As afternoon shadows cast the interior of the carriage into gloom, the most literary of George's sons found his tongue at last.

"Give over the window seat, Ned," Robert said, giving his brother a shove for emphasis. "I haven't enough light to read."

One might have thought, reflected Julia, that four travellers in a carriage might each have a window to himself, but then one would have reckoned without the number of trunks, valises, and bandboxes necessary for transporting the wardrobe Harold deemed necessary for a fortnight's stay in Scotland. Those cases that could not be stored in the boot or tied to the top were of necessity stacked inside the carriage, where they tumbled down onto the passengers every time the driver took a turn too quickly.

"Yes, Edward, surely you can allow your brother a turn by the window," agreed Lady Fieldhurst. "You have been in sole possession of it for the better part of a se'ennight."

Edward's gaze remained fixed upon the passing scenery beyond the glass. "I can't."

"Of course you can, at least until we reach Grantham. It will be quite dark by then, and we will stop for the night."

"I'll be sick if I do," predicted Edward with grim certainty.

Nevertheless, seeing her ladyship would not be dissuaded, he heaved a world-weary sigh and staggered to his feet in the swaying carriage, allowing his brother to slide down the seat to the window. Edward then plopped down onto the middle of the seat, where he derived some satisfaction a quarter-hour later by leaning forward and casting up his accounts onto the floor of the carriage.

"I told you so," he muttered between retches.

"Oh, dear!" Lady Fieldhurst exclaimed, rapping sharply on the ceiling for the driver to stop. She fumbled in her reticule for a handkerchief and a vial of lavender water, then proceeded to bathe the sufferer's brow while his brothers excoriated him for the collateral damage to their boots.

"Dash it, Ned, why must you be such a baby?" demanded Harold, adding as an aside to Lady Fieldhurst, "He always does this."

" 'Always'?" her ladyship echoed indignantly. "You might

have warned me!"

"He's spoken of nothing else since we left London," Harold pointed out. "How were we to know you didn't believe him?" He looked to Robert for support, but that lad had returned to his book and vouchsafed no reply.

After a brief delay while the floor of the carriage was sponged down and Edward restored to his place by the window, they set out once more. The windows had been lowered to disperse any lingering odors, allowing Edward a rare opportunity to amuse himself by dangling his arm out the window.

"Robert, I'm sorry, but you must put your book aside, at least until we reach the posting house at Grantham," Lady Fieldhurst said at last, after watching that young man's book inch nearer and nearer his face until his eyes were nearly crossed. "It is far too dark to read, and trying to do so in such poor light cannot be good for your eyes. Edward, please draw your head back into the carriage before you tumble out onto the road."

Edward obeyed but grudgingly, wailing loudly when he cracked his head on the edge of the window.

"It serves you right," Harold informed him without sympathy.

Robert, rolling his eyes, shut his book with a snap and demanded of no one in particular to know how he was supposed to pass the time until they reached Grantham.

"You might try conversing with your travelling companions," suggested her ladyship with some asperity. "Reading is all very well and good, and I enjoy a novel myself from time to time, but a gentleman is expected to be capable of carrying on a conversation, as well as being well-read."

"Oh, but we're not gentlemen," Harold put in. "Not anymore. We're bastards, didn't you know?"

The words were uttered with a mixture of defiance and pride, and suddenly Lady Fieldhurst knew a great deal that had never been spoken aloud. Bitter experience had taught her how quickly Society could turn on one of its own at the first sign of weakness. She knew, as certainly as if she had witnessed the turn of events herself, the origins of Harold's discolored eye— the knowing looks from his fellow scholars, the taunts that increased in viciousness and volume until Harold had had no choice but to defend his honor with his fists. In spite of her earlier annoyance, her heart went out to these three boys whose place in the world had collapsed so precipitously through no fault of their own. She supposed Harold expected her to express shock at such plain speaking, perhaps even to reprimand him for using such language. She could not find it in her heart to do so. Instead, she smiled kindly at him.

"You have had a difficult time of it, have you not? I think I can understand a little, for it is not at all pleasant to be called a murderess, either. Perhaps it will do us all good to escape London for awhile. By the time we return, perhaps our friends and acquaintances will have had time to grow accustomed to our changed circumstances, and will no longer be shocked by them."

Harold shook his head. "For you maybe, but not for us. Not for me. The stain of illegitimacy will haunt me the rest of my life." He struck his fist against his knee. "God, I could kill Father for this!"

He flushed at the significance of his own words. "I beg your pardon—I should not have spoken so, not after what happened to—under the circumstances," he finished lamely.

It was the eternal tendency of youth, she knew, to dramatize itself, but in this case she feared Harold had spoken no more than the truth. Life must be difficult for any child born outside the bonds of matrimony, but how much worse for one who had supposed himself to be second in line to a viscountcy! She glanced at the two younger boys. They had apparently succumbed to either weariness or boredom, and now sat dozing in their seats, their heads bobbing with each lurch and sway of the carriage. Her gaze traced the curve of Edward's plump cheek, and it occurred to her that, had she conceived shortly after her marriage the heir her husband had wanted so desperately, she might have had a son of her own very nearly his age. They were not really bad children, she thought, merely lost and confused boys, suffering unfairly for sins in which they had played no part.

"Harold," she said softly, so as not to awaken his brothers, "it was very wrong, what your father did to you—to all of you, yourself and your brothers and your mother—and I don't blame you for being resentful. But do your father the justice to admit that his intentions were not evil. His sin was one of weakness, of being unable to resist the pressures placed on him by the expectations of others." *I cannot believe I am defending George Bertram,* Julia thought, knowing that she must do so in order to help this troubled young man find peace. She laid her hand over his clenched fist. "In a way, he has spared you those same pressures and expectations—at great cost to yourself, it is true," she added hastily, seeing an indignant protest forming on his lips, "but he has spared you, nonetheless. For you must know that being a viscount is much more than being called 'your lordship.' There would be several estates to manage, as well as a seat in the House of Lords. Then, too, the viscounts Fieldhurst have a long history of being active in His Majesty's government. Now that you are no longer your father's heir, you are free to pursue any manner of livelihood that interests you. I believe you will find your father eager to make amends by doing whatever he can to help establish you."

Harold shook his head. "Truth to tell, I don't know *what* I might like to do with myself." He cast a sheepish glance at the numerous valises containing his wardrobe. "You may say I care too much for clothes, but I don't know what else to care about. One thing is for sure: I can never go back to Oxford."

He winced at the memory, and his hand went to his discolored eye, confirming Lady Fieldhurst's suspicions.

"Perhaps this trip to Inverbrook will allow you to find some new direction," her ladyship suggested.

"Inverbrook!" he echoed bitterly. "I only wish I could go to India, or Abyssinia, or perdition, so long as no one there had ever heard of the Bertram family! Better yet, I wish I might change my name and start over again."

Privately, Lady Fieldhurst suspected perdition would be well acquainted with the Bertram family, or at least a few of its more shameless members. Still, having felt much the same way as Harold at various times over the past six months, she could find nothing else to dispute in this sentiment. In fact, she pondered it for a long moment in silence, then regarded Harold with a calculating gleam in her eye. "Yes, let's!"

"Let's what?" asked Harold, all at sea.

"Let's not go to Inverbrook after all. Let us stay at an inn instead, one quite a long distance away, where we will be utterly unknown. I can send word to your father's housekeeper and tell her our plans have changed, so she will not sound the alarm when we do not arrive as expected."

"What a capital idea!" Harold exclaimed, smiling for the first time since he had arrived in London. "And may we register at the inn under an assumed name? For there may well be neighborhood gentry, you know, who have sons at Oxford and will be familiar with the name of Bertram."

"Oh, of course," Julia agreed, entering into the spirit of the thing. "I dare not use my maiden name either, for fear someone may remember Miss Julia Runyon and her brilliant marriage to the late Lord Fieldhurst."

"What name shall we use, then? It must be one quite

unknown in Society circles, or else we may find ourselves in the devil of a coil."

It was perhaps inevitable that her imagination should alight on the name of the very one who had unwittingly precipitated her exile to Scotland in the first place.

"Pickett," she said, giving an approving nod at the sound of it. "I shall be Mrs. Pickett."

Two more days of travel saw them cross the border into Scotland, and in another two days they arrived at their destination. This was not, as previously planned, Lord Fieldhurst's estate at Inverbrook, but a modest yet respectable inn located on the western coast. An ancient structure of grey stone, its severe façade was softened by a tangle of roses growing near the front door, a few hardy specimens of which still bloomed, protected as they were from the frigid winds blowing off the Irish Sea.

"Guid e'enin'!" cried the host, a cheerful man with a well-fed belly and a thick red beard. "Whit can I be helpin' ye with?"

"I should like two rooms, if you please," Julia said. "One for myself, and one for my nephews." She and her husband's young cousins had agreed they should alter the relationship slightly as a further way of confounding any suspicions.

"Aye, two rooms, and a fine view of the sea ye'll have, Mrs.—?"

"Pickett," she said. "Mrs. Julia Pickett." Her conscience would not allow her to claim Mr. Pickett's first name along with his last, although she knew he was called John. She could only hope the innkeeper would notice her black travelling costume, deduce that her husband was deceased (which had the advantage of being true), and refrain from asking any questions that he might assume to be painful to her.

He bellowed for a lad apparently a mile away to come and

help with the bags—Cousin George's generosity had not stretched to providing for servants to attend them, a circumstance that in view of their altered plans appeared to Julia to be a very good thing—and led the way upstairs. The bedrooms were small but neat and clean and, just as the innkeeper promised, the windows offered a lovely view of a small garden that gave way to a beach of sand and shingle, beyond which the sea sparkled in the afternoon sun.

"Can we go down to the water, Cous—Aunt Julia?" begged the boys, drawn to the view like flies to honey. "Can we? Please?"

Julia wanted nothing more than to lie down upon her bed, but she was not proof against the boys' pleas. "Very well, for a short while before dinner. Only give me a moment to change my shoes."

The three boys ran for the door amid cheers, all but falling over themselves in their eagerness to oblige her in this request. It remained only for her to locate the valise containing a pair of sturdy half-boots, and soon she joined her "nephews" in the taproom below, where the innkeeper had furnished his young guests with mugs of tart apple cider.

"I wouldna go beyond the headland at this late hour, an I were you," cautioned this worthy, upon learning of their intentions. "Night falls quickly this late i' the year. Ye'll nae want to be benighted."

"Thank you, we shall bear it in mind," Lady Fieldhurst promised to a chorus of groans. "Never mind, boys, we shall have plenty of time tomorrow."

She herded her charges from the taproom, out the rear door, and thence down the garden and onto the beach. As the innkeeper had said, a cliff rose sharply to the south, blocking off the view of the water. They walked in this direction, little Edward making ever more adventuresome forays in the direction of the water's edge, with the predictable result that by the

31

time they turned their steps back toward the inn, he was soaked to the skin and his teeth chattered with the cold.

After pausing at the desk to request hot water and towels for Edward's benefit, the party dispersed to their own rooms to change for dinner. This proved to be a plain but hearty meal served in the taproom. As Julia took stock of her fellow patrons, she noticed with some discomfort that they were almost exclusively male—and that most of them were eyeing her with expressions of marked admiration. For the first time, the perils of being a woman travelling without male companionship— without *adult* male companionship, at any rate—were forcibly brought home to her. In between cutting Edward's meat and correcting Robert's table manners, she dared not let her eyes stray from her own plate, lest any of the men in the taproom mistake eye contact for encouragement. As soon as she could reasonably do so, she laid aside her napkin and rose, signaling to the boys to follow her example. Before going upstairs to her room, however, she stopped to exchange a word with the innkeeper.

"Aye, dinna fash yerself," he said reassuringly, stroking his red beard. "The boys like to stop by for a drop after the day's fishing, and of course they're pleased to take their mutton with such a bonny lass as yersel, but they'll nae do ye any harm."

"Nevertheless, I should be grateful for a private parlor where my nephews and I might take our meals without attracting undue notice."

"Aye, I can let ye hae the breakfast parlor starting tomorrow, but it'll cost ye extra."

After such an uncomfortable meal as she had just spent, she would gladly have paid any price. She readily agreed to the innkeeper's terms, then herded her nephews upstairs and off to bed. After retiring to her own room and checking the lock on the door (despite the innkeeper's assurances, she had no great faith in his "boys"), she collapsed into bed exhausted. She hoped to sleep until noon at the least.

In this hope she was doomed to disappointment. She was awakened at six o'clock the next morning by a pounding upon her door. Snatching up her dressing gown, she thrust her arms through the sleeves, tied the belt about her waist, and opened the door. There stood Edward, fully dressed and hopping from one foot to another in his eagerness.

"You said we might go back to the beach this morning," he reminded her. "May we go now?"

"What of your brothers?" she asked, raising her hand to cover a yawn. "Are they already awake?"

"Oh, yes. Robert is ready to go, too. Harold is still tying his cravat." His scornful tone suggested that this morning ritual was likely to be a protracted exercise. "May Robert and I go now? We won't go beyond the headland until you are there," he promised magnanimously.

"No, indeed! You may wait for me in the breakfast parlor, and we shall all go down together." Seeing his face fall, she added, "You may bespeak breakfast for the four of us, though. That should help speed things along."

With this Edward had to be content. After a filling repast of eggs, bacon, and fried bread, the four set out for the beach. Once there, Edward ran ahead, rounding the headland almost before his companions had reached the water's edge. Robert soon moved ahead (albeit at a slower pace than his younger brother), stopping from time to time to examine some seashell or bit of driftwood washed up on the shore.

"It's smashing, isn't it?" Harold observed to his aunt, his gaze fixed on the far horizon. "One can't help wondering what sort of adventures might await just out of sight."

"Have you never seen the sea before, then?" asked Lady Fieldhurst.

"No, never. Have you?"

"Once." A shadow crossed Julia's face. "My husband and I once spent the summer in Brighton."

It was there that she discovered the late Lord Fieldhurst's affinity for opera dancers, but this revelation could hardly be divulged to her husband's young cousin. There were certain aspects of her marriage that must be kept to herself. She owed the Bertram family that much, at least.

"Did you get to go out on a boat?" Harold asked eagerly. "I should think that would be ripping good fun, going so far out to sea that one couldn't see land."

"No, I fear we were confirmed landlubbers. You would have thought us very dull sticks." Before she could think of some elaboration upon her Brighton trip that would be suitable for Harold's ears, Edward reappeared around the curve of the headland, waving his arms wildly.

"It's Ned," observed Harold, waving back at his brother. "What does he want?"

"He seems to be saying something." Julia shaded her eyes with her hand. "I can't hear him over the crash of the waves."

Harold cupped his hands around his mouth. "We can't hear you!" he bellowed.

It was very likely that Edward could not hear Harold either, but apparently his message was understood. Edward took off across the beach at a sprint, coming at last to a stop before them. His breath came in gasps, his hands braced on his knees.

"There's a woman washed up on the beach," he said when he could speak. "I think she's dead."

CHAPTER 3
IN WHICH A MYSTERIOUS FEMALE IS INTRODUCED

Over the previous six months, Lady Fieldhurst had had too many encounters with death to react to it now with hysterics, or fainting fits, or any of the other responses deemed suitable for a gently bred female. Instead, she hitched her straight black skirts up to her knees and set off down the beach at a run. Harold and Robert were quick to follow her example and, having the advantages of being both young and male, soon outstripped her. By the time she rounded the point, they had already caught up to Edward, and the three boys were assembled around what appeared from a distance to be a large pile of wet rags washed up by the tide.

The woman was not dead, although Edward could be forgiven for believing her to be so. She lay on her belly a scant six feet from the water's edge, so that the incoming waves licked at the hem of her gown. Her long hair, dark and crusted with sand, fanned across the shingle. One arm was flung upward, the hand facing palm up and the fingers curled as if in mute appeal.

"Drowned Ophelia," murmured Harold.

He dropped to his knees before the body. Julia followed suit, wincing as the water-worn pebbles cut into her skin.

"Is she breathing?" Robert asked, leaning toward her so that he cast a shadow over her.

"We must find out," Lady Fieldhurst said. "Robert, Edward, step back. Harold, can you turn her over? Gently, now."

Harold rolled the woman onto her side. She offered no

35

resistance, but flopped limply onto her back. He reached out a tentative hand and brushed back the strands of hair now splayed across her face.

"She's beautiful," he breathed.

"She's alive!" Robert exclaimed, pointing. "Look, she's breathing. Wait until Father hears about this!"

"I found her!" Edward objected. "I get to tell!"

"You thought she was dead," retorted Robert.

"Hush, boys!" Julia chided. "The important thing now is to find help for this poor creature." She glanced up and down the beach, but it was deserted at this early hour. Her gaze took in the distance from the spot where they stood to the point that concealed the inn some distance beyond. Nearer at hand, a path ran roughly parallel to the beach up to the top of the cliff, where the grey slate roof of a house could just be glimpsed above the treetops. Although the path was fairly steep, it was undoubtedly shorter than the trek back around the headland to the hotel.

"Harold," she addressed that young man, who was still gazing at the unconscious woman in rapt wonder, "can you go up there and fetch someone?"

"I found her," Edward insisted. "I should go!"

"You and Robert must stay here with me and, er, stand guard," Julia said vaguely. She had no idea precisely what they were guarding against, but this seemed to suit Edward, who set his jaw, thrust out his chest, and took up his station near the insensible woman's head.

Harold took one last look at the woman, then turned and hurried toward the path. It seemed to Julia that he was gone an unaccountably long time, although in reality it could not have been more than fifteen minutes before he reappeared at the top of the cliff and started down the path, followed by two gentlemen and a pair of footmen. Julia could form no opinion as to which of the gentlemen was the master of the house, for they both appeared to be somewhere between thirty and forty years of age, and both were dressed in the top-boots and tweeds of the country squire. There, however, the resemblance ended. One was tall and willowy with fair hair worn in a fashionable crop, while the other was of medium height and stockier build, with thick black brows and dark hair worn rather longer than fashion dictated.

"Here she is," Harold told them, gesturing toward the woman, who had not stirred in his absence.

The two gentlemen leaned in for a closer look, then the fair one exclaimed, "Good God! It's Elspeth!"

"You know this woman?" Julia asked.

The man nodded. "Our cousin."

Upon closer inspection, Julia could see the family likeness in the storm-grey eyes and hawk-like nose possessed by both men.

The dark gentleman scowled, his heavy brows drawing together in a straight line over his nose. "Impossible! Elspeth drowned almost fifteen years ago."

"But her body was never recovered," the other reminded him.

"I tell you, Elspeth is dead. You cannot mean to foist this female upon Uncle Angus. The shock would kill him!"

"And he would kill us if we neglected to inform him of his daughter's homecoming. In any case, we can hardly leave this poor woman lying here while we debate the matter." He turned toward the two footmen lingering discreetly in the background. "Take her up to the house, and for God's sake, keep her out of my uncle's sight until we have had time to prepare him! Take her inside by way of the kitchen. Mrs. Brodie will know what to do for her."

The scowling man put out his foot and nudged the woman with the toe of his boot. "And if you should accidentally drop her on the way up, it would be so much the better."

The fair gentleman cast his cousin a speaking look, then turned to address Lady Fieldhurst. "You must forgive our lack of manners. As you may have surmised, this has caught us off our guard. Allow me to introduce myself. I am Gavin Kirkbride, and this is my cousin, Duncan Kirkbride."

Lady Fieldhurst sketched a curtsy. "Mrs. Pickett, and my nephews Harold, Robert, and Edward."

"Will you not accompany us to the house?" Gavin Kirkbride asked, gesturing in the direction of the cliff path. "I should like to hear how you came upon Elspeth, and this spot, although picturesque, is hardly conducive to conversation."

Julia glanced uncertainly at his cousin for confirmation.

"Yes, I should very much like to hear the way of it," Duncan Kirkbride growled.

Although his words were courteous enough, his tone suggested he suspected them of perpetrating some hoax. Julia could hardly decline the invitation since the gentlemen, if they were indeed related to the woman, were entitled to an explanation. Still, she resolved not to turn her back on this one. Given half a chance, he would no doubt take pleasure in tossing them all over the cliff.

She took Mr. Gavin Kirkbride's proffered arm and allowed him to lead her up the uneven beach to the base of the cliff path. The footmen and their burden had long since disappeared up the path, and there was no one else in sight. No witnesses, Lady Fieldhurst thought, then chided herself for her morbid flights of fancy. She had been too well-acquainted with violence over the past six months; she was now seeing murderers behind every bush.

By the time the path leveled off at the top of the cliff, she was out of breath and grateful to see the house looming ahead. It was a rather stark-looking residence, made of the same local grey stone as the inn. Its slate-tiled roof bristled with chimneys, and a raven perched on one of these called down a mocking greeting as they approached.

The butler had apparently been watching for their arrival, for in spite of his working costume of apron and silver polishing cloth, he flung open the door as soon as Mr. Gavin Kirkbride's foot touched the front stoop.

"Mr. Gavin, sir, I have been charged with informing you that the other, er, guest has arrived, and that Mrs. Brodie is seeing to her comfort."

"Thank you, Jarvis. And my uncle?"

"Still at breakfast, sir, and none the wiser, if I may say so."

Mr. Gavin Kirkbride nodded. "That's all right, then. You may tell him we have guests, and that we await his convenience in the drawing room."

Jarvis bowed. "Very good, sir."

"Uncle Angus is in delicate health," Mr. Gavin Kirkbride explained as he ushered Lady Fieldhurst and her charges into the drawing room. "My cousin does not exaggerate when he says the shock of Elspeth's return could kill him."

"I tell you, it can't be she!" Mr. Duncan Kirkbride insisted. "It's a cruel prank, no more and no less."

"But to what purpose, Mr. Kirkbride?" Julia asked, seating herself on a straw-colored sofa of ornate yet outdated design. "Why would anyone wish to raise your uncle's hopes in such a way?"

"I'm wondering that myself," he replied, regarding his cousin speculatively.

"And you, Mr. Kirkbride?" Julia appealed to Mr. Gavin Kirkbride. "What makes you so certain this is your cousin, when only yesterday you believed her to be dead?"

Mr. Gavin Kirkbride sat down next to Julia on the sofa. "Look here, before we go further, perhaps you'd best call us 'Mr.

39

Gavin' and 'Mr. Duncan.' I know it is a trifle irregular, upon such short acquaintance, but I fear all these 'Mr. Kirkbrides' will become confusing, especially once my uncle joins us and a third Mr. Kirkbride is added to the mix."

"Very well," Julia agreed, but before she could press him for an answer to her question, the door was thrown open by a footman. A moment later, Mr. Angus Kirkbride entered the room, a shriveled figure in a high-backed Bath chair pushed by Jarvis. The butler positioned his master's chair before the fire and then he and the footman withdrew, closing the door behind them.

"Guests, eh?" The gnarled hands plucked restlessly at the tartan lap robe covering his legs, but his white hair was thick and his eyes, as he studied Julia's face, were bright and shrewd. "We don't entertain often here at Ravenscroft Manor. We've been a bachelor establishment for these ten years and more."

Julia could readily believe that. The drawing room, although clean enough, lacked a woman's touch, as evidenced by the outmoded furnishings, faded velvet curtains, and ornamentation consisting almost entirely of framed hunting prints and stuffed and mounted animal heads.

"Uncle, allow me to introduce Mrs. Pickett and her young nephews." Mr. Gavin's sweeping gesture took in Julia and the three boys.

"How do you do?" she murmured, sketching a curtsy. The boys bobbed awkwardly, cowed into uncharacteristic silence by the frail old man.

"These three lads made a surprising discovery on the beach this morning," Mr. Gavin continued. "We thought you should wish to be informed of it."

"*You* thought," muttered Mr. Duncan under his breath.

"Aye, well, what of it?" demanded the old man. "No Frenchies coming ashore, are they?" He chuckled raspingly at his own wit.

40

"No, sir, no Frenchies," said Harold, finding his tongue at last. "It was—"

"It was a woman, sir," Edward piped up, not to be robbed of his moment of glory. "It was a woman washed up by the surf, sure as I'm standing here."

"Edward is quite right, Mr. Kirkbride," Julia said, shushing the boy with a look. "He had run ahead, around that spit of land between here and the inn where we are staying. He found a woman lying on the beach at the edge of the water. She was unconscious, but appeared otherwise uninjured. I sent Harold to your house for help, since it appeared to be nearer than the inn from which we had come."

"Aye, you did rightly." Mr. Kirkbride's hoary head bobbed up and down. "Glad to offer any assistance we can."

"I gave orders for this woman to be brought to the house," Mr. Gavin confessed. "You must brace yourself for a shock, Uncle. It appears Elspeth has come home at last."

"Elspeth!" The old man's bony hands clenched in his lap, and his gaunt face turned a queer shade of grey.

Mr. Duncan took two swift strides to the bell pull and gave it a jerk. "Jarvis! Brandy for my uncle, and quickly!"

"Elspeth!" Angus Kirkbride's voice was no more than a whisper. "I was informed my daughter was dead. God help me, I wished it so!"

"And so she may be, sir," Mr. Duncan pointed out, taking the brandy the butler decanted and holding it to his uncle's colorless lips. "Just because this woman bears a resemblance to Elspeth does not necessarily mean it is she."

"And she is here, ye say?" The old man ignored Duncan's warning and addressed himself to Gavin. "Ye must take me to her. At once, d'ye hear?"

The woman was awake and alert, as Mrs. Brodie informed them. Apparently the housekeeper had been torn as to the status of this new arrival and, undecided whether to place the unfortunate woman in the servants' quarters or a guest room, had compromised by settling the newcomer in her own bed, where she now sat up against the pillows sipping broth from an earthenware mug. The woman had been bathed and clothed in Mrs. Brodie's own night rail, a voluminous garment of white cotton that seemed to dwarf its wearer. The sand had been washed out of her hair, and her long dark locks now lay in a single thick plait over her shoulder. The effect was sweetly child-like, although Lady Fieldhurst knew from the closer look she'd had at the beach that this woman was at least thirty years old— four years her own senior, and very likely more. Although she smiled at the party crowding around her bed, it was the courte- ous yet distant look one might give a stranger; her fine blue eyes regarded Julia with the same bland expression she bestowed on the man who might be her father.

"Elspeth!" Angus Kirkbride leaned forward, all but falling out of his chair in his eagerness. "Push me up closer, Duncan, and let me look at her."

Duncan obeyed his uncle's command, although his dark scowl indicated that he took no pleasure in the task.

"I believe it is you, sir, whom I must thank for your hospital- ity," Elspeth said, inclining her head in an approximation of a curtsy.

"Dinna ye know me, child?" Old Angus looked stricken at so impersonal a greeting.

"I'm afraid I haven't the pleasure." The smile she gave him held nothing of recognition. "Tell me, where is this place?"

Angus's eyes welled with tears, and the hand he had extended to caress his daughter's cheek now fell uselessly onto his lap. His pain was so evident that Julia was forced to look away. If this was not Elspeth Kirkbride, it must surely be the unhappiest of coincidences. Surely no one could be so intentionally cruel as to cause the old man such suffering.

"You are at Ravenscroft Manor, the home of Mr. Angus Kirkbride." Gavin stepped gamely into the breach, speaking to the woman in the hushed tones so frequently employed by those addressing the gravely ill. "What is your name, ma'am?"

Duncan knew no such qualms. "Who are you and how did you come to be here?"

The woman in the bed blinked up at him. "I—I don't know. I can't remember."

"Hmph!" Duncan muttered. "How very convenient!"

"Dinna ye remember me?" Angus persisted. "And these men, dinna they look familiar to ye?"

"Should they?" Her puzzled blue gaze slewed from Duncan to Gavin and back again.

"You are on the southwestern coast of Scotland, near the village of Ravenscroft," Gavin persisted. "Can you remember nothing of how you came to be here?"

"Scotland, you say? I don't remember—there may have been a boat—" She pressed her hands to her temples with a groan. "Oh, it hurts to think!"

"That's quite enough for one day," interposed Mrs. Brodie. "This poor lamb needs to rest. If there's any change, sir, I'll send word," she added as an aside to Angus, then shepherded the group toward the door.

Lady Fieldhurst cast an uncertain glance at the woman in the bed, then turned toward the door. She was surprised to see Harold, Robert, and Edward clustered just inside, apparently afraid to make a sound lest someone remember their presence and banish them from the sickroom. They met her gaze somewhat sheepishly. Once everyone had reassembled in the drawing room, however, Edward blurted out the question that had been on everyone's minds from the moment the woman had been identified.

"What are you going to do with her now?"

Angus heaved a sigh. "I wish I knew."

"She is very like Elspeth, is she not?" Gavin looked to his uncle for confirmation.

"Aye, that she is. It seems to me we must keep her here until we know for sure."

This suggestion found no favor with Duncan. "If you intend to feed and house her until her memory returns, Uncle, you may be waiting a very long time. With good food in her belly and a soft bed at her back, she may find it more advantageous to remain forgetful."

"Ye think she's here under false pretenses?" The old man slewed around in his chair to look back at his nephew. "What makes ye say so?"

"The whole thing seems a bit too contrived for my liking. With miles of Scottish coastline to choose from, where does she land but on the very beach where a female nearly identical in appearance disappeared fifteen years earlier—with her memory conveniently erased, sparing her the necessity of answering any awkward questions."

"Your point is well taken, Duncan—and yet she looks so much like Elspeth." Angus wagged his white head. " 'Tis God's judgment on an old man's stubbornness."

"At any rate, you need not make a decision at once," Gavin pointed out. "She is not yet recovered enough to be moved. By the time she is on her feet again, her memory may well have returned, and she can tell us herself who she is."

Duncan crossed the room to pour himself a glass of the brandy Jarvis had brought for his uncle. "And what if she tells us she is Elspeth? Do we take her at her word, and kill the fatted calf to welcome the prodigal?"

Angus nodded. "Aye, and try to make up for the years we've lost."

"But Uncle, what if this female is trying to take advantage of you?" Duncan demanded. "Would you let her make a fool of you in an attempt to recreate the past?"

Gavin stepped forward to adjust his uncle's lap robe. "Quiet, Duncan, you are upsetting him."

Duncan lowered his voice. "I beg your pardon, Uncle. I merely do not wish you to be taken in."

Seeing both Robert's and Edward's eyes grow round with undisguised curiosity, Lady Fieldhurst judged it high time to extricate them all from a family drama that was none of their concern. "The boys and I must be going," she said, herding her charges toward the door. Courtesy, however, compelled her to add, "If you will allow it, I should like to return tomorrow and see how the invalid fares."

CHAPTER 4
THE KIRKBRIDES OF RAVENSCROFT MANOR

Having been granted permission to inquire after the invalid's progress, Lady Fieldhurst called at Ravenscroft Manor the following afternoon, escorted by Harold. Robert and Edward did not accompany them on this occasion, an exclusion that gave rise to much indignation until the innkeeper's daughter, a blushing damsel of fifteen summers with more than a passing interest in Harold's *beaux yeux,* stepped gamely into the breach with an offer to teach them how to fish in the surf. Even her best efforts, however, were insufficient to persuade Harold to join them in this exercise; alas, her attractions were no match for the more mature charms of the mystery lady currently in residence at Ravenscroft Manor. And so it was that he and Lady Fieldhurst presented themselves at Ravenscroft Manor unencumbered by the younger set. Here they were ushered into the drawing room, where they were met with the information that the patient was recovering, and that her memory appeared to be returning.

"This is good news," said Lady Fieldhurst, accepting a cup of tea from Gavin's hand. "Has she remembered who she is yet, or anything of her past?"

"She is indeed my daughter, Elspeth," Angus said, beaming. "She has come home at last, and all is forgiven. We'll not waste what time we have left in repeating the mistakes of the past."

Harold leaned forward in his chair, bracing his elbows on his knees. "But how came she to be lying on the beach? Did she say?"

Angus sighed. "Alas, the manner of her return is proving elusive. She remembers nothing of her immediate past."

"She hasn't had a chance to invent it yet," Duncan muttered, helping himself to a scone.

Gavin cast a disapproving glance at his cousin. "If she is an imposter, Duncan, you must admit she is a remarkably well-informed one."

Duncan gave a grunt that might have been agreement. "Aye, she's been well-tutored, I'll not deny that."

"Forgive me, Mr. Duncan," said Lady Fieldhurst, "but what makes you so certain she cannot be your cousin?"

"Elspeth walked into the sea fifteen years ago. The next day, one of her shoes washed up onto the beach."

"Duncan is right," Angus said. "We thought she was lost forever. Her return is nothing short of a miracle."

Lady Fieldhurst thought Duncan would have something unpleasant to say about his uncle's miracle, but instead, he set down his cup and rose to his feet.

"Miracle or not, Uncle, the excitement of the past couple of days is taking its toll on your strength. Let me help you back to your room so you can rest before dinner. You did invite the, er, lady to join us, did you not?"

Angus shooed him away. "Nonsense! I'm not a bit tired. Mrs. Pickett, I would invite ye to dine with us tonight, but I'm selfish enough to want my daughter's company all to myself on her first night with us. I hope ye'll make allowances for an old man's foolishness."

Julia inclined her head. "Of course, sir. Nothing could be more natural."

"As soon as she's strong enough, I'll give a great banquet in her honor. I hope you and your nephew will favor us with your company."

She glanced at Harold for confirmation. "We should consider it an honor, Mr. Kirkbride." She hesitated for a moment, then, choosing her words with care, added, "I see you, at least, are quite convinced of her authenticity."

"Aye, and so would you be, if ye'd known my daughter in her younger days. There's a miniature somewhere—Gavin, you know the one by Lawrence. Show it to Mrs. Pickett."

Gavin rose and offered Julia his arm. "As you wish, sir. If you will allow me, Mrs. Pickett?"

She allowed him to lead her to a small side table on the far end of the room. He picked up a small framed portrait and held it out for her inspection. The subject was certainly younger than the woman she'd seen the day before, but aside from this fact, the resemblance was enough to make her catch her breath. The artist had captured a girl in the first blush of young woman-hood, the sparkling eyes eager for the adventure that surely awaited her, the laughing mouth begging for its first kiss. This young woman would be her father's darling—and, perhaps, would break his heart.

"The resemblance is certainly striking," Julia observed, handing it back to Gavin. "But so much depends on the artist's interpretation. Is this considered a good likeness?"

"Everyone who saw it at the time commented on how he had captured not only Elspeth's likeness, but her essence as well. Her impulsive nature, her sudden bursts of temper, her af-fectionate spirit—all is there on the canvas, just as it was in life."

Julia looked again at the laughing countenance. "Affectionate spirit, indeed. And yet—will you think me impertinent if I ask if there was some unpleasantness between Mr. Duncan and Miss Kirkbride? That is, did they part on bad terms? I should think he would welcome his cousin's return. Instead, it seems he almost hopes to find she is an impostor."

Gavin gave a shrug. "Oh, Elspeth and Duncan were once thick as thieves! In fact, I believe my uncle once entertained hopes of a match between the two of them. No, I suspect Duncan is more concerned about the loss of his inheritance. Elspeth was in fact my uncle's step-daughter. Uncle Angus married her mother when Elspeth was scarcely more than a babe and loved her as his own child, especially when the passing years made it increasingly plain that there would be no issue of his own. You can see how a match between Duncan and Elspeth would have pleased him, uniting as it did the child of his heart with one of his blood. He might have left his fortune to Elspeth yet still kept it in the Kirkbride family. It was not until much later that, supposing his only child to be dead, my uncle had his solicitor draw up a will dividing his assets between his nephews."

"Meaning Duncan and yourself."

"Just so. Now that Elspeth has returned, assuming that it is truly she, Uncle Angus may well cut us out—and rightfully so—in favor of his daughter. In such matters the inclinations of the heart ought to outweigh the accident of birth."

"If that should be the case, Duncan is not the only one who stands to lose a fortune," observed her ladyship. "You, too, would lose your inheritance."

"True, but unlike Duncan, I can afford to be generous. You see, my mother left me, if not a fortune, at least an independence. Duncan has not that advantage."

A faint stirring in the room behind them captured her attention, and Julia glanced back to find Harold staring in rapt attention at the door. The subject of their discussion stood framed in the doorway, dressed in an antiquated gown that the housekeeper had presumably unearthed from some trunk in the attic. Looking at her, Julia had the impression of some ghost from the past returned to haunt the living. She shook off the strange feeling with a shudder.

"My dear cousin." Gavin crossed the room to greet the newcomer with a chaste kiss on the lady's cheek. "How good it is to see you up and about. Let me introduce you to our fair guest. Elspeth, this is Mrs. Pickett and her nephew, Harold. They are visiting from London."

"From London, you say?" Was it Julia's imagination, or was there the slightest flicker of recognition in the woman's eyes? *Nonsense,* Julia told herself sternly. *This unfortunate female has no knowledge of her own identity, much less yours.*

The woman believed to be Elspeth Kirkbride put a hand to the doorframe to steady herself as she dipped a curtsy. "Mrs. Pickett, Harold. I believe I have you to thank for my rescue."

The words were addressed to Julia, who was quick to demur. "Actually, it was Harold who came to Ravenscroft Manor for help after his younger brother found you on the beach. It is to him and his brothers, not me, that you owe your thanks."

Miss Kirkbride bestowed a bewitching smile upon Harold and extended her hand to him. "Mr. Pickett, then."

To Julia, the sound of Harold Bertram being addressed as Mr. Pickett was only slightly less jarring than the sight of that young man bowed deeply from the waist and raising the lady's hand to his lips. It seemed that in addition to her other perceived sins against the Bertram family must now be added the folly of allowing Harold to form an attachment to a female almost twice his age. *To where might they banish me for this new infraction,* she wondered, *the Black Hole of Calcutta?*

With assistance from Harold (whether she needed it or not), Miss Kirkbride sank onto the straw-colored sofa and glanced at the animal heads adorning the walls. "How familiar this room seems!" Her eyes fell upon an ancient deer head over the mantel. "Duncan, you must bag another buck. Poor Jasper is looking quite moth-eaten."

Duncan turned white. Gavin blinked. "Jasper?"

"It was Jasper, was it not?" She looked in pretty confusion from one cousin to the other. "Or perhaps Julian? It was so long ago."

Gavin spoke as one in a daze. "It was Jasper. He was the first buck Duncan ever shot. He was only thirteen years old at the time—Duncan, that is. I've no idea how old Jasper was," he added in a feeble attempt at humor.

Harold set his cup and saucer down with a clatter. "You remember, then? Why, that proves it! You must be Elspeth—er, Miss Kirkbride."

It would certainly appear so, Julia thought. Every family's history contained such minutiae unlikely to be known by outsiders—unless, of course, they were tutored by those in a position to know such things. She couldn't help but wonder what Duncan would make of this newest revelation.

She had not long to wait to find out.

"There's only one thing to do, then," said Duncan, regarding the company with an arrested expression.

Gavin spoke for the group. "And what, pray, is that?"

"We must know for certain." Duncan dropped to one knee beside Angus's chair, the better to look the old man squarely in the eye. "Uncle, you must have this woman investigated."

Gavin nodded. "It can't hurt to send for the justice of the peace."

Angus gave a snort of derision. "Faugh! Sir Henry MacDougall couldn't find hide nor hair of my daughter fifteen years ago, and I'll wager his eyesight hasn't improved in the interim."

"Not the justice of the peace, Uncle," Duncan insisted. "Bow Street. You must send to London for a Runner."

"I'll not have a damned *sassenach* meddling in my family's affairs!" Angus barked.

"English or not, Uncle, the Runners are the best in the realm. If anyone can discover the truth about this female, it is they."

"Perhaps that is so, Duncan, but I fear I must agree with Uncle Angus," Gavin put in, glancing around the room at the woman, who had picked up a book and now thumbed through its pages, seeming oblivious to the hushed conversation of which she was the subject. "Even if we were to send for a Runner by today's post, the fellow would not arrive for more than a se'ennight. Any trail Elsp—er, the woman might have left would have long since grown cold."

Lady Fieldhurst heard scarcely a word of this discussion, so aghast was she at the mention of Bow Street. At any other time, she would have been rather pleased at the prospect of seeing Mr. Pickett again, perhaps even assisting him in his investigation as she had done in Yorkshire. But not here. Not now.

You have nothing to fear, she told herself firmly. It was quite possible that the justice of the peace would get to the truth of the matter, one way or another, and there would be no need to send to London after all. And even if he could not, if the Kirkbrides chose to procure the services of a Bow Street Runner, there were many others besides John Pickett, some of whom had been pursuing lawbreakers throughout the length and breadth of the kingdom longer than he had been alive. If Angus Kirkbride had need of a Runner in Scotland, surely the Bow Street magistrate would send someone older and more experienced than a young man with a mere four-and-twenty years in his dish.

Surely it must be so. It *must* be. For any Runner assigned to the case would wish to interview her and the boys regarding the discovery of the woman on the beach. And she would be obliged to explain to Mr. Pickett how she came to be parading about Scotland under an assumed name.

His name.

★　★　★　★　★

The following morning saw a note delivered to Mrs. Pickett at the Wild Rose Inn, requesting her to call at Ravenscroft Manor at two o'clock that afternoon so that she might be interviewed by the justice of the peace, Sir Henry MacDougall, at the same time he was to meet with the Kirkbride family. Alas, Lady Fieldhurst's hopes for Sir Henry, while never very high, were dashed the moment that revered gentleman entered the Kirkbride drawing room. A stooped little man in his dotage, he wore an old-fashioned (and, she suspected, moth-eaten) frock coat and a bagwig that appeared to be in imminent danger of slipping off the back of his bald head.

Upon being introduced to her, he leaned very close to inspect her through squinting blue eyes, then drew back and announced in the too-loud voice of the hard of hearing, "By Jove, Angus, the gel's an imposter. She don't look a thing like that lass of yours. Elspeth was always dark, and this chit's yaller-haired. Don't know how you came to be so taken in!"

"No, no, Sir Henry," Gavin interposed. "This is the lady who—"

"Don't be daft," Angus chided, not mincing matters. "I never said she was Elspeth! That's Mrs. Pickett. She and her sons found—"

"Nephews, actually," murmured Lady Fieldhurst, hardly sure whether to be amused or insulted at the suggestion that she, at six-and-twenty, might be the mother of the eighteen-year-old Harold.

"Beg your pardon, Mrs. Pickett," Angus interposed. "As I was saying, Sir Henry, Mrs. Pickett and her young nephews found my daughter on the beach."

"What's that?" barked Sir Henry, raising an antiquated ear trumpet to his right ear. "I thought your daughter was dead."

Duncan, viewing the scene from where he stood near the fire

with one arm resting on the mantel, made a contemptuous noise.

"And so did we all, Sir Henry, until this woman turned up," said Gavin, with a speaking look at his cousin. "But the resemblance is quite remarkable, and so we have been forced to consider that she might have met a very different fate than we had assumed. But you must meet her yourself, and tell us what you think."

"Mrs. Pickett, eh?" Sir Henry turned his attention back to Lady Fieldhurst, fixing his quizzing glass on her black bodice in a way that made her feel as if she had neglected to put on her stays. "Tell me, my dear, is there a Mr. Pickett about?" he asked, with a gleam in his rheumy eye.

"I—I believe Mr. Pickett may be joining me very shortly," said her ladyship with perfect truth.

During this exchange (which was conducted at a far greater volume than the mortified Lady Fieldhurst could have wished) Gavin murmured a word to the footman stationed near the door. The servant nodded, then withdrew from the room and returned a moment later with the supposed Elspeth Kirkbride in tow. Once again she wore an outmoded gown presumably unearthed from a trunk in the attic, a nip-waisted, full-skirted frock of stiff brocade that gave her the curiously unworldly air of a woman out of time.

"Here she is now," said Angus, gesturing the woman forward eagerly. "Come in, my dear, and make your curtsy to Sir Henry MacDougall. He once dandled you on his knee when you were little more than an infant, but you won't remember that."

"Sir Henry." The woman did as she was bidden, and achieved a very credible curtsy. Lady Fieldhurst, who remembered hours spent practicing this skill before a mirror prior to her presentation at Court, acknowledged that the woman was very likely of gentle birth. Certainly, she had been taught to curtsy correctly.

"Stap me if it ain't Elspeth, come back at last!" Sir Henry exclaimed. "You've been sorely missed my dear. Don't see what you're making such a mystery about, Angus. It's plain as a pikestaff the girl simply went for a swim and stayed out too long. Young people are often thoughtless, but there's no reason to make a Cheltenham tragedy of it."

"Sir Henry," Duncan put in, "do you mean to suggest that Elspeth has been at sea treading water for *fifteen years*? Why, fifteen minutes would have been too long, if the tide had been coming in at the time."

"Eh?" Sir Henry sought recourse to his ear trumpet. "What's that?"

"Fifteen years, Your Honor," Gavin echoed. "That's how long it has been since Elspeth 'went for a swim,' as you say."

"Has it been that long?" marveled Sir Henry, turning back to Elspeth for confirmation.

"So they tell me," she said. "I confess, I don't remember."

"Why, it seems like only yesterday. And you, my dear! You don't look a day older than you did at seventeen," declared Sir Henry, which only served to confirm Angus's low opinion of that gentleman's eyesight. The supposed Elspeth was certainly a beautiful woman, but that she was in fact a woman, and no longer a girl, could not be disputed by any but the most generous of critics.

"This is getting us nowhere," declared Duncan, stating the obvious. "Sir Henry, we want you to investigate this woman—find out, if you can, who she is, where she came from, and how it was that she contrived to wash ashore practically on our doorstep."

"Certainly, certainly," Sir Henry agreed, wagging his head. "Now, Elspeth, you heard your cousin: how *did* you contrive to wash ashore at virtually the same spot you'd disappeared from all those years ago?"

The woman shrugged in pretty confusion. "I wish I could tell you, Sir Henry, but I fear I cannot remember."

"Eh? What's that?" asked Sir Henry. He leaned closer to the woman, although whether this was to hear her better or to give him an unimpeded view down her bodice was not immediately apparent.

"Good God!" grumbled Duncan. He heaved himself out of his chair and headed for the door.

"Where are you going, nephew?" Angus demanded.

"To pen a letter," Duncan snapped, "to the Bow Street Public Office in London!"

CHAPTER 5

WHICH FINDS JOHN PICKETT
CONSIDERING MATRIMONY

Some three weeks after his encounter with Lady Fieldhurst at the theatre in Drury Lane, John Pickett approached the magistrate's bench in the Bow Street Public Office. Taking a deep breath, he gripped the slender wooden railing that separated the magistrate's raised bench from those lesser mortals who came before him seeking justice or mercy, depending upon which side of the law they found themselves.

"Mr. Colquhoun, sir, if I might have a moment—" he began.

"By all means, Mr. Pickett. In fact, you're a breath of fresh air." The magistrate's scowl lightened at the sight of his most junior Runner. "If anyone had told me twenty years ago that the Metropolis was home to so many pickpockets and petty thieves, I never would have believed them. Sometimes I wonder if there's an honest man in all of London. Perhaps I should take up a lantern and go in search of one, like Diogenes."

As Pickett's education did not extend to classical references, the slight smile with which he greeted this sally was more out of courtesy than amusement.

"But why so solemn, Mr. Pickett? What troubles you this morning?"

"I wonder, sir, if you might speak on my behalf regarding a—" Pickett swallowed hard. "—regarding a rise in my wages."

Mr. Colquhoun's bushy white eyebrows rose. "I seem to recall you were rewarded quite handsomely for that Hollingshead affair. How much does it take to maintain a bachelor establishment these days?"

"There's the rub, sir." Having committed himself this far, Pickett threw caution to the winds. "I am contemplating matrimony."

"Well, I'm dashed!" The magistrate heaved himself to his feet and reached across the railing to shake Pickett's hand. "Never say that viscountess of yours has said she'll have you! Let me be the first to congratulate you."

Pickett saw nothing to amuse him in this attempt at hilarity. "I am preparing," he said with great solemnity, "to make an offer of marriage to Miss Lucy Higgins of Seven Dials."

"John!" The twinkle in Mr. Colquhoun's blue eyes was extinguished, and when he spoke again, there was no trace of amusement in his voice. "You intend to tie yourself to a common strumpet?"

"As you are so kind as to point out, the Viscountess Fieldhurst is unlikely to so demean herself," Pickett said stiffly.

"Yes, but you need not choose one end of the spectrum or the other. If you'll look about you a bit, you'll discover there is a whole range of females who fall somewhere between the extremes of an aristocratic widow and a ha'penny whore!"

Pickett, very much on his dignity, drew himself up to his full height. "I must remind you, sir, that you are speaking of the young woman I intend to marry."

"Fine words, my lad, but the fact remains that the girl is nothing but a prostitute!"

"And what am I but a reformed pickpocket?"

"John?" There was confusion and, yes, pain in the magistrate's voice. "After all you have accomplished here, can you truly think so little of yourself? You are one of the most promising young men it has been my pleasure to know."

Pickett hesitated. He knew Mr. Colquhoun felt a certain sense of responsibility where he was concerned; he sometimes suspected that sense of responsibility was not unmixed with affection. But although he was aware of the debt he owed the magistrate, there were things he could not confide in him. He could not tell him, for instance, that every evening for the past three weeks had found him in the pit of the Theatre Royal in Drury Lane. For twenty-one nights running, Hamlet had pondered aloud whether "to be or not to be" while John Pickett gazed up at the box directly overhead for a glimpse of the widowed Lady Fieldhurst. Not once had his diligence been rewarded; however pleased her ladyship had appeared to be at the opportunity to renew his acquaintance, she had clearly forgotten the encounter. It was long past time for him to do the same.

Unfortunately, in spite of his best efforts, this appeared to be easier said than done. Suddenly weary of his self-imposed celibacy, he saw only one way out of his dilemma. He had decided long ago that he would not be one of those Runners who arrested on Sunday morning the same doxies whose favors they had purchased on Saturday night. For a principled man, there was only one outlet for those urges natural to any healthy, red-blooded Englishman: marriage. Pickett had come to the conclusion that the only way to banish one female from his heart was to tie himself irrevocably to another.

"I will do my best to justify your faith in me, sir, but where would I be had you not intervened?" Pickett asked, seeing the magistrate was awaiting an answer. "Locked up in Newgate, perhaps, or dancing from the end of a rope on Tyburn Tree."

Mr. Colquhoun made a shooing motion with his hands, as if to wave away any suggestion of sentiment. "Nonsense! Cream will rise to the top, my boy—you can't stop it. In any case, they stopped hanging felons at Tyburn before you were born! But ' 'til death do us part' can be a long time if you're wed to the wrong woman. A man wants to be sure his children have his own blood running through their veins."

"I believe Lucy will be faithful to me, once she is assured of a roof over her head and food in her belly. Perhaps all she needs is a chance. Since I can't—that is, since it is impossible—" He broke off and swallowed hard. "I will not try to convince you that I am in love with Lucy, but I am fond of her. I believe I could find some contentment in knowing that I gave her a better life than she could provide for herself. It might not be a blissful marriage, but I think it could be a mutually satisfying one."

The magistrate heaved a world-weary sigh and rolled his eyes heavenward. "There are times," he said, "when I could cheerfully wring the Viscountess Fieldhurst's neck! I'm sure your feelings do you credit, John, but by Jove, you can't marry a female in a fit of philanthropy!"

"But sir, I—"

"You, sirrah, will hold your tongue when you approach the bench!" commanded Mr. Colquhoun at his most magisterial. He picked up a folded sheet of paper and spread it open on his desk. "I fear you will be leaving the Metropolis for a time, Mr. Pickett, so let us have no more nonsense about marriage. I have been thinking for some time now about visiting my native Scotland to harass the local trout population. You will accompany me. We will board the Royal Mail Coach at the Bull and Mouth in St. Martin's Lane first thing tomorrow morning. The Mail departs promptly at eight. Do not disappoint me."

Pickett heard only one part of this speech. "Fishing, sir? In October?"

"Faugh! Has city living made you soft? A fine husband you'd make some poor female, if you can't stomach the prospect of a little cold and damp! Providentially, I have only this morning received a request to send a Runner to Ravenscroft, a village on the southwestern coast of Scotland. Missing person, presumed dead, suddenly reappeared. Family wants to know if it's a hoax. You shall investigate while I indulge in a brief holiday. Do I make myself clear?"

Pickett sighed. "Very clear, sir. And what of my request?"

"Ah, yes. A rise in wages so that you might take a harlot to wife. As to that, Mr. Pickett, you may consider it denied."

Having all the efficiency of the Royal Mail at their disposal, and being unencumbered by the presence of schoolboys, Mssrs. Colquhoun and Pickett accomplished the trip to Scotland with a speed that Lady Fieldhurst might have envied. They reached the seaside village of Ravenscroft a scant three days after their departure from London, at last ending their journey at a quaint old inn of local grey stone whose rear-facing windows offered a fine view of the sea. An ostler hurried from the stables and began unhitching the horses, while a sturdy lad from the inn unfastened the straps securing their baggage to the roof. Pickett, by this time well-travelled enough to know that these persons would expect to be rewarded for their services (and that this reward must be financial in nature), could not but be relieved when Mr. Colquhoun dispatched him on another errand.

"If you'll go inside and bespeak a couple of rooms, I'll square things with these fellows," the magistrate said, drawing a coin purse from the inside pocket of his coat. "I wouldn't say no to a wee drop of something awaiting me in the taproom when I'm done, mind you."

"Yes, sir. I shall see to it," said Pickett, and went inside.

"Guid day to ye, sir," the innkeeper greeted him. "Whit can I do for ye?"

"I have need of two rooms for the next fortnight," Pickett said.

The innkeeper dragged a heavy leather-bound notebook from

beneath the counter and began to write in it with the painstaking scrawl of the unlettered. "Names?"

"Mr. Patrick Colquhoun." Pickett paused to allow the man to catch up. "And Mr. John Pickett."

The innkeeper looked up, stroking his bushy red beard. "Pickett, you say?"

"Yes. P-I-C-K-E-T-T. Pickett."

The innkeeper wrote it down. Curiously enough, he seemed to have no difficulty with "Colquhoun," which, at least in Pickett's opinion, was far more difficult to spell. He could only suppose that, the magistrate's surname being of Scottish origin, the innkeeper had encountered others of that name, while the English Pickett must be a novelty.

Having arranged for a roof over their heads, Pickett wandered into the taproom, ordered two tankards of ale, and sat down to wait for Mr. Colquhoun. He passed the time in observation of his fellow patrons, and decided that most of them were either local fisherfolk fortifying themselves for the afternoon's labors or, like the magistrate, sportsmen on holiday.

"Sorry to be so long," said the magistrate when at last he joined Pickett in the taproom. "Would you believe, it turns out the ostler's sister's daughter is chambermaid to my aunt's grandson?"

"Imagine that," Pickett said obligingly. Deprived of an extended family due to his ancestors' propensity for ending their careers either languishing in a cell at Newgate or dangling from a noose on Tyburn Tree, he had never experienced the charm of finding previously unknown family connections in unexpected places.

"I think I'll step outside and blow a cloud before dinner," said Mr. Colquhoun when the tankards were drained.

Pickett suspected the magistrate was more interested in dredging up further mutual acquaintances, but he bade his mentor a good evening. For his own part, Pickett had a job to do, and before he began his investigations the next morning, he wished to become more familiar with the details of the letter that had summoned him northward. With this end in view, he left the taproom and would have sought his bedchamber, where he might study this correspondence in relative peace and quiet. But as he passed the counter, the innkeeper called out to him.

"Mr. Pickett, sir!"

"Yes? What is it?"

"It appears we have only one room vacant tonight on account of the fine weather bringing all the anglers to the coast for a last bit of fishing ere the winter sets in. That being the case, I've taken the liberty of having your valise sent up to your wife's room. I hope that's agreeable."

"My—my wife, you say?"

"Aye, Mrs. Pickett. You did say that was your name?" the innkeeper asked in some consternation.

"Yes, that's it." Pickett darted a quick, bewildered glance up the staircase.

"You'll think me a regular noddy for not connecting the pair of you at once," the innkeeper continued. "Truth to tell, I had the impression Mrs. Pickett was a widowed lady. Not that I'm not pleased to see you in such good health," he added hastily.

"No, that's quite—quite all right," Pickett assured him, wanting only to be rid of the man so that he might resolve the situation upstairs with the woman whom the innkeeper imagined to be his wife.

And just when he had been noting the lack of people who shared his name! He wondered what sort of female he would find upstairs; a woman of a certain age, apparently, if the innkeeper had assumed her to be a widow. Pickett knew there were young men who married older widows as a way of advancing themselves in the world, but any affront he might have felt at being taken for one of their number was forgotten in the greater concern of placating an elderly widow who, upon discovering a man entering her room, might accuse him of having improper designs upon her person.

Too late, he realized he should have spoken up at once and told the innkeeper he was unmarried, Pickett thought as he climbed the stairs. Since being promoted from the foot patrol, he had developed a habit of being quick to observe and slow to act. It was a practical course to take when conducting an investigation, but less so in other areas of life, as his present dilemma made plain. He continued up the stairs with a growing sense of dread until, reaching the top, he stopped before the room the innkeeper had indicated. He wished he might give the poor woman some advance warning by knocking first but, upon glancing back down the stairs, he saw that he was in full view of his host, who looked up at him expectantly. Taking a deep breath, he grasped the knob and opened the door.

Just as he expected, a high-pitched shriek greeted his entrance, only to be bitten off at once as the lady recognized her unannounced caller. For instead of confronting an outraged dowager, he found himself face to face with the Viscountess Fieldhurst. She was clad in nothing but her shift and stays, and as his slightly dazed brain registered this interesting fact, she snatched up a pink dressing gown lying on the bed and clutched it to her bosom.

"Mr. Pickett!"

"*My lady?*" At any other time Pickett would have nobly turned his back on her *déshabillé,* but such was his sense of shock that gallantry fell by the wayside.

"Sssh!" She started to raise a hand in warning but, as the dressing gown began to slip, apparently thought better of this maneuver. "You must not call me so! Shut the door, and I will explain everything."

Valiantly if belatedly turning away, Pickett closed the door and shot the bolt home. When he turned back to face her ladyship, he was both relieved and disappointed to discover that she had shrugged on the dressing gown and was in the process of tying the belt about her trim waist.

"The innkeeper had my valise brought up to this room," Pickett said, gesturing toward the worn leather bag at the foot of the bed.

"Oh!" exclaimed her ladyship. "Is that yours? I confess, when I saw it there, I thought it must be Harold's. He has so many, it has been difficult to keep up with them all."

"My lady," Pickett said, conscious of having conceived a violent dislike for the unknown Harold, "the innkeeper seems to be laboring under the misapprehension that we are man and wife!"

Lady Fieldhurst heaved a sigh. "An entirely reasonable assumption under the circumstances, I fear. It is a long story, Mr. Pickett, and one that does me no credit. Will you not sit down?"

He took a seat on the room's only straight chair while Lady Fieldhurst perched on the edge of the bed as if poised for flight. It was not the first time he had enjoyed a *tête-à-tête* with the lady; while investigating the Hollingshead incident in Yorkshire, he had posed as her footman and in that rôle had conferred with her privately, usually in her bedchamber, almost every day. Still, there had been subtle differences between those occurrences and this; for one thing, on all those other occasions, the viscountess had been fully clothed.

"I suppose you must wonder why I am in Scotland when I was in London only three weeks ago," she began, her fingers plucking at the quilted counterpane that covered the bed.

"I—yes, I suppose I am." While not uppermost in his thoughts, this home question was far better suited to polite conversation.

"In fact, Mr. Pickett, I am in disgrace with my husband's family—again!" she added with a rueful smile.

"Are you indeed? And what did they find this time to offend them?"

"Can you not guess? I had the effrontery to summon an Undesirable to the family box at Drury Lane!"

"I see. I—I'm sorry," Pickett said. "I should have declined your kind invitation."

She raised an ironic eyebrow. "In fact, you would prefer to offend me than to run afoul of the Bertrams!"

"No, my lady!" exclaimed Pickett, aghast. "I only meant that I would not wish to be the cause of dissension between you and your husband's relations."

"As it turns out, I cannot be sorry, for the incident did allow me to escape London for a time. I have been banished to Scotland, you see, with George and Caroline's three sons in my care."

"Ah!" Pickett's brow cleared at hearing her absence from the theatre so easily explained, to say nothing of the identity of the mysterious Harold. "Then that is why—" He broke off abruptly.

" 'That is why' what?" asked Lady Fieldhurst, puzzled.

Pickett could hardly explain to her ladyship his haunting of Drury Lane Theatre, craning his neck for a glimpse of her in the boxes overlooking the pit. He shook his head. "Never mind. It wasn't important. But why the false name?"

Now it was her ladyship's turn to be embarrassed. "As to that, Mr. Pickett, I am afraid I have behaved impulsively, with disastrous results! Harold Bertram, you see, has been having a most difficult time at school, given his sudden change in status. It is not easy for a young man to go from being the heir to a viscountcy to, er, having the legitimacy of his birth invalidated. On the journey north, he confided a wish that he might go someplace where he would be quite unknown. I confess to having had similar feelings myself over the past six months, and so, since the boys had never seen the sea, we decided on a whim to stop here. When Harold wished to further confound any potential gabble-mongers by using a false name, it seemed amusing at the time to grant his request. And since we needed a name that would be unknown in polite circles, I—well, I chose yours."

"Certainly unknown in polite circles," agreed Pickett somewhat bitterly, more wounded than he cared to admit by this casual reminder of the differences in their respective stations. "My lady, you are more than welcome to make free with my name any time you may have need of it. Still, I'd best go downstairs and square things with the innkeeper. I believe all the rooms are full, but I'm sure Mr. Colquhoun won't object to putting me up."

He rose and would have suited the word to the deed, but she clutched at his sleeve. "Wait! Perhaps I could help you with your investigation, as I did in Yorkshire."

Pickett shook his head. "That was different. You were embroiled in that case from the first. I can't implicate you in this one."

"Can't implicate me?" Lady Fieldhurst echoed, torn between exasperation and amusement. "My dear Mr. Pickett, who do you think it was who discovered the body?"

Pickett fell back onto his chair with a thud. "Do you mean to tell me it was *you* who found the mysterious woman on the beach?"

"Since I am convinced that absolute honesty is imperative when dealing with an officer of the law, I must confess it was Edward, George's youngest, who was first on the scene," admitted her ladyship.

Finding this particular officer of the law temporarily bereft of speech, she added, "So, since it appears I am already involved in the case, you might as well take advantage of whatever help I am able to offer." She smiled. "We made a rather good team in Yorkshire, did we not?"

Yes, they had made a very good team, particularly on that one occasion when they'd been obliged to rifle Sir Gerald Hollingshead's desk in search of incriminating papers. They had been interrupted at this task and, in an attempt to offer some explanation for their presence in an apparently locked room in the middle of the night, had allowed themselves to be discovered in a passionate embrace. Thrusting the memory to the back of his mind (whence it would no doubt return that night to haunt his dreams), Pickett forced himself to concentrate on the present predicament.

"I'll not deny your assistance was invaluable, my lady, but I cannot ask you to pose as my wife for the next fortnight."

"Why not? If I remember correctly, you posed as my footman."

"I'll admit I am no expert on the subject, having never been married, but it seems to me there is a great deal of difference between a footman and a husband!"

"Nonsense! It is not as if we must actually share the same room. You may come to my room to give me instructions as to what you wish me to discover, or to hear what I have learned, and then go back to Mr. Colquhoun's room to sleep once everyone in the inn has settled down for the night. No one need be the wiser."

"And what of the boys—George's sons?"

"Robert and Edward are too young to suspect any impropriety. Depend upon it, to them the whole thing will seem a great lark!"

"And the eldest? Harold?"

Her brow puckered as she pondered the problem of Harold. "Harold is eighteen—certainly old enough to assume the worst, but unless I am very much mistaken, he will be too caught up in his own affairs to spare us a second thought." Seeing his puzzled expression, she added, "Harold, it seems, has conceived a violent *tendre* for the fair Miss Kirkbride."

Pickett's expression devolved from merely puzzled to utterly bewildered. "Is the daughter of the house so young, then? Did she disappear as an infant? Mr. Kirkbride's letter gave me to understand that she was much older."

"Oh, she is thirty if she is a day! But it was bound to happen: a beautiful, mysterious woman unconscious on the beach, a damsel in distress in need of rescue—I daresay it was almost inevitable that poor Harold should succumb."

"And Harold is, what did you say? Eighteen? Whether the woman is who she says she is or not, it will end badly for him."

"Oh, certainly! But tell me, Mr. Pickett, did you never in your misspent youth conceive a grand passion for a wholly ineligible female?"

A rueful smile twisted his lips. "Once."

"So have we all, I believe. When I was fourteen, I was desperately in love with my dancing master."

When she was fourteen, Pickett was twelve, and was serving an apprenticeship of sorts, supplementing his father's earnings (if one could call them that) by picking gentlemen's pockets in Covent Garden. He'd had no thought to spare for the fair sex, all his efforts being concentrated on outwitting—or outrunning—the constable. No, his own impossible attachment was of much more recent date.

"Harold will survive, as we all do, and will be the wiser for the experience," Lady Fieldhurst continued. "In fact, if you can persuade him to take you into his confidence, you might find his insights useful."

Privately, Pickett thought it more likely that a young man with a severe case of calf-love might be far more inclined to

darken the daylights of anyone imprudent enough to cast asper-
sions on his ladylove's character. He made a mental note to
choose his words with care when discussing the woman in
Harold's presence, and to keep a circumspect distance between
himself and that enamoured young man's fists. At the moment,
however, he had a more pressing matter to attend to. Mr. Colquhoun would be finishing his pipe at any moment, and Pickett
would have to break the news to him, first, that they would be
sharing a room; second, that he had acquired a "wife"; and
third, that the wife in question was the very same Lady
Fieldhurst of whom the magistrate so strongly disapproved.

"I'd best find Mr. Colquhoun and inform him how things
stand before he says something to queer our pitch," Pickett
said, crossing the room to the door. "Is there some time and
place where I may speak privately with you and the boys? I
should like to hear about how the woman was discovered."

Lady Fieldhurst thought for a moment, then put forward a
suggestion. "I am sure nothing could be more natural than a
pleasant family stroll along the beach after dinner. We should be
able to walk there and back before dark, and the pounding of
the waves will make it possible for us to speak without being
overheard."

"Excellent! By the bye, how am I related to the boys? Are
they all named Pickett, too?"

"Indeed, they are. And as they are supposed to be my
nephews, I daresay you must have an elder brother whom you
have quite forgotten."

"Of course—how could I be so careless?" Pickett asked, entering into the spirit of the thing. "But then, George and I were
never close."

She smiled but made no response to this sally, instead addressing the more serious aspects of their charade. "I suppose
you had best leave your valise here for the sake of appearances.

Perhaps you can transfer its contents under cover of darkness to the clothes-press in Mr. Colquhoun's room. I hope he will not be too put out by having to share."

Mr. Pickett bade her farewell until their rendezvous after dinner, but inwardly he was convinced that the magistrate would have the room to himself after all. *For once he learns how things stand*, Pickett thought, *he's going to kill me.*

CHAPTER 6

IN WHICH JOHN PICKETT'S
INVESTIGATIONS BEGIN

Pickett had no difficulty in identifying the magistrate's room by the sight of that gentleman's well-travelled trunk placed in the corridor just outside the door. He rapped on the panel and, upon hearing Mr. Colquhoun's voice bid him enter, opened the door and stepped inside.

The magistrate, looking out the window onto the bustling stable yard below, turned to greet him. "Well, Pickett, I confess I had hoped for a view of the sea, but I daresay I shan't be spending much time in my room in any case. I trust you find your room suitable. Is the view agreeable?"

Pickett had found the view most agreeable indeed, but for all the wrong reasons. "Quite agreeable, sir, but I'm afraid there's been a—a slight complication."

The bushy white brows drew together over Mr. Colquhoun's nose. "A complication? Of what sort?"

"I shall have to bunk with you, sir. The inn is full."

The magistrate received this blow with a philosophical shrug. "Well, if there's no help for it, I suppose we will contrive to tolerate one another's company for a fortnight. I trust you've no unpleasant habits? You don't snore, or talk in your sleep, or anything of that nature?"

"No, sir, not to my knowledge."

"Excellent! But where is your valise?"

Pickett sighed. "I was coming to that. The innkeeper had it brought to another room, one occupied by a lady calling herself

Mrs. Pickett. He assumed she must be my wife."

"Oho!" Mr. Colquhoun chuckled. "Have you already been to the room, then? I'll wager you gave her a rare shock!"

"No more than she gave me. The lady calling herself Mrs. Pickett is none other than Lady Fieldhurst."

At this revelation, Mr. Colquhoun fell into a coughing fit so violent that Pickett was obliged to pound him on the back. "Bless my soul!" the magistrate uttered when he could speak at last. "And she is here passing herself off as Mrs. Pickett? To what purpose, pray tell?"

"It seems her ladyship is in the Fieldhursts' black books." Pickett saw no reason to enlighten the magistrate as to the nature of her ladyship's transgressions. "She was banished to Scotland for her sins, to play chaperone for George Bertram's three sons. Somewhere along the route, she and Harold—the eldest of the three boys—decided to kick over the traces and enjoy a seaside holiday, rather than go into seclusion on Lord Fieldhurst's Scottish estate—and more power to them," he added with feeling.

"Your editorial comments are not required," the magistrate replied. "Pray continue."

"Yes, well, they did not dare to use their own names lest word of their indiscretion get back to George—that is, Lord Fieldhurst—or the Dowager Lady Fieldhurst, and so they decided to adopt a false name. And the name her ladyship chose, sir—well—it was mine." Pickett tried without success to suppress the grin that threatened to spread over his face at the thought of her ladyship calling herself "Mrs. Pickett."

"Imagine that," muttered the magistrate.

"She had no reason to believe that I should turn up here, or that anyone outside the four of them ever need be the wiser," Pickett pointed out, feeling some defense of her ladyship's actions was called for.

"Bless my soul!" Mr. Colquhoun said again. "I trust you've had a word with the innkeeper and cleared up the confusion?"

Pickett frowned. "And call the lady a liar? I think not, sir!"

"You don't know what deep waters you are treading," prophesied the magistrate, shaking his head.

"On the contrary, I've come to think it might be a very good thing. It was Lady Fieldhurst and her young charges who found the woman on the beach. She has already become acquainted with the Kirkbride family, and might be in a position to come by a great deal of information that I should have difficulty discovering on my own."

Mr. Colquhoun mumbled something under his breath about playing with fire.

"The only thing that concerns me," Pickett said, having had time to consider the matter, "is how I am to present myself to Mr. Kirkbride. To expect him to believe that the Bow Street Runner he sent to London for just happens to be the husband of the lady who discovered the woman on the beach would be to stretch credibility to the breaking point, do you not think?"

"Oh, unquestionably."

"But if I preserve my incognito and investigate the case clandestinely, as I did in Yorkshire, how am I to account for the absence of the Bow Street Runner, whom the family will be expecting to arrive any day?"

"Perhaps you should have thought of that before agreeing to this farce," barked Mr. Colquhoun, his sudden sternness giving Pickett to understand, having had five years of experience in the matter, that the magistrate was more concerned than he cared to admit.

"And so I would have, sir, but the damage had already been done."

Mr. Colquhoun stuck his unlit pipe between his teeth as he pondered the problem. "I think you should not approach the family at all, at least not immediately," he said at last. "I shall call on Angus Kirkbride myself tomorrow. I'll tell him I was already planning a sojourn in Scotland, and decided his situation was of sufficient importance to look into the matter myself. I can see how much fishing I'm going to accomplish over the next fortnight," he added darkly.

"I'm sorry for it, sir, but there are other kinds of fishing, you know. You might say we are fishing for truth."

The magistrate arched an ironic eyebrow. "Fine words, Mr. Pickett, but they might bear more weight were they not uttered by a man contemplating matrimony with one woman while pretending to be wed to another."

Pickett had the grace to blush. "As to my idea of marrying Lucy, sir, perhaps you were right, and I was a bit hasty."

"Now, I wonder why you would suddenly come to that conclusion?" Mr. Colquhoun marveled aloud. "Still, I suppose I can't complain, since that was my whole purpose in removing you from London. Mind you, while I have no objection to being the face of the investigation, so far as the Kirkbrides are concerned, you will still be the one to do most of the work. So, what is to be your first step on this quest for truth?"

"With your permission, sir, after dinner I should like to go down to the beach with Lady Fieldhurst and the Bertram boys. I want to get a good look at the spot where they found Miss Kirkbride."

"Permission granted. Oh, and John," he called, as Pickett reached the door.

Pickett paused and turned back with one hand on the knob. "Yes, sir?"

"If you will heed a word of advice, I should caution you to be very circumspect in your dealings with that woman."

Pickett regarded him curiously. "I shall bear it in mind, but I don't believe I stand in any real danger from Miss Kirkbride."

He sketched a slight bow and left the room.

"Who said anything about Miss Kirkbride?" grumbled Mr. Colquhoun, apparently addressing the closed door. "I was speaking of Mrs. Pickett."

The sun was low on the horizon by the time Pickett and Lady Fieldhurst, accompanied by the three Bertram boys, were able to slip away from the inn and down to the beach. The boys ran ahead, kicking up sand and frightening the gulls into a shrieking frenzy. The tide was much lower now, exposing a broad expanse of beach littered with seashells, seaweed, and various other forms of aquatic debris deposited there by the receding waters. Out over the sea, the dark waves were capped with red and gold, and in the distance a few hardy fishing boats headed toward the harbor some distance north of the inn. Pickett, though fully alive to the feel of Lady Fieldhurst's hand tucked into the curve of his elbow, knew it was time to set about the business for which Mr. Colquhoun had brought him to Scotland.

"My lady," he addressed his fair companion, "do you think you could call on Miss Kirkbride tomorrow and ask a few discreet questions? I should like to know what happened fifteen years ago to cause the rift between her and her father."

She regarded him curiously. "Certainly, if it will help. But would it not be better for you to ask Mr. Kirkbride yourself? I realize it may be a delicate subject, but surely having sent for you, he would not withhold any information that you might find useful."

Pickett shook his head. "I am limited to investigating from a safe distance, at least for the nonce. Mr. Colquhoun thinks it would be impossible—and I agree—for me to introduce myself to the Kirkbride family as both the Bow Street Runner they requested and the husband of the very lady who discovered their long-lost relative. Instead, he will meet with the family and tell them that, having already planned a trip to Scotland, he decided to take an interest in the case himself." Seeing her alarmed expression, he added, "I could hardly keep our present predicament from him, but you need have no fears on that head. However little he may approve of the charade, he will do nothing to expose it."

"I am sorry," said Lady Fieldhurst, not for the first time. "When I availed myself of your name, I had no thought of inconveniencing you in such a way."

Inconvenient though it certainly was, Pickett could not regret her decision; in fact, it warmed the cockles of his heart to know that, out of all the possible surnames at her disposal, she had chosen his. He would have given much to know the thought processes that led to its selection, while at the same time he cautioned himself against reading too much into what might well have been the unthinking impulse of a moment.

"What's done is done," he said firmly, putting aside her self-recriminations. "Who knows? We may find something useful comes of it."

Having reassured her on this head, he turned to look again at the sea, and regarded the returning fishing boats speculatively.

"I wonder what time the fishermen set out in the morning," he pondered aloud. "Perhaps one of them may have seen something."

"Yes, I suppose they may have done," Lady Fieldhurst agreed somewhat distractedly. She had not taken the time to put on a bonnet, and as a result was obliged to brush from her face those strands of hair pulled free from their pins by the stiff sea breeze.

"I'd best visit the harbor tomorrow and find out," Pickett said. "It might even prove useful to try and see if one of them would consent to take me out on the water—although what reason I could offer him for making such a request, I can't imagine."

"Perhaps we could all go out on a pleasure jaunt," Lady Fieldhurst suggested. "I'm sure the boys would have a marvelous time."

Pickett watched with a jaded eye as Robert and Edward ran down the beach chasing after seagulls, who screamed their displeasure at so invasive a form of entertainment.

"I've no doubt they would enjoy themselves immensely—although whether I could actually learn anything useful under such conditions is another thing entirely."

Lady Fieldhurst, considering the matter further, was forced to abandon this promising idea. "Oh, dear! Yes, I quite see your point. Harold would probably not be so bad, but as for the younger ones—" she broke off as she recalled an earlier conversation with her eldest "nephew." "I have it! You must ask Harold to accompany you."

"Harold? On what pretext?"

"Let us say that Harold has a burning desire to join His Majesty's Navy but, never having been at sea before, wonders if he has the constitution for it. You, being the kindly 'uncle' that you are, wish to take him out on the water and let him test his sea legs, so to speak." She looked up at him. "Besides giving you an excuse to solicit the use of a boat, it would also take Harold off my hands, so that I might speak to Miss Kirkbride without Harold there, ready to take umbrage at any suggestion that the lady is anything but honest."

"I think it might work," Pickett said, much struck. "I thank you, my lady."

"And so you should," she informed him, "for when Robert and Edward discover that their brother is to go out on a boat while they must remain behind, well, let us just say that I do not look forward to breaking the news to them."

"I am sure that you, being the doting 'aunt' you are, will find some way to make it up to them," Pickett predicted. "Now if only I can find some way of making it up to you."

She shook her head. "No, you need not. After all, it is no more than I deserve for putting you in such an awkward situation in the first place by appropriating your name. Speaking of which— " She allowed him to steer her clear of the water as a wave rolled in almost at their feet. "Speaking of which, what are we to call one another? Are we one of those formal couples who refer to one another as 'Mr.' and 'Mrs.,' or shall we be 'John' and 'Julia'?"

Pickett found himself on the horns of a dilemma. On the one hand, he did not think it at all proper for him to call the viscountess by her given name; on the other, to refer to her as "Mrs. Pickett" could only torment him with glimpses of what could never be.

"I think," he said after careful consideration, "that you married beneath your station and now, painfully aware of how far you have come down in the world, you insist upon being called by the honorific bestowed upon you by your first husband. That way, I may continue to address you as 'my lady.' "

"I see!" Lady Fieldhurst arched an eyebrow. "You are willing to traduce my character in order to avoid being made to feel uncomfortable. No, Mr. Pickett, I will not have it! I learned to call you 'John' when you were my footman in Yorkshire, and I am sure that, with practice, you will contrive to call me 'Julia' without choking on the word."

Pickett was spared the necessity of forming a reply by a shout from further down the beach. They had by this time rounded the spit of land cutting off the inn from view of the Kirkbride property, and Robert and Edward were waving their arms wildly.

"Here it is! Here it is!"

Pickett knew, of course, that there would be no physical

evidence of the woman's presence remaining on the beach; footprints or anything else of significance that might have been present at the time would have been long since washed away by the tide. Still, the site itself offered a few clues. Gazing up and down the beach in both directions, Pickett saw that anyone wishing to stage the scene would likely have had ample time to do so: to the north, the jutting spit of land hid the inn and its inhabitants from view; to the south, uninhabited beach stretched as far as the eye could see. Looking inland, he noted that only the brick chimneys of Ravenscroft Manor were visible over the cliff; no one at the house would have a view of the beach unless he (or she) perched on the roof. There remained only the sea itself, which kept its secrets.

"Do you remember how the woman was lying?" Pickett addressed the Bertram brothers. "Can you recall her position?"

"I can!" Edward piped up. "I'm the one who found her. She was lying like this." Without further ado, he flopped down onto the shingle, his head resting on his outstretched arm.

"That's not right, Ned," Harold told his brother. "It was her left arm that was stretched out, not her right. And her face was hidden, until I turned her over."

"And she didn't have a ridiculous grin on her face," Robert added, poking Edward in the ribs with the toe of his shoe.

Pickett looked at Lady Fieldhurst for confirmation. "Is Harold right?"

She closed her eyes, trying to picture the scene in her mind. "I think so. I do know that we couldn't see her face until he rolled her onto her back."

"You touched her, then?" he asked Harold. "How wet was she?"

"I beg your pardon?" Harold asked, bewildered.

"How wet was she? Was she drenched, or merely damp? Or was she completely dry?"

Harold's puzzled expression lifted. "Oh, you're wondering how long she may have been lying there, aren't you? Well, her hair was wet and full of sand, but it wasn't dripping. Her clothes were scarcely damp, and when I turned her over, I believe the ground beneath her was fairly dry."

"She must have been lying there for quite some time, then." Pickett frowned thoughtfully at the prostrate Edward. There was something not quite right about the picture the boy presented, something wholly unrelated to the ridiculous grin rightly pointed out by Robert.

He turned his attention back to the viscountess. "My lady, can you draw? Sketch, I mean?"

"A little. I could never draw hands or faces, though." She wrinkled her nose at the memory. "My governess always said the fingers looked like sausages."

"Hands and faces won't matter. But if you could provide me with a sketch of Miss Kirkbride's position as nearly as you can remember it, it might prove helpful. I could at least study it at my leisure."

"I shall begin work on it as soon as I return to my room," she promised.

Pickett looked out to sea, where the sun was beginning to dip below the watery horizon. Save for the trip to Yorkshire (which had occurred during the summer, when daylight lingered until past ten o'clock), he had never been north of London, and was surprised by how much earlier darkness fell so far north. "Speaking of which, we'd best turn back, if we don't wish to be benighted."

Robert and Edward made only token protests, which were easily assuaged with promises of a return to the shore the following morning. As Lady Fieldhurst had predicted, they were filled with self-importance at the prospect of assisting a Bow Street Runner, and thought it a great lark that they should address this interesting individual as "Uncle John."

For Harold's part, he was all eagerness to do whatever lay in his power to clear his ladylove's name—not unlike Pickett himself had been some six months earlier, when first confronted with the newly widowed Viscountess Fieldhurst. After one last, longing glance at the chimneys of Ravenscroft Manor just visible over the cliff, Harold turned to follow his brothers, who were by this time far down the beach.

Thus Pickett was left to escort his "wife" in blissful solitude. The temperature had dropped with the setting of the sun and the ocean breeze, which had been refreshingly brisk only half an hour earlier, was now quite chilly. Lady Fieldhurst shivered and moved instinctively nearer, tucking her hand more securely into the curve of his arm. Pickett, nothing loth, stopped and shrugged out of his brown serge coat.

"Here," he said, draping this hitherto unromantic garment over her shoulders. "You need this more than I do."

"Oh no, I couldn't," her ladyship protested. "The wind is so brisk, and you only in your shirtsleeves!"

"You would prefer everyone at the inn to think you married a man so careless of his wife's comfort?" Pickett chided. "Now who is traducing whose character?"

"Very well," Lady Fieldhurst laughingly conceded, tugging the front of his coat closed over her bosom. "But how ungentlemanly of you to throw my own words back in my teeth!"

"You knew I wasn't a gentleman when you 'married' me," he reminded her.

"Very true; in fact, it was a large part of your charm."

He took her arm, and together they started back up the beach, hindered considerably by her wind-whipped skirts tangling about their legs. By the time the lights of the inn came into view the sky was fully dark, yet Pickett was conscious of a pang of disappointment at having reached their destination so quickly. It occurred to him that he would not object if the case of the mysterious Miss Kirkbride were to take a very long time to solve.

CHAPTER 7

IN WHICH JOHN PICKETT TESTS HIS SEA LEGS AND FINDS THEM WANTING

The following morning, Pickett and Harold arose early and set out on foot for the village some half a mile beyond the inn. The trek, though not of long duration, was made tedious for Pickett due to the fact that he was obliged to listen to a catalog of Miss Kirkbride's virtues, which were apparently many.

"Oh, I can't begin to explain it!" said Harold after several abortive attempts. "From the moment I saw her lying there on the beach with her hair splayed out over the sand, it was just that—just that—"

" 'That I should love a bright particular star, and think to wed it, she is so above me,' " Pickett paraphrased wistfully.

"That's it!" exclaimed Harold, much struck. "That's it exactly! How did you know?"

"It's Shakespeare," Pickett said, then added cryptically, "he speaks for us all."

"Is that so? I've never thought much of those Elizabethan fellows before—they wore codpieces, you know—*codpieces*! But I see I shall have to pay more attention in the future."

Upon arriving in the village, they chose at random one tavern among several crowded up to the harbor, the better to provide for the liquid requirements of the many men who derived their living from fishing the waters of the Irish Sea. Once inside, Pickett stopped for a moment to let his eyes adjust to the shadowy interior after the brightness of the morning sun sparkling on the waves. As he had suspected, the tavern clearly

84

catered to the fisherfolk, as evidenced by the nets and sea glass adorning the walls, as well as the slate mounted behind the bar with the day's high and low tides written in chalk. The establishment was busy even at this early hour, its patronage being mostly made up of elderly fishermen who had yielded their places at sea to their juniors, whose manners and morals they now spent their days cheerfully bemoaning. One white-haired ancient scarcely looked up from his hands, which appeared to be employed in carving the hull of a tiny boat from the cork of a wine bottle. Four others glanced up only for a moment before resuming their game of cards.

"Good morning," Pickett said, addressing the burly man behind the bar. Suspecting that, as an outsider, he probably had captured the attention of every man in the place in spite of their apparent lack of interest, he launched into the tale that he, Lady Fieldhurst, and Harold had previously agreed upon. "I wonder if there is any man here who would be willing to take my nephew and me out for a pleasure jaunt on the water? Harold here has been offered a berth as a midshipman in His Majesty's Navy, but never having been at sea, he's not certain how well he would take to it."

Some half-dozen old-timers listened to this speech without expression. Just when Pickett decided he was going to be ignored by the lot of them, one rose and shot a stream of brown liquid from his mouth into a battered brass spittoon positioned beside his chair.

"In my day," he said at last, scowling at Harold, "a lad his age was set to work whether he'd a mind to it or no."

"Yes, well, I agree with you there," Pickett said, improvising rapidly, "but his mother would not hear of it, until the young scoundrel got himself sent down from school. For fighting," he added, slanting a loaded glance at Harold's fading bruises.

To his credit, Harold was quick to pick up his rôle in the

little drama. "You should see the other fellow," he put in with some satisfaction.

To Pickett's relief, this demonstration of mettle on Harold's part, far from earning their disapproval, actually served to elevate that young man in their estimation. "Aye, I'd sooner have a lad handy with his fists as some of these mealy-mouthed young'uns one sees these days," the fisherman conceded. "Happen he'd do well in Farmer George's navy, after all."

"Of course, we are prepared to offer compensation to any man with a vessel for hire."

Seeing the tide of public opinion turning in his favor, Pickett offered the price suggested by Lady Fieldhurst. This had seemed outrageously expensive to Pickett for a voyage lasting no longer than a couple of hours at the most, but the viscountess had insisted that a gentleman would not wish to appear niggardly, and so he had allowed himself to be guided by her. And she had apparently been quite correct, for the fisherman, with a gleam in his eye, noted that it was a fine day for sailing.

"Boyd's the name, Elliot Boyd," he said. "I'd be right pleased to hae the pair of you aboard the *Bonnie Prince Charlie.*"

He held out his hand, not to offer a handshake, but palm facing upward, inviting Pickett to pay in advance. Pickett ignored this gesture, knowing from experience that it was wisest to pay for services after they were rendered to one's satisfaction. One of the lessons he had learned at his father's knee, so to speak, involved offering to render, for a consideration, some small assistance to the ladies or gentlemen exiting Covent Garden Theatre, then to flee with one's ill-gotten gain without exerting oneself on behalf of one's patron at all. While Pickett had no doubt that both he and Harold could easily chase the elderly Boyd down, if it should come to that, he knew the wily old fisherman would certainly have other ways to fleece them, should he be inclined to take advantage of a pair of obvious landlubbers. So he made no attempt to reach for his coin purse yet, but turned to follow Boyd out of the tavern.

Halfway to the door, Pickett paused to admire the handiwork of the man carving the wine cork.

"You do good work," he told the man, who was affixing a tiny canvas sail to the mast of his miniature boat. "Do you ever sell them?"

"Aye, sometimes," came the not very enlightening reply.

"Harold has two young brothers who were bitterly disappointed at being left behind," Pickett told him. "How much for two of the boats?"

"A shilling each, and they'll be ready on your return," the man promised him.

"I'll give you a shilling for the pair upon my return," Pickett said, determined not to be taken for a greenhorn.

This offer was accepted (somewhat grudgingly, which assured Pickett that he had not fared too badly), and he and Harold accompanied Boyd out to the pier where the *Bonnie Prince Charlie* was tied up.

"Yessir, a fine day for sailing," Boyd observed.

He stepped aboard the boat with the ease of long experience, and offered his hand to steady his passengers as they boarded the bobbing craft. Then he deftly untied the knot in the thick rope tethering them to the pier. He lowered the sails, which hung limply from the spars, then picked up a pair of oars and held one out to Harold.

"Might as well learn a thing or two about seamanship," he told the boy. "We'll have to row a bit at first, until she catches the wind."

Harold took the oar from Boyd and set to with a will, rowing with such enthusiasm that the boat began to swing about in a sweeping arc.

"Best slow down, lad, or you'll be exhausted before we've

made it past the shallows," Boyd advised with a wink.

Grinning sheepishly back at the older man, Harold let up on the oars, and soon the sails caught the wind, the canvas flapping as the little boat picked up speed, bobbing and dipping as it crested the waves.

"I say!" Harold exclaimed. "I call this capital good fun! Don't you think so?" he asked Pickett, but received no answer. "Mr.— Uncle John?"

He looked back at Pickett, who sat clutching the gunwale with one hand and his belly with the other. "Capital," Pickett echoed with a marked lack of enthusiasm.

"With your permission, I thought we'd go 'round the headland to the south," Boyd said, turning the wheel.

As this was precisely what Pickett had had in mind, he nodded in agreement, thankful to be spared the necessity of speaking. Like Harold, he had never been to sea before. But while that eager young man seemed to be reveling in the experience, Pickett found that his stomach attempted a series of acrobatic moves every time they met a wave.

"Look, Uncle John!" Harold exclaimed, pointing out a building of grey stone on the shore adjacent to them. "There's the inn!"

Pickett nodded in acknowledgment, but found himself scanning the shore in spite of his wretchedness, looking at the inn and trying to determine which of its many windows belonged to Lady Fieldhurst.

In this manner they rounded the headland, Harold glorying in the feel of the salty wind in his hair while Pickett endured the ordeal in quiet misery. But he knew where his duty lay, and so as soon as he saw Ravenscroft Manor atop the cliff, he called to Boyd.

"At the inn there's been talk of a female found somewhere along the beach here."

Boyd nodded. "Aye, old Angus Kirkbride's lass. Quarreled with the old man years ago, and turned up on the shore there with no memory of who she was nor how she came to be there."

"Could she have fallen from a boat and washed ashore?" Pickett asked. He looked at the cliff. "I should have thought she would have been dashed to death upon the rocks."

"Aye, and so she would have been, if she'd come in with the tide. At high tide the waves wash right up to the cliff. See yon path climbing up the cliff to the big house? Can't use it when the tide is high, for the foot of the path is clean underwater."

Pickett remembered the slate in the tavern marking the high and low tides. Clearly an understanding of such things would be crucial to these men whose livelihood depended upon the sea. "And how was the tide that morning? Do you remember?"

"Aye, you'll find everyone on the coast follows the tides right keenly. The tide turned just before dawn that day. I remember it particularly, for my lass Bessie's husband—a good enough lad, though sadly lacking for common sense—was to have delivered a couple of halibut to Ravenscroft Manor that morning. But they weren't biting that day, and he was hard-pressed to catch the fish and get them up to the big house ere the tide reached the full. By the time he got there, the house was all at sixes and sevens with the young lady seemingly come back home. The long and short of it is, by the time he got back down the cliff, the path was cut off, and the boat he'd left on the beach was adrift with no one aboard her." He chuckled at the memory. "Aye, no common sense to speak of, but he's good to my Bessie, so if she's happy, I'm happy."

Pickett knew he had a few mental calculations to make, but he dared not appear to take more than a tourist's passing interest in the case, and in his present state his brain could not seem to hear him over his stomach's protests. Thankfully, Harold asked the questions Pickett couldn't convince his brain to form.

"How far apart do the tides come? That is, how long between high tide and low?"

"About six hours, or a little more," Boyd answered, having by this time recognized Harold as a kindred spirit. "We have two high and two low tides a day, although I believe that may be different in other parts of the world."

"Then the previous high tide would have been around midnight, and the next one would have come about noon," Harold deduced.

"Aye, or a little after."

"Why, she might have been lying there for hours! Only think, if no one had come along and found her, she might have been killed when the tide rose again," Harold continued. "Drowned, or dashed upon the rocks."

Boyd found nothing to argue with in this conclusion. "Aye, she was a right lucky lass."

Lucky, Pickett thought, or very thorough in her planning. But was it possible that a woman unaccustomed to the sea could have calculated the tides so accurately, or would even have known of the need to do so? Pickett had lived his entire life within a mile of the River Thames, into which the North Sea tidal waters flowed, but he was unfamiliar with most of the information that the old fisherman was imparting to the enthralled Harold.

"If she'd been lying there since midnight the night before, surely someone would have seen her," Pickett reasoned. "Someone in a fishing boat must have noticed her, even if no one had come walking along the beach."

"You might think so, but if her clothes were dark, she might have been hard to make out against the rocks, especially around dawn, when the fishing boats set sail." Boyd leaned over and spat into the sea. "Aye, it's a mystery."

"Look, Mr. Boyd," put in Harold, pointing toward a dark

shape in the distance that was breaking the surface of the water at irregular intervals. "What's that? Never mind, it's gone now—no, wait! There it is!"

"Aye, that's a whale, lad. This one's a bit closer to shore than usual, but they're a frequent sight out at sea. There's a spyglass in that sea chest, if you'd like to have a closer look."

Harold clambered over the various ropes and rigging littering the boat, dug in the sea chest, and soon lifted out his prize.

"I say!" he exclaimed, fixing it on the whale. "This is something like!"

"Seems to me you're a natural-born sailor, Master Harold," said Boyd, nodding his approval. "Pity I canna say the same for your uncle, there."

At that moment the boat lifted skyward on the crest of a large swell, then plunged downward. For a brief moment Pickett lost sight of the horizon and thereby his bearings. That one moment was all it took. He leaned over the gunwale and emptied his breakfast into the sea below.

While Pickett and Harold set out to sea (having weathered the storm that had broken over their heads the previous evening, when Robert and Edward discovered their elder brother was to have the pleasure of spending the morning aboard a boat in the company of a Bow Street Runner), Lady Fieldhurst applied herself to the task of providing Mr. Pickett with the sketch he had requested. Fortunately, she had had the foresight to bring a portable writing desk on her journey, thinking to lighten her exile by writing frequent long letters to her dear friend Emily, Lady Dunnington. Now, however, it appeared Lady Dunnington would have to wait, as more pressing concerns took priority. After dispatching the sullen Robert and Edward to the beach under the watchful eye of the innkeeper's daughter, Lady Fieldhurst shut herself up in her room with pencil and paper.

By the time the morning was far enough advanced to permit calling at Ravenscroft Manor, she had produced a draft that, she thought, did not utterly disgrace her as an artist. She closed this up inside the writing desk, resolving to present it to Mr. Pickett at the first opportunity, then changed into an elegant walking costume of the ubiquitous black bombazine. She was just reaching for her gloves and bonnet preparatory to setting out for the Manor when the door was flung open and Pickett staggered into the room.

"Oh, Mr. Pickett! I had just finished—" Her artwork was forgotten as she took in his unsteady gait and slightly greenish countenance. "Good heavens! What has happened to you?"

He gave her a queasy little smile. "I'm afraid Harold has lost all respect for me. It seems I'm not much of a sailor."

She tossed her bonnet and gloves on the room's only chair, Miss Kirkbride and her morning call forgotten. "And so you suffered from *mal de mer*. You poor man! Surely you did not have to walk all the way from the village in this condition! Come in and shut the door."

"No, I didn't have to walk," he said, obeying her behest, "for the greengrocer was making a delivery to Ravenscroft Manor, and Harold prevailed upon him to take us up in his—*bowl*!"

Correctly interpreting this urgent command, she snatched up the bowl from the washstand and thrust it into his arms only just in time, then led him to the edge of the bed, where he might sit down with the bowl upon his knees.

"I'm sorry to impose on you this way," he said, when he could speak again. "But there were people in the corridor, so I dared not be seen entering Mr. Colquhoun's room."

"No, indeed! You did quite right in coming here. Lie down, and you should feel better directly." Anticipating his objection, she added, "I am just going to pay a call on Miss Kirkbride, as you requested, so you shall have the room all to yourself."

He looked longingly at the pillow, then down at his feet. "I shouldn't—my boots—"

"Need I remind you, Mr. Pickett, that I was married for six years? I am unlikely to fall into a faint at the sight of a man's bare feet. I confess, I have never suffered from this particular malady, but I believe it is said to pass soon enough. A little rest and quiet is all that is required. You will be more comfortable with your coat off. Here, stand up so I may help you."

Suiting the word to the deed, she began stripping the slightly dampened coat from his shoulders. Too weak to protest, he submitted meekly to this treatment and withdrew his arms from the sleeves, then sank gratefully back down onto the bed.

"Be careful, my lady, there is something in the pockets," he cautioned as she draped the coat over the back of the chair.

She slid her hand into one of the pockets and withdrew two miniature boats carved from cork, each topped with a tiny sail of real canvas.

"I bought them from a fellow in the tavern," he said. Having removed his boots, he collapsed onto the pillow. "They're for Edward and Robert. Perhaps it will help to make up for the adventure they missed. You may tell them I would have been happy to surrender my place to them," he added with a ghost of a smile.

"You may tell them yourself, after you awaken." She placed the boats carefully on the small table beside the bed. "It was kind of you to think of them."

"Not them. You." His eyes were closed, and she thought his color was beginning to look slightly less green. "I told you I would try to make it up to you."

"Well then, it was kind of you to think of me," she said briskly. He could not have paid more than a couple of shillings for the two boats combined, thus there was no reason, no reason at all, for her to feel so very much affected by so very small a gesture.

She fetched the vial of lavender water from her travelling case and, shaking some of its contents onto a handkerchief, sat on the edge of the bed and bathed his brow, just as she had done Edward's when he had been ill in the carriage. He seemed to relax under her ministrations, and she felt a sudden urge to brush the brown curls back from his brow and press her lips to his forehead. It occurred to her that, while she had indeed been married for six years, it had been a very long time since she had had a man in her bed—and there was something profoundly unsettling about the sight of this particular man there.

Appalled at the direction of her thoughts, she raised herself quietly from the bed, so as not to disturb him, then picked up her gloves and bonnet.

"Sleep well, Mr. Pickett," she whispered, then left the room before she could say or do something she might later regret.

CHAPTER 8
IN WHICH LADY FIELDHURST
RECEIVES A WARNING

Upon reaching Ravenscroft Manor, Lady Fieldhurst was surprised to find the drawing room quite full of visitors, none of whom, thankfully, were previously known to her. Most were relations of the Kirkbride family, all presumably invited to the ball to be held in Miss Kirkbride's honor the following night. Lady Fieldhurst could not but wonder if any of them had their own misgivings as to the woman's identity; if this was the case, they—unlike Duncan Kirkbride—kept to themselves whatever doubts they might harbor. As Gavin Kirkbride introduced her to the rest of his uncle's guests, she identified a few notable exceptions to the family party. The first of these was Mr. Ferguson, the family's solicitor.

"Come from Edinburgh at Uncle's request," Gavin explained. "I believe you are putting up at the same inn—the Wild Rose, is it not?"

"It is, indeed," said Lady Fieldhurst, privately resolving to give Mr. Ferguson a wide berth if she should happen to see him at the inn.

"And here is another distinguished practitioner of the legal profession: Mr. Patrick Colquhoun, the magistrate who oversees London's Bow Street force." He lowered his voice. "Mr. Colquhoun has agreed to investigate our fair guest's unexpected appearance. If anyone can recognize an impostor, it is surely he."

"Oh," Lady Fieldhurst said faintly, offering her hand to a white-haired gentleman with keen blue eyes beneath bushy white brows. Mr. Pickett might assure her of the magistrate's trustworthiness, but she had no such confidence. "I—I'm very pleased to make your acquaintance, Mr. Colquhoun."

He bowed over her hand. "And I yours, Mrs.—Pickett, did you say? I believe we have a mutual acquaintance, ma'am."

"Do we?" She regarded the magistrate warily, but saw nothing in that canny individual's countenance beyond bland interest. Somehow she found his seeming indifference more disturbing than an outright accusation.

"We do indeed, my lady. But let us take a turn about the room while we discuss our mutual friend, and spare poor Mr. Gavin. There is nothing more tedious, you know, than to listen to others exchange reminiscences about a person one has never heard of."

With a nod in Gavin's direction, Mr. Colquhoun took her arm and steered her away. "I confess, I have wanted to meet you for some time—*Lady Fieldhurst.* You will have gathered, I trust, that the mutual acquaintance of whom I spoke is John Pickett."

"I did indeed, sir. Mr. Pickett has spoken of you often. He seems to think very highly of you."

Mr. Colquhoun paused before a large portrait of a younger Angus Kirkbride and, turning his back to the room, pretended to study it with great interest. "But not half so highly as he thinks of you, my lady. Therein lies the problem. I realize there is little you can do about the situation as it now stands. But I hope you will not take it amiss when I ask you, upon your return to London, to drop the acquaintance."

Lady Fieldhurst bristled at such plain speaking. "I understand, Mr. Colquhoun, that Mr. Pickett is answerable to you regarding his activities concerning Bow Street, but surely he may choose his friends to please himself! I fail to see how you should have any say in his personal life."

"Let us just say that there are—reasons—why I take a particular interest in Mr. Pickett's personal affairs."

"I should love to hear them." The words were as much a challenge as they were an invitation.

"As you wish." Mr. Colquhoun tore his gaze from the portrait and paced off a few more steps before stopping to inspect a stuffed and mounted pheasant, its wings spread as if in flight. "The duties of a magistrate are often as unpleasant as they are necessary. In one of my first cases, I ordered a man, a habitual ne'er-do-well, transported to Botany Bay for thievery. It was not until after I had pronounced this sentence that I learned the man had a son, a lad of fourteen, who was already an accomplished pickpocket. Sadly, in such cases the son usually follows the father's example, eventually ending up in Newgate or Botany Bay. In days not so long past, the worst cases ended at Tyburn Tree, where the criminal was hanged by the neck until dead."

Lady Fieldhurst shuddered. "A grisly fate, sir, and one I am sure you must deplore. But where does Mr. Pickett come into it?"

"The fourteen-year-old son's name," the magistrate continued, "was John."

Lady Fieldhurst caught her breath.

"My own father died when I was sixteen, so I know what it is like, to be left to fend for oneself at an early age," Mr. Colquhoun said. "In the hopes of rescuing the boy from a life of crime, I arranged for young John Pickett to be bound as an apprentice to a collier. For the next five years of his life, he hauled coal in exchange for room and board."

One of the other guests, an elderly gentleman in an old-fashioned frock coat and bagwig, approached them with purpose in his step, but Mr. Colquhoun fixed so quelling a stare upon him that the man turned away disappointed.

"Sir Henry MacDougall, local justice of the peace," the magistrate said. "Insufferable bore, and incompetent to boot. We can only hope he will take the hint and leave us alone. Now, where was I? Oh yes, young John Pickett hauling coal. A colossal waste of a fine mind, although I did not know it at the time. He made deliveries to the Bow Street Public Office occasionally, so I was able to follow his progress. At times, when I was in a particularly mellow mood, I would toss him a penny for his pains, and congratulate myself on my Christian charity."

This last was said with such bitterness that Lady Fieldhurst could almost find it in her heart to feel sorry for the magistrate. She dared not interrupt to say so, however, and he once again picked up the thread of his narrative.

"On one such occasion, he was left to cool his heels in the Bow Street Public Office while I wrote out a bank draft for payment. It seems that at some point in his career, our Mr. Pickett had been sent to school (possibly the only decent thing his father ever did for him) and as a result, read anything and everything he could get his hands on. Unfortunately, this was usually not much; the coal business, as you might guess, is not known for the richness of its literature."

"But his speech is not that of the sort of person you describe."

"Ah yes, his speech. It appears that John Pickett has a gift for mimicry—a talent that has served him well in cases involving the aristocracy. By the time we return to London two weeks hence, I have no doubt he will have acquired a fine Scots burr."

"How did he go from delivering coal to investigating crime?" asked Lady Fieldhurst, both fascinated and appalled by this previously unknown history of the young man even now lying fast asleep in her bed at the inn.

"I am coming to that. As it happens, on that particular occasion in Bow Street, there was an issue of *The Hue and Cry* left lying about by one of the other Runners."

"*The Hue and Cry*? I am not familiar with it."

"Nor would I expect you to be. It is a police gazette, published quarterly with information about wanted persons, unsolved crimes—that sort of thing. In any case, John Pickett was not familiar with it either, but that didn't stop him from picking it up to read while he waited on his payment. By the time I had finished writing out the bank draft, he had picked up on the one discrepancy the investigating Runner had missed, and deduced that Mrs. Cranston-Parks's emeralds had not been stolen by her lady's maid, but by Mrs. Cranston-Parks herself, who had fenced them to cover her own gambling debts." He chuckled at the memory. "He was quite right, too, which did not sit well with Mr. Foote, the Runner assigned to the case."

"What happened then?"

"To make a long story short, I met with the collier and bought John Pickett's contract out of my own pocket. I found a place for him on the foot patrol until he got his bearings, at which time he became a Runner. He was not yet twenty-four years old." He scowled at her beneath bushy white brows. "You ask by what right I should presume to choose Mr. Pickett's friends. I might answer that I bought him. If that is so, he is undoubtedly the best investment I ever made."

Lady Fieldhurst regarded the magistrate with a kindlier eye than she had done previously. "And yet I suspect your interest in him is less monetary than it is personal. You would appear to be very fond of him."

He nodded. "Too fond, at any rate, to bear with equanimity the sight of him being hurt for no greater cause than the stroking of your own vanity."

She could not have been more shocked if he had slapped her. "*Vanity?* And what, pray, do you know of my vanity?"

"Only that it would be a very odd female who, finding her name a byword amongst her own set, would not be gratified by the admiration of a personable young man, no matter how lowly his social status."

She stiffened. "Am I to understand, sir, that you believe me to be deliberately toying with Mr. Pickett's affections?"

"What else am I to think? Surely the most democratic of individuals could not suppose you to have a serious interest in securing his regard."

She took a step back, allowing her hand to drop from his arm lest he feel her trembling with rage. "I must confess, Mr. Colquhoun, I find your observations on our mutual friend as bewildering as they are contradictory," she said, controlling her voice with an effort. "On the one hand, you tell me what an exceptional young man he is, while on the other, you seem quite confident that he could not earn my admiration on his own merit."

"Oh, I've no doubt you are sincerely grateful for his efforts on your behalf following the murder of your husband—God knows you should be, for he risked his career for your sake!—but to an impressionable young man, the gratitude of a beautiful woman may be mistaken for something else entirely."

She was spared the necessity of answering (or perhaps robbed of the opportunity to do so) by the appearance of Gavin Kirkbride, who chose that moment to interrupt.

"Mrs. Pickett, have you met Sir Lachlan Malcolm and his wife, Lady Malcolm? They are my uncle and aunt, and are all agog to meet the lady who found Elspeth on the beach."

"No, Gavin, I haven't had the pleasure." She made the stiffest of curtsies to the magistrate. "If you will excuse me, Mr. Colquhoun?"

"I trust Mr. Colquhoun did not bring upsetting news regarding your mutual acquaintance," Gavin said as they crossed the room together. "You look perturbed."

"Mr. Colquhoun's news was unsettling, but nothing more,"

Lady Fieldhurst assured him, and tried hard to believe it herself. "I am sure he is a loyal friend, but I believe his concerns to be groundless."

Whatever Gavin might have said to this assertion was interrupted by a disturbance at the drawing room door. Turning toward the sounds of the commotion, Lady Fieldhurst saw a rough-looking man in homespun attempting to enter the drawing room in spite of the best efforts of the butler and two footmen to prevent him.

"Where is she?" the interloper demanded loudly. "Where is Elspeth? I must see her!"

Lady Fieldhurst instinctively turned toward Miss Kirkbride, along with everyone else in the room, and saw that Elspeth had turned quite pale.

"Elspeth!" The newcomer shook off the footmen holding his arms as easily as he might have swatted away a fly. "I heard you were back."

"Who is *that*?" the viscountess asked, looking back at the man whose unorthodox arrival had clearly cut up Miss Kirkbride's peace.

"Oh, just one of the local rowdies," Gavin muttered. "He used to be employed in our stables, and fancies himself as having a grudge against the family. Depend upon it, Duncan will show him the door quickly enough."

As he had predicted, Duncan strode across the room and seized the fellow by his collar. To Lady Fieldhurst's surprise, Miss Kirkbride left her father's side and joined the two men, placing a staying hand on Duncan's arm. Although the viscountess was not near enough to hear their words, Elspeth was apparently intervening on behalf of the trespasser, for Duncan released his grasp (rather reluctantly, Lady Fieldhurst thought) and the three exited the drawing room together. Two of them returned a scant five minutes later, and although Miss Kirkbride's color was high and Duncan's scowl was even more pronounced than usual, the uninvited guest was no longer with them. Whatever Elspeth had said to him had apparently persuaded him to leave of his own volition.

"Well, that will give the gossips something to stew over with their tea tomorrow," Gavin remarked, dismissing the bizarre incident with a careless wave of his hand. "If you will follow me, my lady, I will present you to my aunt and uncle."

She spent the next quarter-hour curtsying and nodding to various friends and relations of the Kirkbride family, remembering with an effort that since she was masquerading as a mere "Mrs.," she must be presented to even the minor gentry whereas they, as her social inferiors, would have been presented to the Viscountess Fieldhurst. But even as she mouthed the niceties that were *de rigueur* in polite society, her brain was awhirl. Who was the strange man who had interrupted the gathering, and what was his connection to Elspeth Kirkbride? And then, quite aside from the Kirkbrides (and far more disturbing to her mind), there was Mr. Colquhoun's accusation to be considered.

However much Mr. Pickett might respect the magistrate's judgment, Mr. Colquhoun was, at least in this case, quite mistaken. To be sure, an unlikely friendship had sprung up between the widowed viscountess and the Bow Street Runner, first out of gratitude on her part and, yes, perhaps admiration on his. That friendship, once begun, had been strengthened by their shared experiences in Yorkshire. But to suggest that she would deliberately lead him on was as offensive as it was wrongheaded. They were both well aware of the differences in their respective stations and, with the exception of one kiss born of necessity, had no intention of, nor even any interest in, going beyond the bounds of what Society dictated was proper. Indeed, so careful was Mr. Pickett of the gulf between them that he could not even bring himself to speak her name! To suggest that he had succumbed to her fatal charm (if such charm she possessed) was absurd.

"What do you think, Mrs. Pickett?"

Abruptly recalled to her surroundings, Lady Fieldhurst realized that one of the numerous Kirkbride relations, a buxom matron in dark green satin, had asked her a question and was awaiting a response. While she floundered for a noncommittal answer, Gavin stepped into the breach.

"I believe we can expect the fair weather to hold for another week, Lady Malcolm," he said. "What a shame it would be if Elspeth's homecoming ball were to be spoiled by rain or, worse, an early snow."

"How true!" Lady Fieldhurst addressed herself to the matron, who looked rather affronted by her lack of attention. "You must forgive me for my momentary speechlessness, my lady. The idea of Miss Kirkbride's festivities being spoiled is too terrible to contemplate."

This last was said with a smile, which had the happy result of assuaging the lady's sense of ill-usage. "Indeed, it would be quite shocking if anything were to cut up Angus's peace, now that he has found peace at last." Lowering her voice to a conspiratorial whisper, the matron leaned nearer, setting the ostrich plumes in her turban bobbing. "In those first dark days he was quite mad with grief, you know. There were times when we feared for his wits."

The magistrate's accusation was temporarily forgotten as Lady Fieldhurst remembered the original purpose for her call. She glanced at Gavin, and found that his attention had been claimed by Mr. Ferguson, the family's solicitor. She was unlikely to find a better opportunity, or a more obliging source of information. She turned back to the lady in the green turban.

"I have not known the family for long, Lady Malcolm, but I confess, I thought it odd that such a fond father and daughter had ever been estranged." In case the lady needed further encouragement, she added, "I can't imagine what must have occurred to cause such a rift."

"A sad state of affairs, to be sure, and so unnecessary." Lady Malcolm shook her head with much fluttering of plumes. "Angus hoped his daughter would marry one of her cousins, to keep the estate in the Kirkbride family, you know, for Elspeth is actually his step-daughter."

"Indeed?" Lady Fieldhurst raised her eyebrows invitingly, and Lady Malcolm did not disappoint her. "Oh, yes! Elspeth was scarcely more than a babe when Angus married her mother, and when his wife died only a few years later, he raised the child as his own. And to his credit, no father could have loved the child of his own flesh any more. How he doted on the girl! But Elspeth was ever headstrong, and scarcely seventeen years old. She refused to submit to his plans for her future."

"And her cousins? Surely Mr. Kirkbride's plans affected them, too. What were their feelings on the matter?"

"Oh, Duncan was quite willing, even eager, to marry her. Poor Duncan has never had a feather to fly with. His father, besides being a younger son, married a vicar's daughter—a sweet girl, mind you, but not a penny to bless herself with. Gavin, on the other hand, was left a tidy sum by his mother, or so I'm told. He keeps a house in London, in any case, and *that* takes plenty of brass, as they say. In short, Gavin had no need to wed, and apparently no partiality for Miss Kirkbride's company. No, if Angus's plan was to succeed, Duncan must be the one to marry Elspeth."

Lady Fieldhurst, picturing with some difficulty Duncan Kirkbride, even a much younger Duncan Kirkbride, in the rôle of devoted suitor to a girl of seventeen, found her sympathies wholly aligned with Miss Kirkbride. "But she was so young! Surely there was no need for such haste. Given time, the situation might have resolved itself."

"One might have thought so, but then, one had reckoned without the Kirkbride stubbornness. In short, Mrs. Pickett, Elspeth was discovered *in flagrante delicto* with—"

"This will not do, Aunt," interrupted Duncan Kirkbride, regarding Lady Fieldhurst with a bared-teeth expression that might have been a smile, but that somehow put her in mind of a wolf. "I will not allow you to monopolize our fair guest this way. Tell me, Mrs. Pickett, have you seen the cliffside garden? It is widely admired."

Although an avid cultivator of roses, Lady Fieldhurst had little interest in the garden at the moment, and even less desire to explore the side of a cliff with Duncan Kirkbride as her escort. Still, courtesy demanded that she allow him to lead her through the French windows and onto the landscaped terrace that sloped toward the cliff's edge. He stopped before some shrub Lady Fieldhurst could not identify, and ran his fingers through its autumnal foliage.

"Now what, I wonder, can my Aunt Malcolm have been saying to hold you so enthralled?" Duncan wondered aloud.

Although Duncan did not appear to expect an answer, Lady Fieldhurst felt compelled to offer some explanation. "We were speaking of your cousin, Miss Kirkbride. She was merely telling me—"

He raised a hand to silence her. "No, don't tell me, let me guess. My aunt is an incorrigible gossip, and I have no doubt she was eager to impart the circumstances that led to my uncle's and cousin's estrangement." He made a swift, savage motion with his arm, and a branch broke from the stem with a flurry of yellow leaves. "Did she also tell you that my Cousin Elspeth preferred an illicit tumble in the hay with a stable hand to an honorable marriage with me?"

CHAPTER 9

IN WHICH LADY FIELDHURST'S PEACE IS QUITE CUT UP

"As you can imagine, I hardly knew where to look when he said *that,*" recalled Lady Fieldhurst sometime later, when she recounted this scene to Mr. Pickett in the privacy of her bedchamber at the inn. In fact, she hardly knew where to look now, discussing so intimate a subject with a man still flushed and disheveled from sleep. His color was much improved, but he was clad only in shirtsleeves and breeches, and his hair had come loose from its queue and now tumbled to his shoulders in unruly brown waves. Even his bare feet, which she had assured him held no power to move her, now suggested an alarming degree of intimacy in the light of the magistrate's accusations.

But Mr. Pickett's comportment seemed to give the lie to Mr. Colquhoun's claims, for there was nothing the least lover-like in the Bow Street Runner's demeanour. Seated in the room's only straight chair while her ladyship perched on the edge of the rumpled bed, he listened to her tale without interruption, pausing occasionally to make a notation in the small notebook balanced on his knee.

"Duncan Kirkbride offered no further details?" he asked, looking up from the notebook.

"No, indeed!" The viscountess shook her head. "In fact, he turned on his heel and left me abandoned and alone in the garden. I should not have had a chance to press him for details, even if I'd had the audacity. It was shockingly rude on his part, but I confess, I was not sorry to see him go. After all, what reply does one make to such a revelation?"

Pickett, deep in thought, offered no suggestions. "I wonder how I might go about finding this stable hand?"

"I believe," said Lady Fieldhurst slowly, "that I saw him just this afternoon. There was an interruption, a man demanding to see Elspeth. Gavin said he used to work in the family's stables, and fancied himself to have a grudge against the Kirkbrides. Why do you want him? What are you thinking?"

"I'm thinking there are few people more qualified to recognize an impostor than a former lover."

"I see! You are thinking this stable hand might be able to identify Miss Kirkbride by something only known to someone intimately acquainted with her, such as a telltale birthmark on her—er, her—" Finding herself in deep waters, Lady Fieldhurst lapsed into embarrassed silence.

Pickett considered this scenario with a serious expression belied by a twinkle in his brown eyes. "An interesting possibility, although we might have difficulty persuading the lady to disrobe for such an examination. No, my lady, I was thinking of something less dramatic. It seems to me that many of the things Miss Kirkbride has 'remembered' also would have been known by any number of others: her cousins, her father, even the servants might have known these things and tutored her, if they were inclined to perpetrate a hoax. But lovers, surely, must have secrets known only to one another."

Lady Fieldhurst was annoyed to feel her cheeks growing warm, all the more so because there was nothing in Mr. Pickett's words to provoke her blushes. They were not lovers, after all, nor had they any secrets of an intimate nature. Surely Mr. Colquhoun must be mistaken in believing his protégé to have an unrequited passion for her! Else how could they sit here, having been thrown together in the most awkward of circumstances, two reasonable adults dispassionately debating the love affairs of others with nary so much as a blush between them? Well, scarcely a blush, anyway, amended her ladyship, resisting the urge to open the window and admit the cool evening air into a room grown suddenly warm. It was as if that midnight embrace in Yorkshire had never taken place at all. Indeed, she had all but forgotten it, and she supposed he must have done so as well. And yet as he sat scribbling in his notebook, her gaze dropped to his mouth and she remembered as if it had been only yesterday the feel of his lips on hers, and wondered if he ever thought of it . . .

He looked up abruptly. "Do you think you could find out?"

She started guiltily. "I—I beg your pardon?"

"Do you think you could find out how the stable hand might be reached? Where he lives, or where he is currently employed?"

"I—I suppose so," she said, dragging her attention back to the matter at hand. "Although it would be very odd if Mr. Kirkbride were to cast off his daughter and yet remain in contact with her paramour."

He grimaced at the prospect of so abrupt an end to such a promising lead. "True. But the stable hand has obviously kept up with the Kirkbrides over the years, and since he's apparently the sort who wouldn't hesitate to force himself on them if need be, it's always possible that the Kirkbrides have kept a weather eye out for him as well. Perhaps you could find out what became of him, in any case."

"I shall try." Abandoning a losing battle, Lady Fieldhurst rose and crossed the room to throw open the casement, then fetched her portable writing desk from the wardrobe. "Before I forget, here is the sketch you requested."

She opened the hinged lid, drew out the single sheet of paper, and handed it to him. He studied it for a long moment.

"Hmm." He tapped the corner of the sheet with the end of his pencil. "This is very interesting."

"Is it?" the viscountess asked eagerly, far more gratified than the occasion warranted. "What does it tell you?"

"It tells me," he said with great deliberation, "that Miss Kirkbride's fingers bear a marked resemblance to the sausages I had for breakfast this morning."

Lady Fieldhurst tried to be offended, and failed. "Well, I did warn you," she retorted, laughing.

"In all seriousness, my lady, this is very good. God knows I am no connoisseur, but I can almost see her in my mind—" He looked up at her abruptly. "Tell me, my lady, what color is Miss Kirkbride's hair? Is she fair?"

"No, she is dark, like the rest of the family. Why do you ask?"

He gave his head a shake, as if trying to banish an image. "No reason. It was—nothing."

"It is not easy to convey color with only charcoal," Lady Fieldhurst said apologetically, feeling she had somehow failed him. "I could try to do a watercolor, but I haven't any paints."

"You're very kind, my lady, but that won't be necessary." He looked down at the sketch again. "It just seemed familiar somehow, as if I had witnessed the scene myself. Impossible, I know."

"It was probably that Edward's pose was so very like," the viscountess suggested with a mischievous smile.

"No doubt that was it." His answering smile quickly faded. "I wish I could at least *see* the people I'm supposed to be investigating. In the absence of first-hand observation, my mind supplies images that may have nothing in common with the originals. When I looked at your sketch, I could have sworn Miss Kirkbride would be blonde."

Lady Fieldhurst pondered this problem for a long moment. "There might be a way," she said slowly. "Mr. Kirkbride is hosting a ball tomorrow night to celebrate his daughter's return. Harold and I have been invited, as has your Mr. Colquhoun."

This suggestion found no favor with Mr. Pickett. "Unless it is to be a costume ball, I fail to see how—"

"No, no, hear me out! Although I would give much to see you don fancy dress in the line of duty—I suspect you would make a very dashing cavalier, or perhaps a medieval knight—I regret to say it is not a costume ball. Still, there are French windows overlooking the terrace, and a high boxwood hedge from which you might watch the festivities unobserved."

Pickett regarded her with a skeptical eye. "And I suppose Mr. Kirkbride's butler will usher me onto the terrace himself, and install me in the place that offers the best view for spying undetected."

"No, but you might easily reach the terrace yourself by way of the path that runs up the cliff from the beach. You will be in no danger of falling," she assured him quickly, anticipating his next objection, "for the moon is at the full, and the path should be quite visible in the moonlight."

"And how am I to know who I am spying upon? You forget, I have never seen any of the parties involved. I wouldn't know Miss Kirkbride from Queen Charlotte."

"As Queen Charlotte will not be in attendance, her identity need not concern you," retorted Lady Fieldhurst. "The ball begins at nine o'clock. If you will give me an hour to say all that is proper to the Kirkbrides and their guests, I shall slip away and join you for a few minutes, just long enough to point out the principal players."

He frowned. "Surely your presence would be missed, my lady." He added in a curiously flat voice, "Once the dancing starts, I am sure you will be in great demand as a partner."

"You forget, Mr. Pickett, that I am in mourning," she reminded him. "No one will expect me to dance—indeed, they would be very much shocked if I were to do so! In fact, you will be rescuing me from languishing against the wall with the dowagers. I should stand in your debt."

He tapped his pencil against the notebook as he considered the matter. "It might work," he said at last. "I shall have to clear it with Mr. Colquhoun, of course, but I think it might work."

He rose from his chair and began to gather his discarded clothing, presumably to go in search of the magistrate.

"Excellent! I shall meet you on the terrace at ten o'clock, then. If you wish, I shall bring you a plate of refreshments and a glass of champagne."

"You are very kind, my lady, but you'd best leave off the champagne."

"Are you not allowed to imbibe while on duty, then?"

He regarded her with a rueful smile. "No, my lady, but I might develop a taste for things above my touch, and that would never do."

Feeling her face grow suddenly warm, Lady Fieldhurst moved to open the window, and realized it was already open. "Things," he had said. Not "something," but "things," in the plural. To what else might he have been referring? Could it possibly be herself? If that was indeed what he was implying, it would appear Mr. Colquhoun might have been nearer to the truth than she had cared to admit.

And the worst of it was that she hardly knew whether to be sorry or glad.

"Not 'my lady,' but 'Julia,' " she scolded, hating the unsteadiness in her voice. "If I were really your wife, you wouldn't call me 'my lady'!"

"No," he said, his expression unreadable. "If you were really my wife, I would call you *my* lady."

Oh, dear. It appeared that Mr. Colquhoun might have been wide of the mark after all. For as she watched Mr. Pickett tying back his hair with its crumpled black ribbon, it occurred to her to wonder precisely who was toying with whom.

CHAPTER 10
IN WHICH JOHN PICKETT MAKES A SURPRISING DISCOVERY

On the following evening, Lady Fieldhurst arrayed herself in the black satin gown she had worn to Theatre Royal in Drury Lane on the night that had led to her banishment to Scotland. While this garment's short train made it more suitable for dinner or the theatre than for a ball, she was, as she had informed Mr. Pickett, prohibited from dancing in any case. It was one of the more chafing aspects of being obliged to mourn a husband whose absence provoked only relief and a bewildering sense of freedom. Once, in her mad youth, she had loved to dance, until she had quite unexpectedly captured the interest of the Viscount Fieldhurst, and innocent pleasure had soon given way to awe and a dread of displeasing. Sometimes those days seemed so far away it was as if they had happened to another person, a young girl who no longer existed.

Banishing these melancholy thoughts, she summoned the innkeeper's daughter to dress her hair. The girl had an unexpected talent with curling tongs, and by the time she finished her work and stepped back to allow Lady Fieldhurst to examine the results in the small looking-glass over the wash stand, her ladyship's spirits were quite lifted. Her unhappy marriage was in the past, and however uncertain her future might be, for the moment she was still young and attractive, and her unlikely partnership with Mr. Pickett gave her a sense of purpose she had never until quite recently realized that she lacked.

When a knock sounded on the door, she felt a pleasant *frisson* of anticipation, which evaporated when the innkeeper's daughter opened the door to reveal Harold standing there holding a slightly rumpled cravat.

"I can't get the dashed thing tied," he grumbled, giving poor Betsy nothing more than a distracted nod as that damsel curtsied and took herself blushing and giggling from the room. "I never thought I would miss having old Harvey to valet for me! He's a sour old stick-in-the-mud, but by Jove, he can turn out a Waterfall or even an Oriental in style."

"But what about the cravat you wore this morning, or yesterday, or the day before?" Lady Fieldhurst pointed out. "You contrived to tie them all by yourself."

"Those old things?" Harold gave a snort of derision. "Why, those were nothing but a *cravate à la Colin*! They were acceptable for day wear, but for a ball a fellow wants something with a bit more dash."

The late Lord Fieldhurst had refused to let anyone, valet or wife, disturb him while he tied his own cravat, so Lady Fieldhurst's knowledge of men's neckwear was for all practical purposes nonexistent. "I'm afraid I can't help you," she told him. "Perhaps you should go next door and see if Mr. Pickett can offer some assistance."

This suggestion found no favor with Harold. "Mr. Pickett? Why, his cravat is hardly more than an overhand knot!"

Lady Fieldhurst frowned. "It is true that Mr. Pickett does not aspire to the heights of fashion—I daresay he lacks the funds to follow such a pursuit, even had he the inclination—but his appearance is never less than pleasing." Seeing Harold was not convinced, she added, "It is only a country ball, so anything as elaborate as an Oriental would only make you appear gauche."

"Perhaps that magistrate, Mr. Colquhoun, could help," Harold said, brightening at his own stroke of brilliance. "I shall go ask him at once!"

In the light of Mr. Colquhoun's disapproval, Lady Fieldhurst was extremely reluctant to stand in the magistrate's debt any more than was absolutely necessary, but since she could think of no other suggestion that might find favor in Harold's eyes, she had no alternative but to watch as he left the room, determined to put this plan into action.

Apparently Mr. Colquhoun did not disappoint, for when Lady Fieldhurst descended the stairs some quarter-hour later, she found Harold awaiting her there, his cravat tied in a tasteful and age-appropriate *Sentimentale* knot, which showed only the faintest of creases from his earlier attempts.

"Very dashing," she said, smiling her approval. "I hope you remembered to thank the magistrate for his assistance."

"Oh, yes," Harold assured her. "In fact, we have something else to thank him for, as well. He has procured the innkeeper's trap to convey the three of us to the ball. It isn't a natty rig by any means, but it's better than having to go on foot."

Lady Fieldhurst winced at the idea of being further beholden to Mr. Pickett's disapproving mentor, but she was practical enough to admit that accepting Mr. Colquhoun's generosity was better by far than trudging along the road—or, worse, the beach—with her train thrown over her arm. She asked Harold if he had conveyed their thanks to Mr. Colquhoun, but received no answer; that young man's mind had already moved on to more pressing concerns.

"Do you think Miss Kirkbride would be willing to dance with me?" he asked in an off-hand manner that did not deceive the viscountess for a moment.

"I think it very likely." She knew, as Harold did not, that as the guest of honor Miss Kirkbride would be expected to partner as many of her male guests as possible. The only trick would be seeing to it that Harold did not mistake Miss Kirkbride's good manners for encouragement to sit in her pocket all the evening. "But you must remember to seek out other partners as well, you know. It is not at all the thing to dangle after one lady to the exclusion of all others."

"In that case, I hope you will do me the honor, my lady," Harold replied, bowing deeply from the waist with exaggerated gallantry.

Lady Fieldhurst laughed and sank into a deep curtsy. "You are too kind, Mr. Bertram. But I must remind you that I am in mourning, and may not join in the dancing without being thought shockingly forward."

"No dancing? But what will you do instead?"

She shrugged. "I daresay I shall sit against the wall with the dowagers."

"I say, that seems deuced unfair," Harold said with some chagrin. "But if you won't be dancing, then—then I shan't either." This declaration was accompanied by an expression of such noble self-sacrifice that she was hard-pressed to keep a straight face.

"Nonsense! Frederick was only a cousin to you, and not even a close one at that. Besides," she added, seeing he was not convinced, "there are always more ladies than gentlemen at a ball, you know."

"Really?" asked Harold, much struck.

"Oh yes! It is the bane of hostesses everywhere. An eligible gentleman will be expected to assist his hostess by partnering as many ladies as possible, not devote himself to his widowed 'aunt.' "

Harold seemed happy to accept this reasoning, for which Lady Fieldhurst was grateful; she had no desire to keep her terrace rendezvous with Mr. Pickett with Harold tied to her apron strings. And if a little voice demanded to know why Harold's presence at this tryst would be so very undesirable, it was easily silenced with the argument that the fewer people congregated on the terrace the better, as they would be less likely to garner unwanted attention.

As Lady Fieldhurst had predicted, the first hour of the ball kept her far too busy to seek out Mr. Pickett even had she attempted to do so. She was obliged first to say all that was proper to her host, Mr. Angus Kirkbride, then inquire into the health of the guest of honor. Miss Kirkbride, Julia was forced to own, was in exceptional looks, and if her gown was a bit old-fashioned (unearthed from among her mother's things, said Miss Kirkbride, she not having had an opportunity to have anything new made up for the occasion), this circumstance only added to her mystique. Mr. Duncan Kirkbride bowed low over Julia's hand and rather curtly expressed his pleasure at seeing her again, then took himself off to lead out a very young lady in pink satin for the opening set.

"What a pretty girl," Lady Fieldhurst observed as she answered Mr. Gavin's bow with a curtsy. "Who, pray, is Duncan's fair partner?"

"You must be thinking of Miss McFarland," Gavin said, following her gaze. "We are expecting an interesting announcement there any day."

"Indeed? But she seems so much younger than he." Not to mention the fact that the poor girl looked terrified of her formidable suitor. "He must be almost twenty years her senior. Can he truly be happy with such a young lady, or she with him?"

"I see you are a romantic, Mrs. Pickett," observed Gavin wryly. "You must have made a love match for yourself, and now you believe everyone seeks a marriage based on the tender passion. But there are those who haven't the luxury of marrying to please themselves. For them there are other, more pressing concerns."

Indeed there were, such as wealth and land and the begetting of heirs. But Lady Fieldhurst had no intention of carrying on a conversation in which she felt herself to be on very shaky ground. "If we are to speak of pressing concerns, I fear I am keeping you from your duties as host. I must not keep you here talking to me when you should be securing a partner for the Scottish reel."

Gavin was quick to demur, but Lady Fieldhurst insisted upon her willingness, nay, eagerness, to observe the dancing from one of the chairs positioned against the walls. For the next half-hour, she sat amongst the dowagers, tapping her foot in time to the music while she watched the clock and counted the moments until she could seek out Mr. Pickett on the terrace. At length she saw Duncan heading in her direction, having surrendered Miss McFarland to Harold for the next set. Driven as much by boredom as by the desire to assist Mr. Pickett in his investigations, she rose from her chair and contrived to intercept the surliest of the Kirkbride cousins as he crossed the room.

"Oh Duncan, you are just the person I need!" she trilled brightly. "Mrs. Murray has been singing the praises of your uncle's champagne. Can you tell me where I might find a glass?"

Thus cornered, Duncan Kirkbride had no choice but to play the gallant. "Not at all, my lady," he said, baring his teeth in what she supposed must pass for a smile. "You must allow me to fetch you a glass."

She thanked him profusely, and soon he returned bearing two flutes. She accepted one and took a sip.

"Ah! Mrs. Murray was not wrong." Before he could make his excuses and abandon her to the dowagers, she laid her hand on his arm and leaned closer, lowering her voice to a conspiratorial whisper. "I do hope we will not have another visit from that strange man who burst in yesterday. I must say, I thought you handled the situation very well—with Miss Kirkbride's assistance, of course."

"Of course," he agreed sardonically.

"Gavin said the fellow was once employed in your stables. I was never more shocked! I could not help wondering if he was perhaps the person with whom Elspeth—the person to whom you referred during our conversation yesterday."

Duncan tipped up his champagne glass and drained it in a single gulp. "Aye, it was he."

"It must have been most difficult for you, seeing the pair of them together again. At least—" She knew she had to be careful and not overplay her hand. "—At least I suppose it would have been, if you had truly loved her."

" 'If'?" Duncan gave a short, humorless laugh. "I shall love Elspeth until I die."

Lady Fieldhurst almost choked on her champagne. "But—forgive me, but I was under the impression that you had an understanding with Miss McFarland."

"There comes a time in a man's life, my lady, when he tires of pining for things he can't have."

Duncan raised his glass, and seemed surprised to find it empty. Lady Fieldhurst wished she had the means to refill it; the champagne seemed to have the happy effect of loosening his tongue.

"Then you were not courting Miss Kirkbride at your uncle's behest all those years ago?"

"I see the fell hand of my busy Aunt Malcolm at work," he said dryly.

Lady Fieldhurst determinedly held her tongue, hoping Duncan would feel compelled to fill the silence. He did not disappoint her.

"But I can see how my aunt might have come to such a conclusion. She remembers me in my younger days when, like so many very young men, I wanted only to escape the home I had known all my life. I could hardly wait to go to school, to see parts of the world I had only read about." He sighed, remembering. "Within six months, I wanted nothing more than to return. The years that followed were the worst of my life. I felt as if I had been exiled from all I had ever known and loved."

"But your education was eventually complete, and you were able to come back home."

"Aye, and I could not post back to Scotland soon enough! As soon as I passed through the front gates, it was as if I had never left. The house, the land, the sea beyond—everything was just the same." He frowned thoughtfully. "No, not quite everything. When I left, Elspeth had been a hoyden with torn stockings and uncombed hair. I returned to find her grown into a beautiful and desirable young woman, a woman who embodied everything I loved and thought I had lost. Is it any wonder I fell head over ears?"

"Your uncle must have been pleased," Lady Fieldhurst observed.

Again that bitter laugh. "If my uncle had refrained from meddling, he might have had his dearest wish! I believe Elspeth might have come to care for me—nay, I believe she *did* care for me, until Uncle Angus announced his intention of seeing her wed to either me or Gavin. Gavin had always been the smarter one, the richer one, the more dashing one, but Elspeth seemed to prefer me. I could hardly believe my own luck."

The viscountess's eyebrows rose. "Forgive me, but I was under the impression that you and Gavin had grown up almost as brothers."

"Aye, but even brothers can be rivals as well as friends. It wasn't to Gavin that I lost her in the end, though. Elspeth leapt to the conclusion that I had been courting her for the sake of her father's fortune, and nothing I could do or say could convince her otherwise. I believe you can guess what happened next."

"The stable hand," murmured the viscountess.

"She was found in a compromising situation with one of the stable hands—a lad, moreover, with Kirkbride blood in his veins, wrong side of the blanket. I remember it as if it were yesterday: Elspeth standing there with hay in her hair and her clothes in disarray, telling Uncle Angus that if she must needs marry a cousin, Neil would do as well as any other. At that moment I didn't know who I hated the most, young Neil or Elspeth. To this day, I don't know if she had feelings for the lad, or if she simply wanted to strike out in the way that would cause the most pain." He stared down at his empty glass as if he had hoped to find answers there. "And then to have her wash ashore the way she did, ripping the scab off a wound still raw after fifteen years—I wish to God she had never returned!"

"You are satisfied, then, that she is truly your cousin?"

"Aye, I'm satisfied, all right!" he said tartly. "Elspeth always had a rare gift for throwing the household into turmoil. It seems some things never change."

"But why Neil? Why not Gavin?"

Duncan shook his head. "Elspeth wasn't content with ripping my heart out; she wanted to wound her father as well. Gavin never would have suited her purposes, for Uncle Angus would have been just as pleased had she married him. But there was never a possibility of marriage with Gavin in any case; he had hopes of marrying a young lady he'd met in England. He was always more English than Scots, my cousin Gavin. His father held a seat in Parliament, and Gavin spent his school holidays in London."

"I gather his suit did not prosper, else he would not still be a bachelor," she observed.

"Nay, it prospered, all right. His wife died in childbirth, and the babe with her."

Lady Fieldhurst blinked, taken aback by this revelation. Certainly no outside observer would guess that Gavin's urbane manner concealed the tragic loss of a wife and child. "I see. Your family has known more than its share of tragedy."

Duncan neither agreed nor disagreed, but muttered something about having to see to his uncle's other guests and took himself off. It was just as well, thought the viscountess, as it now lacked only five minutes until ten o'clock.

Instead of returning to her chair against the wall, she made up a plate of lobster patties and rout cakes from the spread in the refreshment room. On a sudden impulse, she snagged a flute of champagne from the tray of a passing servant before moving inconspicuously along the wall in the direction of the French windows. Then, in the confusion afforded by the end of the set and the changing of partners, she slipped out onto the terrace.

After the brilliant candlelight of the ball, the darkness of the terrace rendered her temporarily blind. As her eyes adjusted, however, she began to make out the silver trail of moonlight glinting on the sea below and, nearer, the boxwood hedge she had described to Mr. Pickett.

"Hsst! Over here!"

Mr. Pickett's voice came from somewhere in the blackness to the right of the French windows. Lady Fieldhurst took a few cautious steps in that direction, and as she moved out of the bright rectangle of light cast onto the paving stones by the candlelight within, the darkness resolved itself into shapes—the great hedge here, a piece of statuary there, and beyond that, in the gap between the vegetation and the house, a tall young man with his arm held out to her.

"I hope I haven't kept you waiting," she said, moving into the shadows. "I have been having the most enlightening conversation with Duncan Kirkbride! I trust you had no difficulty navigating the cliff path in the dark?"

"Not coming up, but it's getting back down that will be the challenge. I hear the first step is a thumper."

"I hadn't thought of that," Lady Fieldhurst confessed, guilt-ridden. "Should I have smuggled out a candle for you, to light your way down?"

"You look as if you have your hands full already," said Pickett, taking the plate from her. "What is all this?"

"I thought you might be hungry. And thirsty," she added, offering the crystal flute.

"Champagne?" She could not see his face, but his voice was playfully challenging.

She shrugged. "And why not? You only live once."

"You, my lady, are a bad influence, just like Mr.—just like I've always suspected," he amended quickly, but she was not deceived. *Just like Mr. Colquhoun said,* was what he meant. She wondered what else Mr. Colquhoun might have told him. Did he know, for instance, that the magistrate had warned her to keep her distance?

But there were more urgent matters to consider at the moment. "How much have you seen?" she asked. "Have you been able to identify the principal players?"

"Well, Angus Kirkbride is easy to recognize. He's the gentleman in the Bath chair with the tartan lap robe, is he not?"

"Yes, and both of his nephews are dancing at the moment. If you take a step this way, you can see them. Duncan is partnering his aunt, Lady Malcolm, and Gavin is squiring that lady in the blue turban."

He leaned in the direction she indicated, craning his neck to see into the room without stepping into the light. "But which one is our mystery lady? I haven't been able to distinguish Elspeth Kirkbride."

"I am disappointed in you, Mr. Pickett! I should have thought you would have recognized her at once. She is the dark lady in green—the one Harold is practically drooling over."

"*That* is Miss Kirkbride? But that's impossible!"

"I assure you, it is she. Why should it be impossible?"

He looked down at her, and she could see his eyes glinting in the shadows. "Because that is Elizabeth Church, queen of the Drury Lane stage."

Chapter 11

IN WHICH JOHN PICKETT ATTENDS HIS FIRST BALL

"An *actress*?" Lady Fieldhurst leaned past Pickett for a closer look, as if the woman in question should somehow look different in the light of this revelation.

"It makes sense, in a way. Who better to play a part, and play it convincingly, than one who does it every day for a living?"

"Yes, but—Mrs. Church? Are you certain?"

"I'm positive. I've seen her often enough: as Lady Macbeth, as Portia, as Ophelia—" He slapped his forehead. "I'm a fool! Of course your sketch looked familiar. She assumed the same pose in Ophelia's drowning scene, with one arm stretched out beneath her head to cushion it against the hard wooden floor of the stage. You were there, too, on that occasion," he added, looking down at Lady Fieldhurst.

"Yes, but Ophelia was fair," insisted her ladyship. "Miss Kirkbride is dark. The two look nothing alike."

"She wore a wig for the part, but you can see the resemblance in the way she carries herself, the way she moves."

Lady Fieldhurst watched the *faux* Elspeth Kirkbride for a long moment, then shook her head. "I fear I haven't your eye for detail, Mr. Pickett."

"It is a peculiarity of the theatre that the rabble sitting in the pit have a better view of the stage than the aristocrats in their boxes," observed Pickett. "I noticed it that night you invited me to your box. Perhaps that would account for your apparent lack of perception. Or—" His teeth gleamed faintly in the dark, and she could tell by his tone that he was smiling. "Perhaps it is due to the fact that you nobs come to the theatre to see each other and be seen, rather than from any appreciation of drama."

"Guilty as charged," admitted her ladyship, raising her hands in mock surrender. "But confess, Mr. Pickett, had my attention been totally focused on the stage, I should not have seen you seated in the pit below."

"And you would not have summoned me to your box and been banished to Scotland for your sins," he added.

"Very true," she agreed, deriving no small satisfaction from the knowledge that her exile had not proven to be the punishment the Bertram cabal had intended. "In any case, if you are certain of the woman's identity, what will you do now?"

He sighed. "First I must report my findings to Mr. Colquhoun, and either he or I will have to tell Mr. Kirkbride that his 'daughter' is a fraud."

"Then Duncan had it right the first time, although by now she has even convinced him of her authenticity. Will you arrest her?"

"On what charge? So far as I can tell, she's broken no laws—at least, not yet."

Lady Fieldhurst could not agree. "But—but she's perpetrating a hoax, surely, claiming to be someone she is not!"

"Like you, presenting yourself as Mrs. Pickett?" Again that teasing tone, that flash of white teeth.

"That—that's different!"

"In what way?"

"I didn't introduce myself as Mrs. Pickett to anyone who might care who I was, or be hurt by it."

"You didn't think I would care, or be hurt, to discover that you were masquerading as my wife?"

His teasing tone had subtly altered, and Mr. Colquhoun's stern visage suddenly swam before her.

125

"I did not say I was your wife, precisely, I only said my name was Mrs. Pickett," she insisted. "As for your being in any way disturbed, I didn't think you ever need know anything about it. For all I knew to the contrary, you were still in London."

"Perhaps, given the fragile state of the old man's health, Mrs. Church never thought Mr. Kirkbride need know the truth, either," suggested Pickett, steering the conversation back to the matter at hand. "Perhaps she thought she was doing the old man a kindness. Then again, perhaps she was playing a cruel and elaborate prank. Neither is illegal, but I can't know her motives until I confront her directly."

Lady Fieldhurst looked back into the ballroom, where the fiddler struck up the opening measures of "The Wind That Shakes the Barley" as the dancers took their places. "Oh, but must you do so tonight? Poor Mr. Kirkbride looks so happy, and he'll be so crushed to learn the truth. It will be like losing his daughter all over again."

"I suppose it can wait until tomorrow. God knows it will be awkward enough without the added burden of embarrassing Mr. Kirkbride in front of his guests."

"And everyone seems to be having such a good time. Surely it would be a pity to spoil it."

He watched her for a long moment in silence. Her silhouette was limned in gold from the warm candlelight spilling through the French windows, and her head nodded in time to the music.

"You miss it, don't you?" It was a statement, not a question. "Dancing, I mean."

Her sad little smile was just discernible in the candlelight. "Sometimes. It can be very dull, you know, being a widow and unable to participate in pastimes that once brought pleasure." She sighed. "I suppose if I had truly loved Frederick or sincerely mourned his loss, I would not think of such frivolous things as dancing. But it is hard to be sober and staid when I feel like a bird released from a cage. And yet I am still not truly free, for there are the proprieties which must be observed."

Obeying a sudden impulse, he set his plate and champagne flute down on the paving stones. "What is to prevent you from dancing now?"

Turning away from the gaily lit windows, she said in some exasperation, "You think I should march back into the ballroom and solicit some poor gentleman to dance with me? It would certainly distract everyone's attention from Miss Kirkbride, I'll grant you that."

"No, not in there; out here. Who is to see you?"

"No one, I suppose. But in case you haven't noticed, there is the small matter of a partner."

"Will I do?"

Lady Fieldhurst was annoyed to find her heart pounding in her chest as if she had run all the way up the cliff path. "You, Mr. Pickett? Can you dance?"

"Probably not the way you are accustomed to, but I am willing to be taught."

The idea was too absurd to contemplate; the temptation was too great to resist. She hesitated only a moment before shoving Mr. Colquhoun and his warning to the back of her mind. "Very well, then, Mr. Pickett. Stand facing me, and take two steps to your right." She picked up the train of her dress to allow for more freedom of movement. "Now we each take four steps forward, circle each other, and back—no, don't turn around, keep facing forward. Of course, we should change partners at this juncture, but we shall have to make do with each other. Now turn to your left—no, Mr. Pickett, your *other* left—"

Between her giving instructions and the time it took for him to put them into practice, they were of necessity a full beat behind the music. Still, she had never enjoyed a dance more. Here there was no aristocratic suitor to impress, no Bertram family honor to uphold. In fact, she thought as they laughed over a misstep that left Mr. Pickett half standing in the hedge, Frederick would no doubt be spinning in his grave at the thought of his viscountess in her widow's weeds, dancing in reckless abandon with a man as far beneath him socially as the earth beneath the heavens. The very thought of such a thing made her want to throw back her head and laugh out loud at the sheer absurdity of it all.

And then he took a wrong step—or was it she?—and they found themselves breast to chest. She looked up at him to make some clever rejoinder, and her smile died aborning. Their eyes met and held, their noses almost touching and their lips scant inches apart, lips that had been joined, however briefly, only months ago in the darkened study of a Yorkshire country house . . .

Afterwards, neither one could have said who made the first move, but suddenly they were in each other's arms. As he was quite tall, she had to stand on tiptoe to raise her face to his, a circumstance that caused her to sway unsteadily on her feet and lean against Pickett for support, to that young man's evident satisfaction. They kissed eagerly, hungrily, a man and a woman who had kissed as a matter of expedience some three months earlier and who now realized that their lives since then had merely been marking time until they could find (or make) an opportunity to kiss again. At last they drew apart, breathing heavily and staring deeply into one another's eyes in awe and wonder for a long moment before collapsing into another embrace and taking up where they had left off.

This process might have gone on indefinitely, had a slight sound from the darkness beyond the terrace not compelled Pickett to pull Lady Fieldhurst deeper into the concealing shadow of the boxwood, from which vantage point they could see the terrace without themselves being observed.

A moment later a man emerged into the light. At first Lady Fieldhurst thought it must be Duncan, and wondered at his sudden appearance on the terrace from the direction of the cliff when he had been in the house dancing with his aunt only a few moments ago. Then he moved closer to the French windows, and the light from the ballroom fell full on his face. Although there was something of Duncan's appearance about him, and the two men were of a similar size and build, this was not Duncan Kirkbride, but a man she had seen only yesterday, a man clad in the rough homespun garments of the common labourer.

Lady Fieldhurst looked up at Pickett, his attention now fully engaged by the newcomer. "Neil, the stable hand," she started to whisper, but he laid a finger on her lips to silence her. It seemed to her that there was nothing personal, nothing of intimacy, in the gesture; whatever madness had seized him a few minutes earlier had now passed, and his thoughts were fully fixed on the scene being played out before them.

The stable hand stared intently into the ballroom, but made no move to enter the house as he had done the previous day. A moment later the French window was opened from within, and Miss Kirkbride—or rather, Mrs. Church—stepped out onto the terrace.

"I got your message," she said in an undervoice that carried in the still night air to the hedge where Pickett and Lady Fieldhurst hid in the shadows. "What are you doing here?"

"I hae to speak wi' ye." He gripped her shoulders. "E'er since I heard ye'd come back, I've waited for ye. Why dinna ye come to me, Elspeth?"

"For God's sake, Neil, will you leave me alone?" said the actress playing Miss Kirkbride. "I haven't come this far only to have you spoil it for me! It's been fifteen years! Did you think nothing had changed in all that time? How could you be such a fool?"

He gave her a little shake. "Ye said ye were goin' to marry me!"

"I would have said anything to hurt my father and Duncan. You knew that." She shrugged out of his rough embrace. "Have you waited for me all these years? I'm afraid you've wasted your time."

"Ye dinna care for me at all! Ye were only usin' me!"

"Yes, I was. God knows I'm not proud of it, but I was little more than a child myself. What other weapons did I have at my disposal?"

He shook his finger in her face. "Ye owe me, Elspeth. I'll nae leave it be until ye've paid the debt."

"We'll speak of this later, Neil, but this is not the time. I must go back inside before Father begins to wonder at my absence."

"When, then?" Neil demanded. "If nae now, when?"

"Tomorrow," she said in some exasperation. "Don't come to the house. I'll meet you in the stables."

"Aye, I'll come in the morn. What time?"

"I don't know—make it ten o'clock." She gestured toward the cliff path. "Now go, quickly, before someone sees you here!"

He took a backward step in the direction she indicated, his expression filled with loathing. "Aye, I'll go for now, Elspeth, but I'll be back tomorrow at ten. Dinna forget!"

And then he was gone, swallowed up by the darkness beyond the terrace. Mrs. Church waited until the sounds of his departure faded, then schooled her features into an expression of serenity just as the door opened once more and Duncan Kirkbride stepped out onto the terrace.

"Still indulging a taste for stable hands, Elspeth?" he observed sardonically. "Some things never change."

"And what does it matter to you, Duncan? You lost any right to dictate to me fifteen years ago."

Under the cover of her answering retort, Pickett whispered against Lady Fieldhurst's hair. "This place is busier than Bow Street on a Saturday night."

His breath was warm against her ear, and Lady Fieldhurst felt a brief stab of resentment toward the Kirkbrides for making such frequent use of their own terrace. With an effort, she pushed aside her more amorous inclinations and focused her attention on the quarreling pair.

"If you will excuse me," Elspeth was saying, "I must be getting back to the ballroom. Father will be wondering where I have gone."

She would have brushed past Duncan and returned to the ballroom, but he seized her arm.

"Why did you have to come back, Elspeth?" he demanded. "Why couldn't you have stayed dead, where you belonged?"

Without waiting for an answer, he pulled her roughly into his arms and covered her mouth with his own. Lady Fieldhurst, watching from her hiding place in the shadows, felt her face grow warm as she recalled her own part just moments earlier in a similar scene. Then again, she was forced to own, perhaps it was not so similar. For while Elspeth neither resisted nor returned Duncan's embrace, the viscountess recalled her own rôle as a far more active participant.

"So cold, Elspeth?" Duncan challenged, releasing her at last. "I can remember a time when you weren't so—"

"Duncan, there are things you don't know," Mrs. Church interrupted him. "I can't tell you—"

Whatever she might have revealed was lost as the French window opened yet again. Lady Fieldhurst felt rather than heard Pickett's huff of annoyance as Lady Malcolm swooped down on the quarreling lovers. She recalled that Pickett was not yet acquainted with Angus Kirkbride's gossipy sister, but dared not identify the woman to him until they were alone; it would not do to be discovered at this juncture, even less so by this particular person.

"So this is where you've been hiding!" exclaimed Lady Malcolm, regarding Mrs. Church with an arch smile. "What can you have been doing out here, my dear? Your poor father is beside himself!"

"I beg your pardon, Aunt. Like you, Duncan had just come outside to fetch me. I confess, so much has happened over the last few days, I sometimes find it overwhelming. I am sorry Father was distressed by my absence; I had merely stepped outside for a moment to collect my thoughts."

"Well, collect them inside, before Angus worries himself into an apoplexy!"

Without giving the younger woman an opportunity to protest, she steered her nephew and her supposed niece toward the French window. As Duncan and Elspeth returned to the ballroom, Lady Fieldhurst relaxed and breathed a sigh of relief at their having so narrowly escaped discovery. Alas, her relief was premature, for her black satin train brushed against Pickett's empty champagne flute and knocked it over. The crystal did not shatter, but it did roll, tracing a long, shallow arc as it moved slowly across the paved terrace to rest at last against Lady Malcolm's skirts.

"Why, what have we here?" Lady Malcolm asked of no one in particular, bending low to pick up the glass. "Who is there? Come out at once!"

Thus caught out, the fugitives had no alternative but to step forward.

"Good evening, Lady Malcolm," the viscountess said, painfully aware of the lock of hair brushing her cheek, pulled loose, no doubt, by Mr. Pickett's exploring fingers. "I trust you are enjoying the ball?"

"Very much, Mrs. Pickett, but apparently not nearly so much

as you are," said that too-astute lady, her attention fixed on some point beyond the viscountess's shoulder. "It seems that all the real festivities are taking place on the terrace tonight! I gather this must be Mr. Pickett? But of course it is! Newly wedded couples always look just alike."

Mr. Pickett, unaccustomed to moving in polite society, nevertheless stepped forward and made a very credible bow. "How do you do, ma'am?"

Lady Malcolm dipped a curtsy. "Pleased to meet you, I'm sure, Mr. Pickett. But I confess, when I saw our lovely Mrs. Pickett dressed all in black, and no husband in sight, I assumed she must be a widow. So many of our young women are, these days, what with that Bonaparte wreaking havoc all over the Continent! But tell me," she continued, her curious gaze darting from one to the other and back again, "if not for her husband, then for whom is Mrs. Pickett in mourning?"

"My mother."

"Her father," said Pickett at the very same time.

The "newlyweds" exchanged a brief, panicked glance before Lady Fieldhurst plunged ahead. "Both, actually," she told Lady Malcolm, with a silent apology to her parents, both of whom were still very much alive and living in Somersetshire. "My mother succumbed to a consumptive disease six months ago, and my father followed soon after. The doctor said he died of a broken heart."

Lady Malcolm made suitably sympathetic noises, then brightened perceptibly. "But there is nothing to be gained in dwelling on your loss when this evening's entertainment is meant to be a celebration! Will you not come inside and join the festivities, Mr. Pickett?"

"I—I'm not dressed for evening," Pickett protested, painfully aware of the shabbiness of even his best black serge coat against this glittering company.

"Nonsense!" Her ladyship dismissed this argument with a wave of one plump beringed hand. "What are such things as clothing among friends?"

"Nor am I a friend," insisted Mr. Pickett. "In fact, I have never met any of the Kirkbride family before in my life."

"My husband arrived in Scotland some time after me," Lady Fieldhurst explained, coming to his rescue. "He has not had the pleasure of making Mr. Kirkbride's acquaintance."

"There you are, then! No time like the present, I always say."

"In fact, I had only come with a message for, er, Mrs. Pickett. As you may have heard, we have our three young nephews in our care, and poor Edward, the youngest, is complaining of a stomachache," Mr. Pickett explained, rising to new heights of invention. "I am not much of a nurse, so I had hopes of a woman's advice."

"Then you came to the right place," Lady Malcolm declared, not to be denied, "for I have reared four sons of my own. You may depend upon it that children are stronger than most of us give them credit for. I daresay little Edward's stomach will improve on its own once he sees that his uncle and aunt do not intend to drop everything and fly to his aid. Now, come inside and let me introduce you to my brother."

Thus adjured, there was nothing Pickett could do but take Lady Fieldhurst's arm and allow himself and his "wife" to be led inside.

"You have come at a very opportune time, Mr. Pickett," Lady Malcolm continued placidly, having had her way at last, "for I believe my brother is about to make an interesting announcement."

"I wonder if I might retire to the ladies' withdrawing room and tidy up a bit," put in Lady Fieldhurst, all too painfully aware of her disheveled appearance. She tucked a vagrant strand of hair behind her ear. "The—er, the wind off the sea is very keen tonight, is it not?"

Lady Malcolm eyed her shrewdly. "Aye, and it's not the only thing that's keen tonight, I trow. You need not blush, my dear Mrs. Pickett; after all, I was a young bride too, once upon a time."

"If you will excuse me," murmured the viscountess, scarlet with mortification. Pickett shot her a look of such agonized appeal that she felt compelled to assure him, "I shan't be gone a moment longer than necessary, I promise."

He swallowed hard. "I shall be counting the minutes, my la— dear."

Alone in the small room set aside for the ladies' personal needs, Lady Fieldhurst stared aghast at her reflection in the mirror. Her hair, so carefully dressed by the innkeeper's daughter only a couple of hours earlier, now tumbled over her shoulders, the aigrette of dyed ostrich plumes that had adorned this coif now tilted at a drunken angle. Perhaps worse, her lips were rosy and swollen, and her face was flushed. She looked, in fact, like a woman who had just been thoroughly kissed.

Plucking out the few hairpins that remained undisturbed, she twisted her hair into a loose chignon and anchored it to the back of her head. As for the rest of the evidence, there was little she could do. Finding a bowl and pitcher provided for the ladies' use, she bathed her face in cool water in the hopes of dispelling the rich color that stained her cheeks. She could only hope the commotion caused by the announcement of Duncan's engagement would draw so much attention to the unhappy Miss McFarland that her own indiscretion would be overlooked.

She returned to the ballroom to rescue Mr. Pickett and found him in the center of the Kirkbride clan, looking woefully ill at ease. Indeed, she could hardly blame him, for just as he had predicted, his black serge coat, breeches, and top boots looked glaringly out of place.

"There now," she said brightly, coming up beside him and taking his arm. "Didn't I say I wouldn't be long?"

"Every moment without you was an agony," he declared. No lover had ever spoken more sincerely.

"Of course, you think we should all be as careless of our appearance as you are," she scolded, straightening his cravat with a proprietary air before addressing the rest of the company. "As you can see, Mr. Pickett cares nothing for fashion."

Pickett might have been wounded by her seeming mockery, had he not realized that she had just given the group an explanation for the obvious differences in the quality of their respective wardrobes.

He gave her a grateful smile. "You would do well to follow my example, my l—dear. Surely a beautiful lady decking herself out in silks and satins is a case of gilding the lily."

"Very prettily said, Mr. Pickett," applauded Lady Malcolm. "I believe we can see how you contrived to win your fair lady without the trappings of fashion."

Fortunately, Pickett's blushes were spared at this juncture by Angus Kirkbride, who chose that moment to command the notice of all his guests.

"If I may have your attention, please," he called in a surprisingly strong voice.

The fiddler ground to a halt, and the dancers crowded nearer to hear their host's words. Lady Fieldhurst noted that the prospective bride and bridegroom stood nowhere near each other: Miss McFarland had been dancing with Harold, while Duncan was now positioned against the wall near the French window beyond which he had only moments earlier been kissing another woman. No, thought the viscountess, she could not be optimistic about the match.

Seeing that all eyes were now fixed upon him, Angus Kirkbride extended his hand to Mrs. Church, who stepped forward to clasp it.

"It has long been my dearest wish to ensure that my estate will remain the home of the Kirkbride family," he said. Angus extended his other hand to his nephew and Gavin stepped up to take it. The trio stood together, a living chain with the frail old man as its central link. "Tonight my daughter has made my happiness complete. I am pleased to announce the betrothal of my dear Elspeth to my nephew, Gavin Kirkbride."

The silence that followed this pronouncement seemed to fill the room. Lady Fieldhurst could only suppose that the other guests, like herself, had expected Mr. Kirkbride's announcement to concern the nuptials of Duncan, not his cousin. Her gaze darted to that surly gentleman. Duncan stood as if turned to stone, his face drained of all color. Without warning, he turned on his heel and flung himself from the room, shutting the French window behind him with enough force to rattle the panes. The sound seemed to break the spell. The assembled guests politely applauded the betrothed couple, and the moment of tension passed.

"But there is more," added old Mr. Kirkbride. "As most of you know, many years ago I cast off my daughter in a fit of foolish pride. I then rewrote my will, dividing everything between my two nephews. Tonight, as a wedding gift to the bridal pair, I intend to rectify my error. I have sent for my solicitor, Mr. Ferguson—" He nodded at the little man from Edinburgh. "And in the morning he and I will draw up a new will, one in which everything I own will pass at my death to my daughter, Elspeth."

With a growing sense of dread, Lady Fieldhurst glanced at Mr. Pickett. The furrow puckering his brow was sufficient to inform her that they were thinking the same thing.

The purpose of Mrs. Church's charade had just become abundantly clear.

CHAPTER 12

IN WHICH A VIOLENT DEATH
IS REVEALED

"She doesn't love him!" Harold insisted, not for the first time, as the trap rattled along the short stretch of road between the Kirkbride house and the inn. "I know she doesn't!"

"Mrs.—Miss Kirkbride is a grown woman," Lady Fieldhurst reminded him. "No one can force her to marry against her will." In fact, she was rapidly losing patience with Harold's adolescent histrionics. There were far more significant, and sinister, implications to be taken into account, had she only the luxury of discussing them with Mr. Pickett in private. Instead, he now made up a fourth in the borrowed conveyance. She was glad he was spared the necessity of navigating the cliff path again in the dark, but there was no denying the fact that they were uncomfortably squeezed as a result.

"But when she danced with me, I thought—I thought she liked me," Harold confessed forlornly.

"I daresay she likes you very well," said Lady Fieldhurst, readily conceding the point. "But a lady may enjoy a young man's company, even flirt with him a little, without having serious intentions toward him."

"Listen to your aunt," recommended Mr. Colquhoun from his seat on the opposite side of the carriage. "She knows whereof she speaks," he added cryptically, drawing a sharp glance from the viscountess.

"I confess, I had supposed the 'interesting announcement' would concern Mr. Duncan Kirkbride, rather than his cousin," her ladyship continued, hoping to give Harold's thoughts another direction. She noticed Mr. Pickett did not volunteer the information that "Miss Kirkbride" was not whom she appeared to be, and she was quick to follow his lead; aside from the possibility that divulging too much information at this juncture might hinder Mr. Pickett in his investigation, she suspected Harold would not take kindly to any slur against his beloved. She only wondered what Gavin's reaction would be when he learned the truth about his betrothed.

At last the trap drew to a stop before the inn, and the four disembarked. Harold flung himself off to his room at once, no doubt to mope over the loss of his ladylove. Mr. Colquhoun lowered himself ponderously to the ground, then turned to offer his assistance to Lady Fieldhurst. Pickett, for his part, suspected this show of chivalry on the magistrate's part to be motivated by no nobler instinct than depriving himself of the opportunity to clasp her ladyship's hand. In any case, there was no chance to speak privately with the viscountess, for Lady Fieldhurst bade both men goodnight and then followed her recalcitrant nephew into the inn.

Alone in the stable yard with Mr. Colquhoun, Pickett found himself on the receiving end of an all too keen stare.

"Yes, sir?" he asked the magistrate.

The wily Scot merely shrugged. "I didn't say a word."

Pickett sighed. "You didn't have to. You are wondering how I came to be discovered, when I assured you of my discretion. I can offer no explanation, sir, except to say that I was—distracted."

"Yes, and a very fetching distraction she is, I'll grant you that."

Pickett neither confirmed nor denied it, but hurried to give the magistrate's thoughts a happier direction. "I think you will be pleased to know that my efforts were not wasted. I contrived to get a good look at Miss Kirkbride. It seems Mr. Kirkbride's long-lost daughter is in fact Mrs. Elizabeth Church, the Drury Lane actress."

Mr. Colquhoun's scowl lightened at once. "Is that a fact? Well done, John, well done indeed!"

"It does seem a pity to have to tell the old man, though. He was so happy to have his daughter back."

"Aye, but this business of ours is not all sweetness and light. You should know that by now." Mr. Colquhoun yawned. "Well, there's nothing to be done about it until morning, in any case. Might as well turn in. Are you coming up?"

Pickett shook his head. "I'll be up later. Right now I should like some time alone to think."

"Try not to dwell on it," advised the magistrate. "Mr. Kirkbride knew when he sent to Bow Street that there was a chance his daughter was not on the up and up."

"Yes, sir."

Pickett saw no reason to inform his mentor that it was not Miss Kirkbride, much less her father, who filled his thoughts to such a degree. Long after Mr. Colquhoun had trudged up the stairs to their chamber, Pickett paced back and forth before the dying fire in the taproom, reliving those moments when he had held his goddess in his arms and tasted paradise. He knew he must apologize in the morning for his behavior; he still could not quite believe he had taken such liberties, but he could not find it in his heart to regret them. How did one apologize for the most magical experience in a decidedly mundane existence? He sat down on the settle before the fire and stretched out his long legs. If he closed his eyes, he could almost feel her in his arms again, almost . . .

He must have dozed off, for he awoke with a start to find a grey light filtering through the windows and a lad no older than Robert Bertram shaking him by the shoulder.

"Bow Street?" the boy asked urgently. "Be you the Bow Street Runner what's staying here at the inn?"

Still groggy with sleep, Pickett forgot to defer to Mr. Colquhoun. "Yes, I am. What's wrong?"

The boy jerked his thumb in the direction of Ravenscroft Manor. "They want you at the big house. It's the old man, Mr. Kirkbride. He's dead."

"Dead?" echoed Pickett, now fully awake.

"Aye, I just come from there. Doc's still with him. Says he'll nae leave until you get there."

Pickett shot to his feet. "I'm on my way." Seeing the lad was undecided whether to go or stay, Pickett shooed him toward the door. "You need not wait for me. Go back to the house, and tell them I'm coming."

"Aye, sir." The boy tugged his forelock and quitted the room.

Pickett took the stairs two at a time and burst into his own chamber, where the sleeping magistrate lay snoring with relish.

"Mr. Colquhoun!" He shook the magistrate by the shoulder in much the same way the boy from the big house had shaken him. "Mr. Colquhoun, sir, wake up!"

Mr. Colquhoun's snores ended abruptly. "Eh, what the devil—?"

"There's been a messenger from the Kirkbride house, sir. We're needed there. Angus Kirkbride is dead."

"Bless my soul!" Mr. Colquhoun flung back the covers and sat up in bed. "You don't say! Well, don't just stand there, lad—hand me my boots!"

Pickett was quick to oblige, and as soon as the magistrate had flung on his clothes, they were on their way. The doctor, as promised, was still there, as was an elderly gentleman in an old-fashioned frock coat and bagwig, whom Pickett had no difficulty in recognizing from Mr. Colquhoun's description as Sir Henry MacDougall, the local justice of the peace. Also in attendance at the patriarch's deathbed were Gavin Kirkbride and his supposed fiancée; of Duncan Kirkbride there was no sign. Gavin stood beside the bed and looked down at his uncle, his face white and strained, while Elspeth sat in a chair drawn up to the head of the bed and wept silently, her tears running down her face and falling on the frail, still hand clasped in hers. Pickett, knowing what he now knew about her, felt a cynical urge to applaud a moving performance.

Hard on the heels of this thought came another, far less welcome one. The messenger who had awakened him at the inn had asked for the Bow Street Runner. Not the magistrate from Bow Street, but the Bow Street Runner. Either the boy had misunderstood his instructions, or someone at the house knew who he was.

But there would be time to consider this possibility later. For now, the doctor was shooing the family from the room, the better to speak to the Bow Street contingent alone.

"Thank you for coming so promptly," said the doctor, closing the door behind the pair as Gavin led Mrs. Church from the room. He turned to the magistrate and offered his hand. "Mr. Colquhoun, is it? Mr. Wallace Reid. I'm sorry to disturb you at such an hour."

"Not at all, not at all." Mr. Colquhoun waved the doctor's scruples aside.

"I believe you are acquainted with Sir Henry MacDougall, justice of the peace?"

"Aye, we've met." The two dispensers of justice shook hands.

"I've just been pointing out to the good doctor that Angus Kirkbride was old, and his health not the best," said Sir Henry. "Tempest in a teacup, if you ask me. Can't be murder; we don't hold with that sort of thing in these parts."

The magistrate turned to address Mr. Reid. "By your summons, I assume you have reason to believe his death was not of natural causes?"

The doctor glanced uncertainly at Pickett. Mr. Colquhoun, correctly interpreting his concerns, hastened to reassure him. "My colleague, Mr. John Pickett."

The doctor scowled at the young Runner. "I've got boots older than you."

Seeing Pickett bristle, Mr. Colquhoun stepped in to pour oil on troubled waters. "Mr. Pickett may be young, but I trust him implicitly. Pray do not hesitate to speak freely in front of him."

The doctor gave Pickett a doubtful look, but addressed the magistrate. "Mr. Kirkbride's heart was not strong, but there was no reason to suppose that, with proper care, he mightn't have had several more years out of it."

"His life has undergone quite an upheaval in the past fortnight," observed Pickett. "Might not the strain have hastened his death?"

"Aye, it might have," the doctor concurred. "And it's my belief that is what our murderer is counting on."

Mr. Colquhoun's bushy white brows drew together over the bridge of his nose. " 'Murder' is a harsh word, doctor."

"Aye, I'm aware of that. But look here."

He crossed the room to the bed and, bending over the old man's body, drew back one eyelid with his forefinger. The lifeless eye was almost entirely black, with only the slenderest ring of blue along the outer edge to indicate the color.

"Dilation of the pupils is an indicator of digitalis overdose," the doctor explained.

"Digitalis?" Pickett echoed, scribbling in his notebook.

"A plant derivative often used for the treatment of heart ailments." The doctor picked up one of two black bottles on the small table beside the bed. "Mr. Kirkbride takes this to regulate his heartbeat. It is an infusion of dried plant matter mixed with sherry to make the bitter taste more palatable. Observe, if you will, the level of liquid in the bottle."

He handed the bottle to Pickett, who held it up to the window, through which the dawn light was beginning to penetrate. Pickett shook it slightly and saw that the bottle was about one-third full.

"I brought him this bottle only last week," the doctor continued. "It should still be at least half full, and very likely more."

"Plain as a pikestaff what happened," Sir Henry put in. "Angus knocked over the bottle and spilt the stuff. Done it myself a time or two."

Of that, at least, Pickett had no doubt. He had suspected Mr. Colquhoun's blistering assessment of Sir Henry's mental acuity to be an exaggeration; after meeting the man, however, he could see that his magistrate had in fact understated the case.

"If any of the medicine has been spilled, Mr. Kirkbride's valet will know of it, or the maid who cleans his room," Pickett noted.

"I don't need you to tell me my business, boy," said Sir Henry, very much on his dignity. "I shall speak to the chambermaid myself."

With a gleam in his eye that suggested this interview would very likely take place in a dark corner of the butler's pantry, he took himself from the room, leaving the doctor to let out a sigh of relief as the door closed behind him.

"Sir Henry's position requires that I summon him," the physician told Mr. Colquhoun, "but I fear he has long since outlived any aptitude he may once have had for the work. I would feel better knowing the case is in your hands."

"Yes, but even if the cause of death is overdose, it doesn't necessarily follow that the lethal dose was deliberately administered," Pickett pointed out. "Is it possible that Mr. Kirkbride accidentally took too large a dose himself? With all he has been through over the past week, he might have felt his heart needed all the help it could get."

The doctor shook his head, unconvinced. "Tell me, are you gentlemen familiar with an English wildflower called foxglove?"

"Aye." Mr. Colquhoun nodded.

Pickett, whose knowledge of botany extended no further than the flowers sold by girls in Covent Garden, looked from one man to the other, all at sea.

"Mr. Kirkbride's medicine is made from the dried leaves of the foxglove plant," said the doctor. "The plant is also indigenous to Scotland, where it is more commonly known as—"

"Dead man's bells," Mr. Colquhoun put in. "In other words, Mr. Kirkbride would not have risked giving himself an overdose, being fully cognizant of the plant's lethal qualities."

"If what you are telling me is correct," Pickett said slowly, "it means that every schoolchild in Scotland would know of the plant's potential as a poison."

The doctor nodded. "Precisely. No special medical knowledge would have been needed to bring about Mr. Kirkbride's death. Anyone with motive and opportunity might have done the deed." He looked from Mr. Colquhoun to Mr. Pickett and back again. "Can either one of you think of anyone who might want the old man dead?"

Pickett and the magistrate exchanged a loaded glance, but Pickett answered the doctor's question with one of his own. "What about the other bottle? What is in it?"

Mr. Reid glanced at the other bottle beside the bed and shook his head in dismissal. "A paregoric draught I gave Mr. Kirkbride for those occasions when he had trouble sleeping."

"Is it poisonous, too?"

The doctor frowned, considering the question. "Almost any medicinal concoction is dangerous if given in large enough doses. But the symptoms of paregoric overdose would be very different—the pupils of the eyes, for instance, would contract rather than dilate—and would take much longer to appear, possibly as much as two hours or more."

"Tell me, doctor, when were you called in? Was Mr. Kirkbride still alive?"

"He was alive, but barely conscious. When I realized what had happened, I attempted to flush the digitalis from his system by giving him water to drink, but my efforts were in vain. He was beyond reason at that point, and I could not compel him to swallow the water that might have diluted the poison. He died shortly afterwards."

"Who found him, did they tell you?" Secondhand testimony would be inadmissible in court, but it would be interesting to determine whether the Kirkbrides' accounts squared with the doctor's.

"Apparently Miss Kirkbride heard her father retching and rose to check on him. For what it's worth, nausea and vomiting are also symptoms of digitalis poisoning."

"And so she sent a footman to fetch you?"

"Yes, and she was most urgent in her summons. The footman had instructions not to return without me."

Pickett could not doubt it. Despite her dishonesty in the matter of her identity, no one had a greater reason to keep Angus Kirkbride alive, at least until the will could be changed. Duncan, on the other hand, was quite another matter. Pickett would be most interested in hearing an account of that gentleman's evening activities.

"Have you any idea what time you were summoned, Doctor?"

"You are trying to fix the time the poison must have been administered, I presume," the doctor observed. "I fear I can be of little assistance. I do recall hearing a single peal of the clock as I was shown upstairs to Mr. Kirkbride's room, but that offers very little information. One stroke might indicate any half-hour. I do think the one o'clock hour may be ruled out, for the guests would hardly have been gone long enough for the necessary sequence of events to transpire."

Pickett looked up inquiringly from his notebook. "And what events, in your professional opinion, would have been necessary?"

"Well, let alone giving time for the household to settle down after the evening's festivities, the killer must have had time to administer the fatal dose, then time for it to take effect."

"How much time?" the magistrate put in, anticipating Pickett's next question.

"The first symptoms—headache, nausea—would occur shortly after ingestion as the heart rate begins to fluctuate. More severe symptoms—vomiting, blurred vision, delirium, and eventually death—would follow in anywhere from twenty to thirty minutes. In a man with an already weakened heart, I would guess nearer to twenty."

"And yet he was still alive when you arrived? You must live quite near the Kirkbride house, if you were able to get there so quickly," Pickett observed.

"Aye, I've a house on the other side of the manor from the inn."

"May I call on you there, if I have other questions?"

"Certainly you may, although you might not find me in. A message left with my housekeeper will always reach me, however."

"Thank you," Pickett said. "You've been most helpful."

Having concluded his interview with the doctor, Pickett sought out Mrs. Church and found her downstairs in the drawing room. The room appeared somehow disreputable in the early morning light, the furniture still pushed back against the walls to allow room for dancing, the rugs still rolled up.

"Let me say, Miss Kirkbride, how sorry I am for the loss of your father," said Pickett, making his bow. He had made up his mind not to confront Mrs. Church with her charade; better by far, he decided, to allow her to play her part and see what, if anything, she might let slip.

"Thank you, Mr. Pickett." She sank gracefully onto the sofa positioned against the wall and gestured for him to join her. "Father's health was not good, so his death should not come as a shock, but it does so nevertheless."

To any outside observer, it might have appeared that Pickett seated himself beside Mrs. Church on the sofa, but in his mind he was many miles away, watching his father board a ship for Botany Bay. "I doubt if any of us are ever ready to say goodbye to a parent, no matter how unsurprising that parent's end." He shifted uncomfortably, then dismissed the memory and regarded Mrs. Church with what he hoped was a disarming smile. "Miss Kirkbride, I fear I have enjoyed your family's hospitality under false pretenses. My name is indeed John Pickett, but I am not in Scotland on a pleasure jaunt. I am the Bow Street Runner your father requested."

She nodded, curiously unsurprised by this revelation, but showed no inclination to confide in him in return. "I knew, of course, that Duncan had persuaded my father to send for one." Her answering smile was enigmatic. "I believe he doubted whether I was truly his cousin Elspeth."

"Can you imagine any reason why he might harbor such doubts?" Pickett asked. He had a sudden image of a boxing match, the two combatants circling in the ring, each one attempting to size up his opponent before throwing the first punch. He was forced to admit that Mrs. Church was the most attractive pugilist he had ever seen.

"When I was young, Mr. Pickett, I was given to histrionics. When I left home fifteen years ago, I staged my own death, thinking to make them all sorry for using me so shabbily." She smiled sadly at the memory. "I suppose I made a better job of it than I realized. There were reasons, too, why Duncan might not be delighted to see me again."

"You are thinking of your father's intention of changing his will?" Pickett guessed.

She shrugged, dismissing Duncan's inheritance as of no importance. "That, among other things. But tell me, now that Father is dead, will you shift the focus of your investigation? The doctor believes he was hastened to his death."

Pickett nodded. "So he told me. I am no medical man, but his reasoning appeared sound."

"So am I now a murderess as well as a fraud?" There was a hint of fear as well as a challenge in the words.

"Everyone must be considered a suspect at this point, but I confess, I can see no reason why you should murder Mr. Kirkbride now when you might have waited twenty-four hours and inherited the lot. Now, can you tell me, as nearly as you can recall, what happened last night?"

She stared unseeing at the opposite wall, her gaze unfocused as she cast her mind back. "It was quite late by the time we sought our beds. Father, although exhausted, was agitated from the evening's festivities, and took a paregoric draught to help him sleep."

Pickett withdrew the notebook from the inside breast pocket of his coat and began to write. "Did he take this draught often?"

"I believe 'often' may be too strong a word, although my cousins tell me he needed it frequently in the days following my return. Let us say, rather, that it was not unusual for him to require some sort of soporific."

"And did it have the desired effect on this occasion?"

She frowned thoughtfully. "It certainly seemed to, at least at first. My bedchamber is next to his, and after his valet prepared him for bed and left the room, there were no sounds that might lead me to suppose he was having difficulty sleeping. Unless—" She broke off abruptly.

"Unless?" Pickett prompted.

"I heard a door close," she said slowly. "I had not thought of it before—I had assumed it was Ramsay, Father's valet. But he would have taken the servant's stair."

Pickett knew, from his investigation into Lord Fieldhurst's murder as well as his own brief stint as Lady Fieldhurst's foot-man in Yorkshire, that the bedchambers of the wealthy had discreet servants' doors tucked away in the wall that allowed the servants to come and go without cluttering up the corridors. The best servant, he knew from experience, was an invisible one.

"And when was this?" he asked, pencil poised above the page.

"It was past one o'clock when I sought my bed, and I could hear Father's conversation with Ramsay for some minutes after, although I could not distinguish the words spoken," she said, glancing at the long-case clock as if she might still read the crucial times on its face. "It was probably a quarter of an hour before the sound from Father's room ceased. One-thirty, per-haps?"

"Do you recall hearing the clock chime?"

"No, but then, I wouldn't have heard it in any case. My bedroom is on the opposite end of the house from the drawing room."

"And after the room grew quiet, how long was it before you heard the door?"

"Not long. Ten minutes, perhaps. Early enough that I was not yet asleep."

"You heard no other sounds from the corridor? No footsteps, no voices?"

"Not at that time. It was some time later that I heard sounds of distress from Father's room. Alas, I can give you no idea of the time, as I was awakened from a sound sleep."

Pickett shook his head. "Never mind that. What were these sounds, and what did you do when you heard them?"

She grimaced. "They were groans and—and retching noises. I threw on my dressing gown and ran to Father's room, to find him out of bed on his hands and knees, becoming violently ill all over the carpet. I rang the bell for Ramsay, and he came at once, so apparently it was early enough that he was not yet asleep, although he was wearing his nightshirt. Gavin heard the commotion and came running as well."

"But not Duncan?"

She shook her head. "When Duncan did not appear, I dispatched Ramsay to awaken him." She looked up at Pickett, her face pale and strained. "When Ramsay came back, he said Duncan was not in his room, and his bed had not been slept in."

Pickett jotted down this information in his notebook. "And your father? Was he conscious? Did he know you?"

"He seemed to," she said thoughtfully. "He didn't speak to me directly, but then, he was so very ill."

"You say he didn't speak to you 'directly.' Did he say anything intelligible at all?"

"Yes." She took a deep breath. "He said 'Gavin.' "

Chapter 13
THE TRAGICAL HISTORY OF ELSPETH KIRKBRIDE

"Gavin?" echoed Mr. Pickett. It would be convenient, of course, if Angus Kirkbride identified the killer with his dying breath, but in his admittedly limited experience, such things only happened in Gothic novels. In any case, the doctor had said that delirium was among the symptoms of advanced digitalis poisoning, so it was quite possible that the old man's singling out his nephew meant nothing at all. Still, any lead was worth pursuing. "Why Gavin? Was Mr. Kirkbride particularly close to his nephew?"

"He was pleased at the prospect of having Gavin for a son-in-law, but I should have said he was closer to Duncan, particularly in view of certain things that are now ancient history."

Pickett had his doubts that anything relating to the Kirkbride family was ancient history; in fact, he was convinced the events of fifteen years ago, whatever they were, still controlled the Kirkbrides today.

"Forgive my candor, Miss Kirkbride, but I feel as if I am fencing in the dark. Ever since I arrived, I have heard vague references to a scandal fifteen years ago. I realize the memories may be painful to you, but I should like to hear a candid account of those events, if you please."

"Of course, if you feel it will help."

Mrs. Church rose from the sofa and walked slowly across the room to stand before the French windows overlooking the terrace, her gaze fixed upon the sea beyond. Had he not known the lady's true identity, he might have supposed her to be recalling old memories; knowing what he did, however, he suspected she was most likely rehearsing her lines.

"We grew up together, Duncan, Gavin, and I," she said at last. "Their parents were still alive then, my aunts and uncles, so it was a large, happy family living here. Then the time came that the boys were sent to England to be educated, while I stayed here with my governess. Things were never the same after that. Duncan's father died, and his mother returned to Edinburgh to be closer to her own family. Gavin's father held a seat in Parliament, so Gavin spent his school holidays in London with his parents."

"You must have missed your childhood companions," Pickett observed.

"Oh, I did! I thought it terribly unfair that they should be able to go abroad, as I thought of England in those days, while I was kept at home merely because I was a girl. When I next saw them, they were twenty-one years old, and had completed their studies at Oxford." She chuckled at the memory. "I was seventeen, and quite dazzled by my handsome, grown-up cousins. Duncan, especially, was most flatteringly attentive."

Her smile faded. "It was exactly what Father had expected, nay, had counted upon! By this time both of his brothers were dead, and he was very much aware of his own mortality. I don't know if you are aware of this, but he was actually my stepfather. He had married my mother, a war widow, when I was hardly more than an infant. The disposal of the estate was much on his mind after the deaths of his brothers and, unbeknownst to me at the time, he had conceived the happy notion of marrying me off to one of my cousins, and letting that cousin inherit the lot—thus providing for me and at the same time keeping the property in the family, so to speak. No, Mr. Pickett, there would be no Season in London for me, no presentation at Court, just marriage to whichever of my cousins was desperate enough for money to tie himself to a seventeen-year-old bride." Her voice shook and she controlled it with an effort, that magnificent voice that carried all the way to the back rows of Drury Lane Theatre. "Suffice it to say that I did not take the news well. I felt twice played for a fool, once by my father, and again by Duncan."

"So what did you do?" Keeping the skepticism from his voice presented no problem; so convincing was her performance that Pickett found it hard to believe she had not actually experienced the events she recalled. Whoever her tutor had been, he (or she) had done the job well.

"There was another cousin, a distant one whom we did not talk about. Apparently my great-grandfather Kirkbride was a bit of a lad, as they say. Certain physical characteristics of the Kirkbrides are not uncommon amongst the general population of the village. One possessor of said characteristics was employed in the Kirkbride stables. I contrived to be found in a compromising position with Neil." Her lips twisted in a cynical smile. "My intention, of course, was to enrage Father. I succeeded beyond my wildest dreams. He cast me off without a farthing."

"And Duncan?"

"Duncan, quite understandably, lost all interest in marriage to me." She leaned forward and placed her hand over Pickett's. "I was very young, Mr. Pickett. I acted without thinking, acted out of pain and injured pride. In truth, Neil and I did not—did not do nearly as much as I allowed Father and Duncan to think we had. But when I realized I had pushed Father too far, it was too late. The damage had been done. My protestations of innocence fell on deaf ears, and why not? I had done my work only too well."

"What did you do then?"

"What else?" she asked, with a cynical twist of her lips. "I proceeded to make matters worse. In the time-honored tradition of youth, I resolved to make them all sorry. I staged my own death by walking into the sea, even making sure to take off my shoes so that they might wash in on the next high tide. In fact, I rounded the point and, once out of sight of the house, managed to tread water until a fishing boat came to my rescue. It was low tide, so I was never in any real danger. As luck would have it, the fisherman who plucked me out of the sea had recently quarreled with Father over fishing in the shallows adjacent to the house. He was only too happy to take my part against Father."

"And this man's name?" asked Pickett, scribbling furiously in his notebook.

"Muir, but it won't do you any good. He's dead." Seeing Pickett's skeptical expression, she added, "It has been fifteen years, you know."

"Fifteen years for a woman, little more than a girl at that, to make her way in the world all alone," Pickett remarked. "How did you survive?"

Her gaze fell to the carpet. "I don't know." She raised a trembling hand to her forehead. "There is still so much I don't remember."

Very convenient, thought Pickett, unconsciously echoing Duncan's sentiments.

"I am only thankful I was able to reconcile with Father before he died," she said, raising misty eyes to his.

"Yes, your timing was providential, was it not?" Pickett agreed. "Tell me, now that you know Mr. Kirkbride intended to leave everything to you, do you intend to challenge the will?"

She stiffened. "File a legal claim against my father's estate before he is even underground? Is that what you think of me, Mr. Pickett?"

Pickett shut his notebook with a snap and tucked it away in his coat pocket, then rose to his feet. "Shall I tell you what I think of you, Miss Kirkbride? I think you are playing a very dangerous game, and I only hope I am not called upon to investigate another death before it is over. Now, if you will excuse me, I should like to see what I can discover about the strange disappearance of Mr. Duncan Kirkbride."

He had scarcely left the room when a door further down the corridor opened and Gavin Kirkbride emerged. "Ah, just the man I wanted to see. It's true, then, that you are the Bow Street Runner my Uncle Angus sent for?"

News apparently travelled fast in the country. "It is," Pickett said, nodding in acknowledgment.

Gavin plunged into speech. "I realize it looks bad for me, Uncle calling my name with his dying breath."

"Not at all," Pickett assured him. "It is true that everyone must be considered a suspect at this point, but the doctor assures me that those in the final stages of digitalis poisoning are usually delirious. Mr. Kirkbride's last words might mean anything, or nothing at all."

"I believe he had a message for me." Gavin dabbed at his eyes with a black-bordered handkerchief, appearing not to have heard Pickett's assurances. "I believe he was asking me to take care of his daughter."

This assertion, true or not, raised a question Pickett had not yet considered. "Where does that leave the wedding plans, now that the family is in mourning?"

Gavin shook his head. "Elspeth and I have not yet had time to discuss the matter. It hardly seemed the time to—but I shall, of course, defer to her wishes in the matter."

"I should think she would be thankful for the comfort of a husband's presence in her time of loss," Pickett suggested.

"Perhaps, but it was her father's wish that she wed one of her cousins," Gavin confessed. "His wishes were not necessarily hers. I have always been fond of my cousin Elspeth, and was naturally delighted when she returned to us very little the worse for whatever adventures she must have endured. Given that those adventures must render her an ineligible wife for most gentlemen, I was happy to please my uncle and provide for my cousin by taking her to wife. But now that Uncle Angus is dead, God rest his soul, Elspeth may choose to marry according to her own inclinations."

"Might those inclinations lean toward stable hands?"

Gavin's hand checked, and his handkerchief fluttered to the carpet. "I see our family's closets have been flung open to reveal their skeletons. My aunt Malcolm's doing, I daresay."

"Not at all," Pickett protested. "I had it from the lady herself. Your cousin told me of her youthful peccadilloes."

"I see. In truth, I was speaking of Duncan when I suggested that Elspeth might wish to wed another. They were once well on the way to having an understanding."

"Perhaps Duncan is reluctant to share his wife with the stable hands," Pickett suggested. "I must say, it is remarkably broad-minded of you not to hold her past indiscretions against her."

Gavin dismissed these accolades with a wave of his hand. "Bah! Who among us has not committed youthful follies we would be reluctant to have made known? I have always thought it grossly unfair that the same behavior which in males is considered no more than a rite of passage is deemed ruination in females." He sighed. "Poor Elspeth must find it a comfort to know that she and her father were reconciled before he died. It is appalling that, reconciliation notwithstanding, she must still be cut out of his will. For that reason, if no other, I will be glad to honor the betrothal so desired by my uncle or, if Elspeth prefers, yield my place to Duncan. She would be wise to choose one of us, for otherwise she must lose her inheritance completely."

"And so after fifteen years, nothing has changed," Pickett observed. "Still, an entire roomful of people heard Mr. Kirkbride state his intention of changing his will. I am no lawyer, but I should think she might have grounds for contesting the will, and stand some chance of success."

"Hmm, I wonder if she would do such a thing? Good God, what an awkward situation Uncle Angus has placed us all in! For one of us to gain a fortune, another must lose it. I should not mind so much for my own sake, but I do feel sorry for Duncan. It appears to me that he, as much as Elspeth, has been caught in the middle of all this."

"Speaking of Duncan, I should like to have a word with him. Have you any idea where he is?"

Gavin shrugged. "I haven't seen him since the ball last night—good God, was it only six hours ago? It seems an eternity! But to answer your question, I know Duncan left the house in a high dudgeon when my engagement to Elspeth was announced. Ramsay says he wasn't in his room, and his bed hasn't been slept in. But surely you don't think Duncan killed Uncle Angus! Why, he was always my uncle's favorite."

"I don't know what I think yet," Pickett said, "but it appears that Duncan certainly had the most to lose by your marriage to Elspeth."

"Yes," Gavin said slowly, "I can see how it might appear that way. First by losing Elspeth a second time, and then by losing his share of Uncle Angus's fortune when the will was changed. Shall I send out a party of servants to look for him?"

"No, not yet. He can't go far without being recognized, and I am still hopeful that he will turn up on his own. In the meantime I should like to have a word with your uncle's valet—Ramsay, was it?"

"Of course." Gavin reached for the bell pull.

"If you please," Pickett put in, raising a hand to stay him, "I should prefer to speak to him in the servants' quarters." His own brief stint as a footman had been sufficient to inform him that the servants had their own particular society below stairs, and they were likely to be more forthcoming if interviewed in their own sphere, so to speak, than they would be if summoned to the more rarified heights above.

"Certainly, certainly." Gavin walked with Pickett as far as the door, then called to the footman in the foyer to direct Pickett to the servants' quarters. "And if my cousin Duncan should perchance reappear," he promised Pickett, "I shall send word to you at once."

Chapter 14
THE FURTHER INVESTIGATIONS
OF JOHN PICKETT

Pickett followed the footman down the stairs and through the green baize door to the servants' quarters. The housekeeper had offered up her sitting room as a place where Pickett might interview the servants, and it was in this small but comfortably furnished chamber that he was introduced to Ramsay, Angus Kirkbride's valet. Pickett was expecting a willowy, somewhat foppish fellow like those who so often served London gentlemen in that capacity; great, therefore, was his surprise to find himself confronted with a burly, broad-shouldered specimen who looked as if he would be more at home with a carriage horse than a curling iron.

"I believe you served Mr. Angus Kirkbride as valet?" he asked this worthy, trying not to let his surprise show.

"Aye."

"How long have you been employed in that capacity?"

"Twenty years. Ere that, I worked in the Kirkbride stables."

Pickett paused in his scribbling and looked up. "Forgive me, but is it not unusual for gentlemen to hire their personal servants from the stables?"

Far from being offended, Ramsay chuckled. "Aye, in London t'would be unheard of, but nae so much here. Mr. Kirkbride had no ambitions to cut a dash, as the saying goes. So long as his linen was clean and his boots shined, he was satisfied. Besides, there was a young lad just come to Mr. Kirkbride's attention, apparently a by-blow of the old gentleman. Mr. Kirkbride—Mr. Angus Kirkbride, that is—wanted to give the boy a place in the stables, as a way of providing for him."

"Generous of him," Pickett remarked, keeping to himself the observation that Mr. Angus Kirkbride's generosity fell short of countenancing a match between the bastard stable boy and the daughter of the house.

"Aye." The valet nodded. "The Kirkbrides always take care of their own."

"You got along well with Mr. Kirkbride, then?"

"Aye, and he wi' me. He said he'd leave me twenty pounds in his will." A shadow crossed the man's ruddy countenance. "I was that grateful, mind you, but I never thought to collect it so soon."

"It came as a shock, then, Mr. Kirkbride's death?"

"His health had nae been so good for several years, but the doctor said there was no reason to suppose he might not live a good many years yet."

"Tell me about last night," Pickett urged.

"It was much later than usual when Mr. Kirkbride rang for me, on account of Miss Elspeth's party," Ramsay began. "Mr. Kirkbride should have been tired out—aye, he *was* tired out, but too agitated to rest easy. Agitated in a good way, mind you, on account of Miss Elspeth and Mr. Gavin marrying, but agitated nonetheless. I suggested to Mr. Kirkbride that he might benefit from a dose of the paregoric draught the doctor gave him to help him sleep, and Mr. Kirkbride agreed. Just as well, too, as he was so nigh asleep that he took no notice of the sounds from Miss Elspeth's room."

"Sounds?" echoed Pickett, his attention fully engaged. He was quite certain Mrs. Church's account of the evening's events had contained no mention of such a thing. "What sort of sounds?"

"Sharp, quarrelsome voices. I'd have said Miss Elspeth was

merely cross with her maid, but it sounded like a deep voice, and Rosie, the lass what waits on Miss Elspeth, has a voice like a bird a-twittering. The housekeeper, Mrs. Brodie, has a deep, booming voice, mind you, but what reason she'd have to be in Miss Elspeth's room at such an hour is beyond my ken."

"Could it have been a man's voice?" Pickett suggested.

"Are you suggesting that Miss Elspeth is the type of female that entertains men in her bedchamber?" demanded Ramsay, the personification of outraged propriety.

Pickett resisted the urge to point out that the young Elspeth had seemingly been caught in a very similar situation. "I meant no slur upon Miss Kirkbride's virtue," he said, choosing his words with care. "But she and Mr. Gavin were newly betrothed and, well, betrothed couples have been known to anticipate their marriage vows."

"I'll not argue with you there, but if they was that eager, why would they be quarreling?"

"Perhaps the lady was unwilling to submit to her fiancé's, er, ardor," Pickett suggested.

"Aye, that'll be it, no doubt." Ramsay nodded, quick to seize upon any opportunity to acquit Miss Kirkbride of any wrongdoing. "Mind you, I never did hold with Mr. Gavin's London ways."

"Or perhaps the visitor was not Mr. Gavin at all, but Mr. Duncan, hoping to persuade her to change her mind. I believe he had a lot to lose by Miss Kirkbride's marriage to his cousin."

"I suppose it could have been," Ramsay conceded begrudgingly. "Me, I think it's a great pity Miss Elspeth and Mr. Duncan couldn't reconcile their differences after so many years. To my mind, they'd be better suited than her and Mr. Gavin."

"Back to the events of last night," said Pickett, curtailing a line of questioning that he could see would lead to nothing but idle speculation. "Was Mr. Kirkbride asleep when you left him?"

"I'd have said so. Sleepy enough, as I said, that he took no notice of the voices next door. If he weren't asleep, he was near enough as made no odds."

"And how much later was it when you were summoned to his room?"

Ramsay's brow puckered with concentration. "Fifteen minutes, perhaps twenty. I'd had time to seek my own bed, but wasn't yet asleep."

"Less than half an hour, then?" Pickett asked, jotting down notes.

"Oh, certainly nae so long as that."

"And what did you find when you reached Mr. Kirkbride's room?"

"Mr. Kirkbride was on the floor, retching, and Miss Kirkbride was cradling him in her arms." He grimaced at the memory. "Mr. Kirkbride had been ill, and she was trying to lift him out of the puddle, if you'll forgive my plain speaking."

Pickett nodded. "Of course."

"Between the pair of us, Miss Elspeth and I were able to get him back into bed and into a clean nightshirt."

"What of Mr. Gavin and Mr. Duncan? Where were they during all this?"

Ramsay shook his head. "They hadn't arrived yet. Well, and they wouldn't have, would they? Their rooms were too far to hear the commotion. I wouldn't have heard it myself, but for Miss Elspeth ringing for me."

"I see. But I trust both his nephews were able to see their uncle before he died?"

"Mr. Gavin did, but there was no sign of Mr. Duncan. I remember thinking how queer it was that he slept through all the hullabaloo, being as we were all at sixes and sevens. He could hardly have failed to be wakened by the noise, what with servants running to and fro with hot water, and Jem dispatched to fetch the doctor, and what all. And then when Miss Elspeth sent me to fetch him, there was Mr. Duncan's room empty and his bed with nary a wrinkle on the sheets." He paused and yawned widely behind one beefy hand. "Begging your pardon, Mr. Pickett, but it's been a long night for us all."

"I'll not argue with you there," Pickett said, suddenly aware of the fact that he had never made it to bed at all. "One last question, and I'll let you go. You mentioned a stable hand of Mr. Kirkbride's, a distant relation born on the wrong side of the blanket."

Ramsay nodded. "That would be young Neil. I remember him well. A regular hothead he was, resentful of the family although Mr. Kirkbride tried to do right by him."

"I understand he has made a couple of attempts to see Miss Kirkbride, so I assume he still lives in the area."

"Aye, though not for lack of trying to get away." Ramsay leaned closer and lowered his voice. "Between you and me and the lamppost, he thought to turn that affair with Miss Elspeth to his own advantage. Came to Mr. Kirkbride after she'd gone and offered to hold his tongue about the whole business—for a price, mind you."

Pickett's eyebrows rose. "What did Mr. Kirkbride have to say about that?"

"Dismissed Neil and threw him out on his, er, ear."

A former employee who had been nursing a grudge for fifteen years might prove to be a valuable source of information. "Can you tell me where I might find him?" Pickett asked.

"You'd best try Sir Henry MacDougall, the justice of the peace," Ramsay recommended. "For the last several years, Neil has worked in his stable. Failing that, he's often to be found hoisting a pint at the Mermaid Tavern."

Pickett recalled seeing this establishment during his jaunt to the village with Harold. He made a notation of the name and then dismissed the valet. He next sent for Miss Kirkbride's maid, Rosie, a pert young lass with classic Scottish features of flame red hair, sparkling green eyes, and an upturned little nose liberally sprinkled with freckles.

"You served as Miss Kirkbride's maid, is that correct?" he asked her.

"Aye. Mind you, there was no lady's maid on staff, there being no ladies in residence. I was a laundry maid until Mrs. Brodie called me up to do for Miss Kirkbride, me being that handy with a needle that I could alter some of her mother's things to fit my mistress."

Pickett, with his recently acquired knowledge of the servants' domain, recognized this as an elevation of no small degree. "Quite a step up for you, wasn't it?" he remarked, letting his admiration show.

She grinned back at him, revealing a bewitching pair of dimples. "Aye, that it was, sir, I'll not deny it."

"And how do you find Miss Kirkbride as a mistress? Is she very demanding?"

Rosie was quick to rise to her mistress's defense. "Oh no, sir! She's right grateful for every little thing what's done for her. 'Tis a sad life she's had, and no mistake. And now to come back home and lose her father that way—" She shook her head at the tragedy of it all. "It don't bear thinkin' on."

"At least she has the happy memories of her ball last night," Pickett suggested. "Both she and her father seemed to enjoy that."

"Aye, it were a fine party! When she came upstairs, Miss Kirkbride told me she was quite worn out with dancing."

"I don't doubt it, for she was much in demand as a partner. Very tired, was she?"

"Aye, sir, but in a good way, if you take my meaning."

"I do, indeed." He hesitated for a moment, then observed,

"Mind you, I worked for a short time as a footman, and it's been my experience that even the kindest of mistresses can be cross and ill-humored when she's worn herself to the bone with gaiety." He added a mental apology to Lady Fieldhurst for this blatant attack on her character.

"Aye, so I've heard, but not Miss Kirkbride. When she dismissed me, she told me she had no desire to be awakened early, and that I might stay abed until six o'clock if I wished, which I thought was right kind of her." A shadow crossed her cheerful countenance. "Mind you, things didn't work out that way for neither one of us, now, did they?"

Pickett agreed to this pithy observation and, having confirmed that no cross words had been uttered between mistress and maid, allowed Rosie to return to the somber task of dyeing blacks for her mistress. He then questioned each of the three footmen who had been in service at the ball on the previous evening. Two of the three remembered seeing Duncan leave the house following the announcement of the betrothal (the third, under further questioning, confessed that he had been indulging in a bit of slap and tickle with Rosie in the butler's pantry), but not one recalled seeing Duncan at all after that point.

At last he rose from the table, returned his notebook to the inside pocket of his coat, and thanked Mrs. Brodie for the use of her sitting room. He then returned to the library, where he found Elspeth exactly as he had left her, seated on the sofa with her hands clasped tightly in her lap. Gavin was there as well, prowling back and forth before the fireplace like a caged animal. From the sudden silence that descended upon the room as Pickett entered it, he had no difficulty in surmising the subject of their discussion.

"I'll take my leave of you now," he told the pair, "although I may be obliged to return, if more questions should occur to me." Of that, at least, he had no doubt; his sleepless condition was hardly conducive to astute inquiries.

He emerged from the house to find the sun well above the horizon, the morning now far advanced. Hoping the fresh sea air might clear the cobwebs from his brain, he took the cliff path down to the shore, focusing on each step lest in his sleep-deprived state he should pitch headlong over the edge. As he rounded the promontory, he discovered he was not the only one enjoying the bracing ocean breeze: farther down the beach, Robert and Edward Bertram raced one another to the water's edge, followed at a more sedate pace by Harold and Lady Fieldhurst. As if of their own accord his feet moved faster, eager to intercept the viscountess before she reached her young charges.

She called to him as he approached. "Good morning! Are you returning from your morning constitutional? You must have been out and about early." Her smile faltered as he drew nearer. "Good heavens, you look dreadful! Have you been out all night?"

She wore no bonnet, but sheltered her complexion with the aid of a black-ribboned parasol. The stiff breeze off the sea tugged at her golden curls. In fact, she looked so lovely and carefree that it came as a shock to Pickett to realize she did not yet know about Angus Kirkbride's death.

"Good morning, my lady. Yes, I've been at Ravenscroft Manor for most of the night. There has been an accident—" He glanced uncertainly at Harold.

As he had hoped, Lady Fieldhurst caught that glance and understood it at once. "Harold, will you please run ahead and see that your brothers do not drown one another? I shall be there directly."

For a moment it appeared Harold might protest this dismissal, but something in Pickett's expression must have made him think better of it, for he swallowed whatever protest he might have made and trotted down the beach after his brothers.

"What is it, Mr. Pickett?" Lady Fieldhurst asked once they were alone. "What has happened?"

"It's old Mr. Kirkbride. He died in the night."

One black-gloved hand flew to her mouth. "Oh, how dreadful!"

"It gets worse. The doctor who attended him believes he was murdered, and after hearing his reasons, I am forced to agree. A bottle of medicine which he took for his heart should have been almost full, but it was two-thirds gone, and Mr. Reid says Mr. Kirkbride's symptoms were consistent with an overdose of that same medicine. And Duncan Kirkbride," he concluded, "is missing."

"Missing?" echoed Lady Fieldhurst.

"His bed hadn't been slept in, and no one can recall seeing him since he left the house following the betrothal announcement." He frowned thoughtfully. "At first glance, Duncan seems to be the most likely suspect, for he stood to lose everything once old Angus changed his will. And yet something doesn't seem to fit, although I can't think what it might be."

"Perhaps you will think of it once you've had a little sleep," she suggested. "But in the meantime, who else does that leave? Who else do we know who might have a grudge against Mr. Kirkbride? The real Elspeth might have been nursing resentment over her father's treatment of her so many years ago, but we know our Elspeth is a fraud."

"There's always Neil, the stable hand. By the valet's account, he was a hothead who took umbrage at the fact that a mere accident of birth was all that separated him from a fortune. Apparently he tried to extort money from Mr. Kirkbride after the business with Elspeth, and we know he's shown up at the manor twice trying to see her. But I don't really see him as the murderer. For one thing, I can't imagine how he could gain access to Mr. Kirkbride's room, let alone persuade a man who disliked him to take medicine from his hand, overdose or no."

"Which leads us back to the obvious choice," Lady Fieldhurst concluded. "Elspeth Kirkbride, also known as Mrs. Elizabeth Church."

Pickett prodded at the pebbles on the beach with the toe of his boot. "As easy a target as she makes, I'm afraid we may have to eliminate Mrs. Church as a suspect," he said. "She may be a fraud, but she would have no reason to kill the old man, so far as I can see. In fact, no one would have a better reason to want him alive, at least until he'd had a chance to change his will in her favor. But whether or not she is guilty of murder, she is certainly being less than honest with me, for Mr. Kirkbride's valet mentioned hearing the sound of quarreling voices coming from her room, and she made no mention of any visitor to her room at all, much less a quarrel taking place there."

"Perhaps Mr. Kirkbride finally recognized her as a fraud," suggested her ladyship. "Might she not kill him to prevent being exposed?"

"I suppose she might, but I should think it much simpler to merely return to London with all due haste," Pickett pointed out. "If he had indeed recognized her as a fraud, it must have surely put paid to Mr. Kirkbride's plan to change his will. Having failed in that scheme, I can't imagine what reason she would have had for staying on."

"Marriage to Mr. Gavin, perhaps?" suggested her ladyship.

"If her only ambition was making an advantageous marriage, she might have done far better for herself in London, and under her own name. It seems to me there is never any shortage of gentlemen searching for paramours amongst the actresses. With her reputation, Mrs. Church might have reserved her favors for a man willing to put a ring on her finger." Pickett frowned. "Now that I think of it, much has been made of Mr. Gavin's fondness for London. It is surprising that he never came across her while he was in Town. Surely he must have taken in a performance or two, at the least."

"Perhaps he chose to patronize Covent Garden Theatre instead, or the Theatre Royal Haymarket. Or," she added with a mischievous gleam in her eye, "as you yourself have noted on more than one occasion, perhaps his oversight was due to that deplorable tendency of my class to frequent the theatre for mere social purposes, rather than a true appreciation for the dramatic arts."

Pickett's cheeks assumed a rosy glow that owed nothing to the crisp sea breeze. "I meant no disrespect, my lady—"

"Or perhaps Gavin knew exactly who she was, and knew his uncle would never countenance so unequal a match," continued her ladyship, her eyes growing round as she expounded upon this theme. "Depend upon it, Gavin knew Uncle Angus would leave his entire fortune to Duncan if he—Gavin, that is—were to take a bride off the London stage. Therefore the lovers hatched a scheme, not only to gain Angus's blessings on the marriage, but to snatch Duncan's share of the inheritance as well. Poor Duncan! I have never liked him above half, but now I feel quite sorry for him. He has been shamefully used!"

"My lady—"

"I can see a condolence call is in order. Shall I pump the illicit lovers for information?"

"I can't deny you have a way of ferreting out information that I should be hard-pressed to duplicate, but as for their being illicit lovers—"

Lady Fieldhurst abandoned her theory with a shrug. "No, theirs does seem to be a rather bloodless attachment, does it not? I fear the truth, whatever it is, will prove to be something far more mundane, and probably far less interesting. But it cannot hurt, can it, for me to ask a few discreet questions? All wrapped in the warmest sympathy, of course!"

"No, it certainly cannot hurt, and it might help a great deal. But unless the lady chooses to confide in you, do not let Mrs. Church suspect that you know she is not whom she appears to be! Remember, our murderer has already killed once, and he—or she—may not hesitate to kill again, should it become necessary. I would not want you to put yourself at risk."

"Nor should I, I assure you! And now, if you will excuse me, I had best see to Robert and Edward before they drown themselves or one another. And you, I think, should seek your bed."

Pickett cleared his throat. "One more thing, my lady." He laid a hand on her arm to detain her, but having achieved this modest goal, struggled to know where to begin. The wind tugged at his shallow-crowned hat, and he released the viscountess's arm in order to snatch the hat before it was whisked away down the beach. He did not put it back on his head, but clutched the brim with both hands until his knuckles turned white. "About last night—I sincerely regret—I was out of line. It was unpardonable of me."

He flushed crimson, giving Lady Fieldhurst to understand that his embarrassment sprang not from any circumstances surrounding Angus Kirkbride's death, but rather the little scene they had played out on the terrace several hours earlier.

" 'Unpardonable,' Mr. Pickett? Surely not! Indiscreet, certainly, and possibly ill-advised, but as I recall, you were hardly alone in your indiscretion. I was an active participant, and must be equally culpable."

"You are too kind, my lady." Pickett looked down at his modest headgear with apparent fascination. "I assure you, I will not—that is, you need not fear—" He looked her squarely in the eye and set his jaw. "I beg your pardon, my lady. It will not happen again."

She inclined her head and responded with the same stiff

formality. "Very well, Mr. Pickett. Your apology is accepted."

He executed an awkward bow, then turned up the path toward the inn.

"Oh, Mr. Pickett—"

He paused and turned back. "Yes, my lady?"

"Do you, in all honesty? Regret it, I mean."

He hesitated only a moment before giving her a rather uncertain smile. "In all honesty, it was the high point of my existence."

He bowed once more and continued up the path. She did not call to him again, but stood on the beach and watched him go.

It was the high point of my existence. Good heavens, thought Lady Fieldhurst, what sort of life must he have led, if a stolen kiss on the terrace earned such a tribute? If one kiss (well, more than one, if one were inclined to keep count) held a place of such high regard, she could only imagine what his reaction might have been had they—

She slammed the door of her mind on a line of reasoning far too improper to pursue. And yet the thought, once admitted, would not be so easily dismissed.

CHAPTER 15

IN WHICH LADY FIELDHURST MAKES A MOST UNPLEASANT DISCOVERY

As she followed her young relations down toward the beach, Lady Fieldhurst tugged at Harold's sleeve.

"There is bad news from Ravenscroft Manor," she told him once his younger brothers were safely out of earshot at the water's edge. "Old Mr. Kirkbride died in the night, and Mr. Pickett has reason to believe his death was not from natural causes. Once we return to the inn, I must change my clothes and pay a condolence call on Miss Kirkbride."

Harold brightened at once. "I'll go with you," he volunteered with an eagerness far out of proportion to what the sober task demanded.

"No, no, you must not!" Noting the mulish set of Harold's mouth, she realized the necessity of acquainting that young man with certain unpleasant facts. "I understand how much you admire Miss Kirkbride," she continued gently, "and I had hoped to spare you this, but you must know that Miss Kirkbride is not whom she appears to be. In fact, she is Mrs. Elizabeth Church, a fixture of the London stage."

"An—an *actress*?" Harold stumbled as the pebbles shifted beneath his feet. "Are you certain?"

"Mr. Pickett recognized her at once. He assures me there can be no mistake."

"An actress," Harold murmured, pondering the significance of this revelation.

"Mr. Pickett is not ready to confront the woman with his

173

knowledge, so you must understand the need for the utmost discretion," she added.

After extracting a promise from Harold that he would prevent his younger brothers from inflicting bodily harm on themselves or each other in her absence, Lady Fieldhurst excused herself from the beach excursion as soon as she might reasonably do so. She then left the trio to examine the various specimens of flotsam and jetsam deposited on the shore by the ebbing tide, and made her solitary way back up the path to the inn.

The low murmur of conversation in the taproom told her the death of Angus Kirkbride was now public knowledge, the hushed voices of the villagers their only concession to the tragic nature of the latest gossip. Of John Pickett there was no sign; Lady Fieldhurst could only suppose that he was asleep in his bed—an unfortunate assumption, as it called to mind images of tangled sheets and unclothed limbs.

With a little huff of annoyance at her wayward imagination, she climbed the stairs to her own room and inspected her meager wardrobe for a gown suitable for making a condolence call. There was no shortage of these, thanks to her own status as a mourning widow; everything she had brought with her from London was dyed in shades of black, black, and yet more black.

It had not been this way during the summer just past, when she had travelled to Yorkshire with her trunks filled with new gowns in subdued but less funereal hues of half-mourning, including greys, lavenders, and even the occasional muted striped pattern. If such garments had been suitable in Yorkshire, she wondered, why had she deemed them inappropriate for Scotland?

The unwelcome answer came unbidden to her mind. She had not worn half-mourning in Scotland because she feared the Bertram boys might tell their father, who would lose no time in passing the news of her indiscretion on to the dowager viscountess, her late husband's mother. Good heavens! Aside from the unlikely chance that three schoolboys on holiday should care the snap of their fingers for a lady's wardrobe, was she truly such a coward? One might have supposed that with her husband's death, she would finally have the freedom to do as she pleased without the cloud of his disapproval hanging over her head. Instead, was she to spend the rest of her life trying to appease his family? When was she to have the freedom to live according to her own desires?

She looked at the black bombazine in her hands, then held it up to her shoulders and turned to regard her reflection in the looking-glass. As she cast a critical eye over the effect of flat black fabric on fair hair and skin, she thought longingly of certain gowns in her wardrobe in London. There was a particular satin of celestial blue, she recalled, which was said to match her eyes, and an ethereal white silk, which had so flattered her figure that two gentlemen had very nearly come to blows over the privilege of leading her in to dinner. What would Mr. Pickett think if he could see her in them? Would he find her attractive, or would the rich fabrics merely serve to emphasize the social gulf between them?

Shoving aside the questions that there seemed to be little point in asking, she turned away from the mirror. However much her husband's family might disapprove, it appeared she possessed a certain talent for investigations. At least for now, she would concentrate on that. And if a small voice in her head asked if she would be quite so eager to assist Mr. Pickett if he were, say, of the same age as Mr. Colquhoun, or senile like Sir Henry MacDougall, this voice was easily silenced by her insistence that it was surely the duty of all good English citizens to see that the laws of the land were upheld, no matter how winsome the instrument of that law might be.

She arrived at Ravenscroft Manor to find the house displaying all the trappings of mourning. The hatchment had been mounted over the door, a wooden panel displaying the black shield and silver cross of the Kirkbride coat of arms, and the door knocker had been swathed in black crape as if the sound of the knocker might somehow disturb the dead. The footman who opened the door to her wore a black armband over the sleeve of his livery. When she asked to see Miss Kirkbride, the footman glanced upward—toward heaven or the deathbed upstairs, Lady Fieldhurst could not begin to guess.

"Miss Kirkbride is not seeing visitors," he said in hushed tones, "as she is occupied at the moment."

"Mr. Gavin, then?" her ladyship persisted, disappointed but not defeated.

"Mr. Gavin is out riding."

"How long will he be gone?"

"He did not say." Seeing that the visitor did not intend to be turned away, the footman opened the door wide to admit her. "If you will allow me to show you into the drawing room, I shall inform Miss Kirkbride of your arrival."

With this Lady Fieldhurst was forced to be content. As she waited in the drawing room, she reflected that, whatever Mrs. Church had hoped to gain by her charade, the actress had undoubtedly got herself into far more than she had bargained for. These thoughts were confirmed when her hostess appeared ten minutes later, looking so haggard that she could hardly be recognized as the reigning beauty of the Drury Lane stage. Lady Fieldhurst imagined this was how Mrs. Church might have appeared on stage as Lady Macbeth, whose own ambitious schemes had also ended in tragedy.

"My dear Miss Kirkbride," she said, rising and extending her hands in greeting. "I came as soon as I heard the news. Allow me to express my condolences on the loss of your father."

Miss Kirkbride's hands seized hers and gripped like talons.

"Pray forgive me for keeping you waiting. I was obliged to meet with the village woman who will—who will lay out Father's body."

"A sad task, indeed," observed Lady Fieldhurst. She wondered if she should mention Mr. Pickett's suspicions concerning Angus's death, and when the lady raised the subject herself, she hardly knew whether to be sorry or glad.

"A sad task, as you say, and according to Mr. Pickett, a task which should not have been necessary," the actress answered bitterly. "He will have told you, I suppose, that my father was very likely murdered."

"He did, and I am sorrier than I can say. To lose your father so suddenly, and in such a way . . ." She let the sentence trail off, hoping the *faux* Miss Kirkbride would feel compelled to fill the silence.

She was not disappointed. "In such a way, indeed! You cannot know what it is like, living in this house, not knowing—" The actress broke off and collapsed onto the sofa, raising one trembling hand to her eyes.

Not knowing—what? *Not knowing who did it? Not knowing whether I shall be arrested?* Or, perhaps, *not knowing if or when I shall die next?* With startling clarity, Lady Fieldhurst realized that Miss Kirkbride's distress was in fact stark terror. She should have known it at once; she had known such fear herself not so long ago, following the murder of her husband. She, too, had feared for her own life, albeit at the hands of an avenging Law. Quite against her will, the viscountess found herself feeling a certain kinship with Mrs. Church in spite of the woman's duplicity. However wicked it might be, fraud was surely undeserving of death. She sank onto the sofa next to the actress and covered Mrs. Church's hand with her own.

"Miss Kirkbride, you may rest assured that Mr. Pickett will do all he can to discover the truth about your father's death. In the meantime, if there is anything you can do to assist him, I urge you to confide in him. I can assure you of his competence and his discretion."

Mrs. Church shook her head. "You are a loyal wife, I am sure, but I have nothing to confide."

Lady Fieldhurst was somewhat taken aback by this unexpected reference to the late Lord Fieldhurst, until she realized Mrs. Church referred to her hasty "marriage" to Mr. Pickett. So much had happened in the twelve hours since they were discovered on the terrace that she had quite forgotten her own charade.

"I suspect all who have had professional dealings with Mr. Pickett will share my confidence in his abilities," she insisted. "Believe me when I say that in spite of his youth, he is not without experience in such cases."

"I shall remember it, if I should recall anything that might have a bearing on the case," promised Mrs. Church, gently but firmly closing the subject.

The conversation progressed to the more innocuous topics common to bereavement: earlier, happier memories of the deceased, the arrangements being made for laying him to rest, and his daughter's sense of gratitude that they had reconciled before his passing. And yet the actress's fear was like a living presence in the room, shading even the most commonplace observations with sinister meaning. When she rose to take her leave, Lady Fieldhurst felt obliged to try one more time.

"It cannot be comfortable for you, being the only woman in the house at such a time," she said, reclaiming her bonnet from the butler and tying its black ribbons under her chin. "Shall I come and stay with you, at least until after the funeral?"

"You are too kind, my lady, but I can't take you from your young nephews at such a time."

"Nonsense! Harold is very nearly grown, and there is always

the innkeeper's daughter, whose assistance has been invaluable to me throughout our stay. I am sure she would be only too glad to help in looking after the younger boys. If you have need of my company, you have only to say the word."

"I shall bear it in mind," promised Mrs. Church with such a dismissive air that Lady Fieldhurst was quite certain the offer would be forgotten before the door was closed behind her. "Now, I beg you will excuse me, Mrs. Pickett, but I should like to lie down for a bit before meeting with the vicar about the funeral service. I've sent the groom in the trap to fetch him, and they should be returning very shortly."

And that, Lady Fieldhurst reflected, was that. Seeing that nothing she might say would change Mrs. Church's mind, she allowed herself to be ushered out of the house, then turned and started down the cliff path toward the beach.

The farther she walked, however, the less satisfied she became. It appeared that the Kirkbride cousins had closed ranks. Against outsiders, she wondered, or against each other? Perhaps both. In any case, it was clear she would get little information from any of them. But there was another, in the family yet not of it, who might be more forthcoming. She resolved to have a word with Neil, the bastard Kirkbride once employed in the family's stables. Mr. Pickett had not mentioned where Neil might be found, but the head groom might know where he was currently employed.

She turned and trudged back up the path. When she reached the top, she skirted the house and made for the stables. All was quiet; apparently the groom had not yet returned with the vicar, and Gavin had not yet come back from his ride.

"Hello?" she called, expecting someone, anyone, to emerge from the large wooden structure.

Receiving no response, she grasped the heavy iron door handle and pulled. Sunlight slanted through the increasingly widening gap, revealing rows of recently mucked-out stalls and filling the air with the sharp tang of fresh hay. Lady Fieldhurst stepped inside, blinking as her eyes adjusted to the dark interior. Within the stalls, horses stamped and snorted nervously as they regarded her with rolling eyes.

"Hello?" she called again. "Is anyone there?"

She spotted a roughly dressed figure in the dimness ahead, but even as she moved toward it, she realized something was terribly wrong. At that moment a gust of wind pushed the stable door open wide and the sunlight spilled in, revealing the body of Neil dangling by a rope from an overhead rafter.

Chapter 16

WHICH REVEALS THE SURPRISING TRUTH ABOUT MRS. ELIZABETH CHURCH

Pickett was awakened all too soon from his slumbers by the arrival of Mr. Colquhoun, who sat down heavily on the edge of the bed and began removing his boots.

"Arise, slugabed, and greet the dawn," said the magistrate with a cheerfulness Pickett found disgusting. "Or the afternoon rather, for the morning is all but gone. I nabbed a couple of fine trout, which our host's wife has kindly agreed to cook for our dinner."

Pickett rolled over with a groan. "I am pleased to hear it, sir, but I should be happier to nab a murderer."

"Perhaps you should try wetting a hook," suggested Mr. Colquhoun. "I find that many times it calms the mind and clears the head. But as I was saying, this morning I had the good fortune to meet up with a fellow angler on holiday, an Oxford don by the name of Basingame, who told me of a prime fishing spot on the burn beyond the kirk—"

Pickett massaged his temples to clear his sleep-deprived brain. He knew by Mr. Colquhoun's own admission that that worthy had left his native land at the age of sixteen to seek his fortune abroad. But now that Mr. Colquhoun had returned to the land of his birth, he seemed to grow more Scottish by the day. Pickett feared that if he did not solve the Kirkbride mystery soon, he would not be able to understand a word that issued from his magistrate's mouth.

"Begging your pardon, sir, but the 'what' beyond the 'what'?"

"Damned *sassenach*," the magistrate muttered, although the twinkle in his eye robbed the words of the insult Pickett suspected lay hidden there. "The brook beyond the church, my boy."

Pickett dragged the counterpane over his head, grumbling under his breath. "Well, why didn't you—?" He suddenly bolted upright in bed, all vestiges of sleep vanished as the significance of Mr. Colquhoun's words sank in. "Do you mean to tell me that 'kirk' is the Scottish word for 'church'?"

"Aye, didn't I just say so?"

"And," Pickett continued with growing certainty, "I would wager 'Elspeth' is the Scottish form of 'Elizabeth.' "

Mr. Colquhoun nodded. "You would win that wager, if you could find anyone foolish enough to accept it. I should have thought it was obvious."

"Then she is exactly who she says she is," Pickett marveled.

The magistrate's eyebrows rose. "I trust you are going to enlighten me?"

"Tell me, Mr. Colquhoun, are you familiar with the Theatre Royal in Drury Lane?"

The magistrate's bushy white eyebrows drew together in bewilderment at this seeming *non sequitur.* "I know where it is, of course, but when I go to the theatre—which is not often, I confess—I prefer to see Grimaldi at Covent Garden."

Pickett flung himself off the mattress and began to pace the room, the bare feet that had so cut up Lady Fieldhurst's peace now slapping against the scrubbed wooden floor with every step he took. "When I first saw the supposed Miss Kirkbride last night, I was convinced she had to be a fraud. In fact, I recognized the lady as Elizabeth Church, the actress who treads the boards at Drury Lane. I made the mistaken assumption that she must be either Miss Kirkbride or Mrs. Church. It never crossed my mind that the two women might be one and the same."

Mr. Colquhoun nodded. "It is my understanding that those in the theatre often assume a stage name."

"Yes, and in the case of Miss Kirkbride, she simply took the English equivalent of the name she'd been called by ever since her mother married Angus Kirkbride."

"I take it, then, that Miss Kirkbride did not drown fifteen years ago," observed Mr. Colquhoun.

"Precisely. She somehow found her way to London, where she has made a name for herself on the stage. Although," Pickett added, "why she chose this particular time and manner of staging a homecoming, I should like to know."

"I wish you luck in prevailing upon her to tell you," was the magistrate's dour reflection.

"Oh, I doubt she would tell me anything worthy of mention." Pickett stopped pacing and stared fixedly at the far wall, as if he could see through it and the several rooms beyond into Lady Fieldhurst's chamber further down the corridor. "I wonder if Lady Fieldhurst might have more success with her? Miss Kirkbride might be more forthcoming with a member of her own sex."

"An excellent notion," seconded Mr. Colquhoun with exaggerated approval. "And it has the added benefit of necessitating yet another *tête-à-tête* between her ladyship and yourself."

Pickett refused to take the bait. "It is unfortunate that I should be obliged to impose on her ladyship yet again, sir," he remarked with an innocence that deceived no one, "but needs must when the devil drives."

Here, however, he was to be disappointed. He rapped on her ladyship's door (a bit sheepishly, as the hotel management supposed him to be sharing this chamber with his "wife"), but there was no response. He rapped a second time, debating the wisdom of opening the door and entering unannounced, when a door opened further down the corridor and young Edward Bertram's head appeared in the crack.

"Hullo," he called. "If you're looking for Aunt Julia, she's not here."

"Where is she?"

Edward shrugged. "She's gone to visit that 'bride' lady."

"Miss Kirkbride?"

"That's the one," said Edward, idly swinging back and forth on the door.

"Did she say when she would return?"

Another shrug. "I don't remember."

"You don't remember if she said, or you don't remember what time she said she would be back?"

"I don't remember," Edward said again. "Harold said old Mr. Kirkbride is dead. Is that true?"

"Yes."

His interest piqued, Edward abandoned the door and joined Pickett in the corridor. "Did somebody kill him? Can I help you catch the fellow that did it?"

"You can help me by telling me about your Aunt Julia—what time did she leave? Has she been gone long?"

A third shrug, and a fourth, were his only answers. "When you catch him, are you going to shoot him?" Edward asked eagerly. "Can I watch?"

Giving up a lost cause, Pickett thanked the boy (for what, precisely, he wasn't sure) and made his way down the stairs. If Lady Fieldhurst had only recently set out, he might be able to overtake her. At the foot of the stairs, however, he paused. Angry voices issued from behind the door of the private parlor—and one of the voices was female. His chivalrous instincts aroused, Pickett flung open the door, ready to rescue Lady Fieldhurst from whoever might be harassing her.

But the lady in question was not Lady Fieldhurst, nor did she appear to have any need of his assistance. Elspeth Kirkbride struggled in the ardent embrace of Harold Bertram, but even as Pickett moved forward to her aid, she delivered a ringing slap to her youthful swain's face.

"Harold! Release Miss Kirkbride at once!" Pickett commanded unnecessarily, for Miss Kirkbride's violent reaction had the effect of cooling Harold's passion to such an extent that he dropped his arms from his *inamorata* so that he might press one hand to his stinging cheek. "You owe the lady an apology."

" 'Lady?' " Harold echoed a bit breathlessly. "But Aunt Julia told me you said she was an actress!"

"As it turns out, she is both. But even if she were a scullery maid, her position would not entitle you to force unwanted attentions upon her."

"But I wasn't—I didn't mean—I love her!" Harold turned to face the unwilling object of his affections. "When you danced with me, I thought—I thought you liked me!"

"I like you very well, Harold, but I cannot say I like being mauled," replied Miss Kirkbride with spirit. "If granting a dance also entitled one to take liberties, well, it would make for some very interesting balls," she added with a hint of a smile.

Thus chastened, Harold hung his head. "I beg your pardon, Miss Kirkbride. I only thought, if you were indeed an actress— well, one hears things about actresses, and I thought perhaps you and I could—I know you are older than I, so perhaps you might—might teach me—" He broke off, flushing crimson.

"I know what you are saying, Harold, and while I daresay you meant your overtures as a compliment, your assumptions are not true of *all* actresses, and even those who are open to such arrangements as you suggest are not generally in the habit of corrupting schoolboys."

"But—well, how is one to—that is, I seem to be the only one

at Oxford who isn't—who hasn't—" Lapsing once more into incoherence, Harold at last fell into an embarrassed silence.

"I believe I understand your dilemma," Miss Kirkbride said. "Let me assure you, I have some knowledge of gentlemen, and of one thing you may be certain: those with the most talk generally have the least action, if you take my meaning."

Although Miss Kirkbride's words were not intended for himself, they called to mind some previously overlooked thread of evidence that flitted through Pickett's brain only to vanish before he could catch hold of it.

"Then the stories the lads tell at school," Harold said with dawning comprehension, "they're not true?"

"Oh, there might be a grain of truth to some, but I would wager most are exaggerations, if not outright lies," Miss Kirkbride assured him.

"I meant no insult, Miss Kirkbride, but you must—" Harold gave Pickett a glance that clearly wished him at the devil. "You must know how I feel about you," he continued, his voice scarcely above a whisper.

"I think I do," she said gently. "Tell me, Harold, how old are you?"

"Eighteen. But it is only a matter of a few months before I shall be nineteen," he added hastily.

Miss Kirkbride nodded wisely. "I thought as much. It may not seem so now, but somewhere in England at this very minute, there is a young lady in the schoolroom who is stitching samplers and practicing the pianoforte and nursing a grand passion for her dancing master. She is preparing herself for you, Harold, and when the time is right you will meet her."

"Much good it will do me," Harold muttered. "I can never pay court to a lady who needs her father's permission to marry, for he would shut the door in my face. I bear the stigma of illegitimacy, you know."

"Oh, better and better! As a matter of fact, I did *not* know, but I can assure you that nothing appeals to very young ladies quite so much as the prospect of a forbidden romance. You are clearly destined to break hearts." She extended her hand to him. "Come now, let us cry friends, and when you return to school for the autumn term you may tell your cronies that you kissed the hand of the celebrated Mrs. Church."

Harold was quick to do so, and Pickett was pleased to note there was nothing but the deepest reverence in his demeanor.

"Miss Kirkbride, I congratulate you," Pickett observed, once the blissful Harold had left them alone. "That was well done."

She shrugged. "Ah well, first love can be painful. Perhaps if my own father had spoken so to me, instead of flying up into the boughs—" She shook her head. "But it is all water under the bridge now. In any case, I see you have penetrated my guilty secret. Tell me, Mr. Pickett, have you spoken to your wife this afternoon?"

He shook his head, a bit taken aback as always to hear Lady Fieldhurst so described. "Edward tells me she has not yet returned from calling on you."

"Has she not? How very odd! She set out some minutes before I did, so I should have thought she would have arrived before me. I daresay she took the cliff path and stopped along the way to admire the prospect from the beach. Very wise of her, for this pleasant weather cannot last much longer."

Pickett's eyebrows drew together in a thoughtful frown. Miss Kirkbride's demeanor, so easy and natural with Harold only a moment ago, had undergone a sudden change. Now she seemed nervous and excessively talkative. Pickett was quite certain she had not come all the way from Ravenscroft Manor to make inane observations about the weather.

"Miss Kirkbride, is there anything I can do for you? I'm sorry my, er, Mrs. Pickett is not here, but if you will accept my escort, perhaps we might meet her on the beach—"

"No, no, that will not be necessary," she assured him hastily. "In fact, it was to speak to you that I came. Mrs. Pickett assured me that I might safely confide in you."

At last, it seemed, Miss Kirkbride was ready to talk. As he led her to the settle before the fire, Pickett found himself in the unlikely position of hoping Lady Fieldhurst might linger on the beach a bit longer; it would not do if she were to interrupt just as the mysterious Elspeth Kirkbride decided to unburden herself.

"Very well, Miss Kirkbride, what is it you wish to tell me?"

She sank onto the settle, arranged her skirts, and clasped her hands tightly together in her lap. Then, taking a deep breath, she began. "It all started with my recent appearance as Ophelia in *Hamlet,* and an unexpected visitor to my dressing room following my performance one evening . . ."

CHAPTER 17

WHICH OFFERS MORE UNPLEASANT SURPRISES FOR LADY FIELDHURST

Lady Fieldhurst stood as if rooted to the floor, staring dumbly at the body turning gently with the slight air current, its eyes and tongue bulging hideously. She knew she should inform Mr. Pickett at once of the stable hand's death, but she could not seem to force her feet to obey her mind's commands. Then the roan mare in the nearest stall nickered as if seeking consolation, and the sound released her from her horrified trance. She turned and ran blindly from the stable, hardly knowing or caring where she went until, rounding the corner of the building, she ran full tilt into Gavin Kirkbride.

She smothered a shriek as she recognized the hands bracing her shoulders. "Oh, thank heavens! Gavin—in the stable—it's—it's—"

He gave her a little shake. "Yes? What is it?"

Her breath came in great sobbing gasps, making coherent speech impossible. "The stable hand—Neil. He—he—"

"Calmly, Mrs. Pickett. He what?"

"He's dead. He—he's hanging from the rafters." She covered her face with her hands as if she might somehow blot out the ghastly image.

"Good God!"

"We must—we must tell Mr. Pickett. He will want to examine the—the body," she concluded, shuddering.

"Of course Mr. Pickett must be informed at once," Gavin nodded. "But you must allow me to escort you back to the inn.

The cliff path will be quicker, but I dare not let you attempt it alone in your present agitated state."

"Yes, yes, of course. Thank you." She allowed him to tuck her hand into the crook of his elbow, and together they started down the narrow footpath skirting the sheer plunge to the beach.

"But how came you to be here, Mrs. Pickett?"

Although her heart was still pounding, her breathing was a bit steadier now, making it easier to answer his questions. "I came to pay a call of condolence on Miss Kirkbride—you must allow me to express my condolences to you, as well, on the death of your uncle—and when I left the house—" She realized she could hardly confess to searching the stables for information regarding the whereabouts of the stable hand whose body was even now hanging from the rafters. "When I left the house I found the wind had grown rather keener, so I stopped by the stables thinking to ask if someone might be spared to drive me back to the inn. But when I entered the stable, I found no one but the horses and—and—" Her voice broke, and her trembling began anew.

"A most distressing sight, I am sure," he said, then sighed. "I very much fear that I may be in some way responsible for the poor fellow's death."

"You, Gavin? In what way?"

He paused to steer her past a rock jutting into the narrow pathway. "I daresay you have heard enough of our family's history to know that he was once caught in what is commonly called a compromising position with my cousin Elspeth. Of course she was merely using him to goad her father, but I believe he thought she truly cared for him. Once her betrothal to me was announced, I fear he could no longer live with the knowledge that he had lost her a second time."

Lady Fieldhurst's mind had become so attuned to murder that the possibility of suicide had not occurred to her. "You believe he died at his own hand, then?"

"I believe it is the only explanation that makes sense. Who would have reason to kill a stable hand?"

"But a stable hand who tried to force his way into the house—"

"There is no denying that he made a nuisance of himself, but most of us deal with annoying people every day without having any overwhelming urge to kill them. Besides," he added, "Elspeth was the one being harassed, and I doubt she would have the strength to do such a thing, even had she the inclination."

"I suppose you're right," she said slowly. "I had not thought—and yet—"

"Yet what, Mrs. Pickett?"

Not for the first time, she wished she had not been so hasty in assuming Mr. Pickett's name; hearing herself thus addressed, and at such a time, was much too great a distraction.

"I am far from expert at such things, but would he not have needed a chair, or a stool, or something to—to reach the beam overhead and then to step off—" she shuddered at the more grisly details of doing away with oneself by hanging.

"I believe you may be right," Gavin said, much struck. "And was there no such chair or stool in evidence?"

She shook her head. "No, I am quite certain there was not."

"Perhaps it was merely out of sight, in the shadows," he suggested. "Forgive me for being so graphic, but I daresay that in his death throes he might have kicked it quite some distance."

Lady Fieldhurst frowned thoughtfully, seeing once more the horrific scene that was surely burned into her brain for all eternity. "No, there was no chair or stool. Even if there had been, and Neil had kicked it as you say, it must have come to rest against one of the stalls." She recalled once more the nervous, stamping horses, and glanced up at her escort as a new thought occurred to her. "What did you do with your horse, Gavin?"

His arm stiffened beneath her hand. "I beg your pardon?"

"The footman said you had gone out riding. When you returned you must have—" Too late she realized the terrible truth. Of course Gavin would have led his horse back into the stable for grooming, and then—what? Had he discovered Neil's body before her? Surely, then, he must have said so—unless he had found a very much alive Neil waiting to confront him over his marriage to Elspeth. Or had Neil had bigger fish to fry than the mere blighting of a fifteen-year-old love affair? Mr. Pickett had said that Neil had once before sought to profit from the misfortunes of the Kirkbride family; had he gained some hold over Gavin that he thought to turn to his advantage? And what secret would be more worth paying to keep than the truth regarding one's part in a murder?

She picked up her pace, suddenly eager to escape the narrow confines of the path and the precipitous drop to the sea. "But Gavin, what a shocking way to treat your horse!" she exclaimed brightly. "You must have abandoned the poor creature in the stable yard, for if you had entered the stable you surely must have seen poor Neil. It is too kind of you to accompany me, but you must not neglect your horses on my account. I could have found my way back to the inn without your escort. You must give him an apple or some extra oats when you return, to repay him for his patience. Or do you ride a mare?"

She was babbling. She knew it, but she could not seem to stop. All she could do was keep talking in a desperate attempt to banish the sudden suspicion from Gavin's eyes. Then his fingers closed around her arm, and she realized that all the talking in the world would do her no good. She had no doubt that she would soon be taking a shortcut down the cliff path, and that her self-appointed escort intended that she would not survive the fall.

"A valiant attempt, my dear, but your every word condemns you," Gavin said, confirming her worst fears. "Yes, I returned to the stables following my ride and, as you suspect, I found Neil waiting for me there, the fool."

"You are a better man than this, Gavin," she said cajolingly, in a desperate attempt to appeal to his better nature—if in fact he possessed such a thing. "Surely much must be forgiven a man disappointed in love not once, but twice, and over the same woman. He did not deserve to die."

Gavin gave a snort of derision. "Believe me, ardor for the fair Elspeth was the last thing on his mind! He offered to sell me his silence, the blackguard! After the ball he was waiting on the terrace like a moonling, awaiting a glimpse of his lost love, when what did he see instead but the figure of a man silhouetted against the curtain in Uncle Angus's window—a man, he was persuaded, whose stature was too slender to be Duncan, and whose movements were too nimble to be Uncle Angus's manservant. When Neil learned the next day that the old man was dead, he put two and two together and saw a way—or so he thought—to extort money from me in exchange for keeping quiet."

The path widened a bit some twenty or thirty feet ahead. If she could only keep Gavin talking until they reached that point, she might be able to hitch up her skirts and run. It was a slim chance, but at the moment it appeared to be the only chance she had. "Then it was you who killed him?"

"My dear girl, do you truly think I would admit as much? Ah well, I suppose it matters little. It is not as if you will live long enough to pass the information along to the intrepid Mr. Pickett. Well then, since you will have it, I did silence Neil, and permanently. When in London, I box frequently with Gentleman Jackson, so I am stronger than I look. Neil probably outweighed me by at least two stone, but whatever I lacked in size, I made up for in technique. Once I had rendered him unconscious, I had only to slip the rope around his neck, toss the loose end over the beam, and hoist the body off the ground."

"And—and Mr. Kirkbride?"

"Neil was quite right; I did indeed hasten my dear uncle off to his heavenly reward. Hmm, I wonder if there is a word for the murder of one's uncle? We have patricide for the murder of a father, and fratricide for the murder of a brother—we nefarious nephews should be immortalized in the lexicon, as well. I must look into it."

Fifteen feet to go, twelve—"But why, Gavin? He was prepared to entrust his beloved daughter to you in marriage. What could he possibly have done to you that should warrant his death?"

"Why, nothing, at least not to me personally. But have you any idea how much it costs to maintain a fashionable existence in London?"

"But Elspeth was to be her father's sole heiress, and you were to be Elspeth's husband! You would have eventually controlled his entire fortune," she pointed out. "Or was that the problem—the fact that she was not Elspeth at all, but the actress Mrs. Church?"

Gavin stopped and stared at her, a maddening ten feet short of her goal. "So you know about that, do you? It appears your Mr. Pickett is rather more clever than I gave him credit for. But there is where I made my fatal—no pun intended—error. The actress I hired to play the part of my long-lost cousin was, in fact, my long-lost cousin. It seems Elspeth survived after all, and found fame as the toast of Drury Lane Theatre."

"You *hired* her?"

"I did indeed, and tutored her rigorously in the history and mannerisms of my dear departed cousin. And she, damn her, was careful not to prove too apt a pupil. How she must have laughed at me!" He ground his teeth at the thought. "And just when things were going so well—old Angus over the moon at her return, and all eagerness for us to be joined as man and wife—I went to her room that night after the ball to give her the first installment of the payment we had agreed upon, and she informed me of her true identity. She said she had no intention of marrying me, and even thanked me for effecting a reconciliation between her and her father, curse her impudence. She told me she planned to break off the engagement the next morning, as soon as she could speak to her father in private."

"If that was her intention all along, I wonder why she went through with the betrothal announcement at all?" Lady Fieldhurst marveled. If she could only keep him talking long enough, surely someone would come along. The wrongly suspected Duncan might yet turn up, or perhaps even Mr. Pickett, if he were not still sound asleep at the inn.

"I can answer that. She went through with the ball so that all the neighboring gentry could see that her father accepted her fully, the prodigal child returned at last to the fold. Even though the broken engagement must undoubtedly cause some speculation, it would not be her reputation damaged by it, but mine. Breaking an engagement is, of course, a lady's prerogative. Then, too, she might not have stopped with merely breaking the engagement. She might have decided to make a clean breast of it and tell Uncle Angus of my part in the little drama. I could not take that chance."

Lady Fieldhurst made what she hoped was a sympathetic noise, although it sounded even to her own ears like a pitiful whimper.

"Acting on the theory that half an inheritance was better, so to speak, than no bread, I resolved to do in the old man before he could carry out his plan to change his will in Elspeth's favor. It was easy enough to accomplish, thanks to the foxglove derivative he takes for his heart."

"Good God, you must be mad!" breathed Lady Fieldhurst.

"Mad? Not at all. Merely at low tide financially, and with no other way of righting the sinking ship. I console myself with the knowledge that Elspeth's return, while undeniably a happy event to Uncle Angus, put a significant strain on his already weak heart. He probably would not have lived much longer in any case, and his sufferings were brief. So shall yours be, my dear, I assure you."

And with those final words of comfort, he seized her by the arms and dragged her to the edge of the precipice. Lady Fieldhurst fought with every ounce of strength she possessed, but Gavin's lithe form concealed a surprising strength.

"You are wasting your energy, Mrs. Pickett." Gavin was hardly even breathing heavily. "As I told you before, I box regularly with Gentleman Jackson in London. Not to boast, but I even beat him on one memorable occasion."

"I'll bet—you—cheated!" Lady Fieldhurst retorted, still struggling to free herself.

Gavin chuckled. "If you are thinking to shame me, you are wasting your breath. You would be better served in saying your prayers."

She was already doing that, although whether those prayers were directed toward the Almighty or John Pickett, even she could not have said. She could no longer spare the breath to speak, not even to scream for help. Her foot found Gavin's instep, and she kicked and stamped for all she was worth. She might have saved herself the effort, for his iron grip never slackened.

At last, when her strength was almost spent, she knew what she must do. She knew, just as surely as if she had read the account in the newspaper, what would happen in the days following her plunge over the cliff. Her death would be deemed a tragic accident, the sad consequence of her taking the path too quickly in her impatience to reach the inn and report the stable hand's suicide. Duncan would no doubt hang for the murder of his uncle, since he stood to lose his inheritance, and indeed his very absence seemed to confirm his guilt. Elspeth was too frightened for her own life to come forward, or perhaps Gavin would find some way to kill her next, and there would be no one to see that he paid for his crimes.

In that moment of clarity, she knew that if she could not prevent Gavin from throwing her off, she could at least make certain he went over with her, thus ensuring that some rough sort of justice was done. Sooner or later Mr. Pickett would be called upon to examine their bodies at the foot of the cliff, and perhaps he would deduce the rest; her sacrifice would at least prevent him from having Duncan's innocent blood on his hands. Her mind made up, she stopped struggling against her captor and instead flung herself against his chest. Thrown off balance, he released her abruptly, windmilling his arms.

His scream joined with hers as they went over the precipice together.

CHAPTER 18
IN WHICH JOHN PICKETT ASSUMES
THE RÔLE OF ROMANTIC HERO

"Are you telling me," Pickett asked incredulously, "that your cousin Gavin hired you to portray *yourself?*"

"Yes, although of course he did not realize I was in fact his cousin Elspeth," Miss Kirkbride answered. Her gaze was fixed on the view outside the window of the inn's private parlor, but Pickett suspected that, instead of seeing the busy inn yard, she saw her dressing room backstage at Drury Lane Theatre and the cousin, now approaching middle age, who had called on her there. "Recall that Gavin had not seen me in more than a decade, and he thought I was dead, so he would naturally not expect to see me. And then there was the heavy theatrical *maquillage* I wore as Ophelia. Alas, it takes a liberal application of cosmetics to transform a woman of more than thirty years into Shakespeare's innocent young heroine."

"And yet Gavin never recognized your name? I confess, I only this morning became aware of the connection between your birth name and your stage name, but Gavin grew up in Scotland. Surely he must have noticed it was the English equivalent?"

"You are clever, Mr. Pickett, but there is a difference between being clever and being merely crafty. Gavin prided himself on the former when instead he was only the latter."

"What of that little scene on the beach? Your recent success as Ophelia helped you out a bit there, I believe."

Miss Kirkbride looked puzzled. "I beg your pardon?"

"Mrs. Pickett drew a sketch showing you lying in the position in which they found you," he explained.

"Oh, did you recognize my Ophelia?" She smiled, and for a moment the shadows in her eyes were banished. "Yes, the position was the same, although I can assure you the boards of the Drury Lane stage are much more comfortable than the shingle on the beach!"

"Yet you lay there for how long before you were discovered?"

"Actually, not as long as you might think. Gavin had given me funds for passage on the mail coach from London, but I dared not disembark at Ravenscroft for fear of being recognized. I had the coach set me down at the next village over. Between that village and this, there is a stretch of isolated beach where my cousins and I used to swim, until they went off to school and my father decided I was a young lady and too old for such things. I waited until the afternoon, and then walked to this stretch of beach. There was a moon that night, and the beach has not changed much in the intervening years, so I was in no danger. In fact, I passed a very peaceful night gazing at the moon and swimming beneath the stars."

"Swimming?" Pickett echoed, appalled. "At this time of year?"

"You forget, Mr. Pickett, that I am Scots bred. I find the cold water bracing."

"But Harold said your clothes were scarcely damp!"

Miss Kirkbride arched a mischievous eyebrow. " 'Clothes,' Mr. Pickett? I don't recall having said anything about swimming in my clothes." Seeing him blush crimson, she added, "As I said, it is a very isolated strip of beach, so there was little chance of my being discovered. Then as dawn approached, I put on my clothes and walked on to the beach adjacent to the house, where I arranged myself on the shingle, just as Harold and his brothers found me."

"But why the beach? Why was such an elaborate ruse necessary?"

"The beach scene was Gavin's idea. He thought Father would be much more inclined to take pity on a familiar-looking stranger with no memory than on a returned prodigal who sails into the drawing room after fifteen years with no explanation or apology, clearly prepared to resume her place in the family. It may sound cruel, Mr. Pickett, but I welcomed the opportunity to gauge my family's reaction to my return before deciding whether or not to reveal myself to Gavin."

"It seems to me that Gavin was as much a pawn in your scheme as you were in his," Pickett remarked.

"Yes, I confess that while speaking with Gavin I began to form a plan of my own." She gave a wistful sigh. "I wanted to go home, Mr. Pickett. I suppose I'd always wanted to go home, but I didn't realize how much until Gavin came to me with his proposition. I had not seen my father in more than a decade, and I knew he must be getting on in years. Gavin seemed certain that he would welcome me, and if it turned out that Gavin was wrong, well, I would be no worse off than before. Either way, I would be five thousand pounds the richer—a comfortable retirement, when the time came. Then, too, there was Duncan. In spite of the bitterness of our parting, I had never truly forgotten him. If I were to come here and find him happily married with a quiver full of children, perhaps I could finally lay the ghosts of the past to rest."

"I understand, and I wish you every success. But I still don't see why your cousin Gavin should conceive of such a scheme in the first place."

"And here I was only moments ago calling you clever!" Miss Kirkbride chided him archly. "I fear I shall have to take back my words."

"Look here," Pickett said in some exasperation, "the only

reason I can see, particularly in the light of your betrothal, is that he was trying to get at your father's fortune."

Miss Kirkbride inclined her head. "Precisely. My faith in your intelligence is restored."

"But why? Gavin didn't need it half as much as Duncan did, by all accounts—" He broke off as he recalled a snatch of conversation between Miss Kirkbride and Harold. "I see! You said it yourself!"

Now it was her turn to be confused. "What did I say?"

"As you told Harold—those who talk the most generally have the least. I've heard a great deal about 'poor Duncan,' whose need for funds was so much greater than his cousin's, and what a pity it was that he was to be disinherited. But the source of those comments was not Duncan bemoaning his loss, but Gavin expressing his supposed remorse at cutting out his cousin. Lady Malcolm said much the same thing, but I would wager Gavin was her source of information as well. Hmm," Pickett pondered aloud, "if I were to pay a visit to Gavin's banker, I wonder what tale he would tell?"

"I daresay you would discover that Gavin's late wife's dowry was not so large as he was led to believe, or perhaps he ran through it more quickly than he expected. Gavin enjoys a way of life in London that is frightfully expensive to maintain. Certainly he must have an urgent need of funds to hatch such a scheme as the one he proposed to me." She looked down at the hands in her lap. "Poor Catherine! We have never had any reason to suppose that her death was anything other than childbed fever, but now I shall always wonder."

"And yet, believing your cousin to be capable of murder, you said nothing last night when I was summoned to examine your father's body." Pickett's voice assumed a harder edge. "Why did you not tell me of your suspicions then?"

"Quite frankly, Mr. Pickett, I was terrified! I knew my cousin to be capable of perpetrating a hoax for financial gain but, disgraceful as that may be, it is a far cry from murder! Until my father was dead and the doctor voiced his suspicions, I had not suspected Gavin to be capable of that. I feared for my own life. Would he kill me next, in order to ensure my silence? Lady Fieldhurst offered to stay with me, and I wish now that I had accepted her offer. I may still do so, when she returns to the inn."

Pickett hardly heard the last part of this speech, so taken aback was he by Miss Kirkbride's casual reference to "Mrs. Pickett's" true identity.

" 'Lady Fieldhurst'?" he echoed, feeling uncomfortably like a recalcitrant schoolboy caught in a lie.

Miss Kirkbride's lips twisted in a wry smile. "Come now, Mr. Pickett, even theatre people read a newspaper occasionally! The details of Lady Fieldhurst's brush with the law, and your heroic efforts on her behalf, made for the most lurid reading! It was quite enthralling, I assure you. I know of at least one aspiring playwright who has the fixed ambition of adapting the story for the stage."

Pickett put his hand to his head and let out a groan.

"Never fear, if it is anything like his previous masterpieces, it will never be published, much less performed. And as for my telling anyone here of her identity, I assure you her secret—and yours—is safe with me. But tell me, do you have enough evidence to hold Gavin for murder?"

"Not at this point," he admitted. "In fact, unless Duncan has returned with a very good explanation for his prolonged absence, I fear it is he, not Gavin, who appears to be the most likely suspect."

"I feared as much. I daresay I should go back to the house and await his return, but I cannot rest easy staying under the same roof as Gavin, and I am sure it would arouse all his

202

suspicions were I to remove to the inn indefinitely. If only Lady Fieldhurst would return!"

Pickett hated to break the news to Miss Kirkbride, but he had no intention of allowing Lady Fieldhurst to remove to a dwelling that in all likelihood housed a murderer. In fact, her continued absence was beginning to make him more than a little uneasy.

"Surely she should have returned by now, no matter how compelling the view of the sea," he remarked. "Shall I accompany you back to the manor? I should like to satisfy myself that nothing has happened to her. The cliff path is quite steep, as I recall."

"Indeed it is, and I shall be happy to accept your escort," Miss Kirkbride said, rising and shaking out her skirts. "Shall we go now? I do hope you will forgive me for not confiding in you sooner, when her ladyship assured me that I might." She slanted a look at him from beneath her lashes. "You should know that she has the highest opinion of you."

Having reduced poor Pickett to stammering demurrals, she took his proffered arm and allowed him to lead her down the sloping path to the beach. As they traversed the long stretch of sand and shingle, Pickett looked in vain for any sign of Lady Fieldhurst. There was no solitary female form gazing out to sea, but there was a bank of dark clouds piling up on the horizon; apparently Miss Kirkbride had spoken the truth when she predicted a turn in the weather.

As they rounded the headland, however, the weather was forgotten as Pickett caught sight of two figures near the top of the cliff path. The smaller, a fair-haired female in a black mourning gown, struggled in the arms of a man too lithe to be Duncan Kirkbride. Pickett dropped Miss Kirkbride's arm and set out at a run for the foot of the path.

"Halt!" he shouted breathlessly. "Halt in the name of the King!"

But even as he spoke, both figures went over the side of the cliff, the man's arms flailing in a futile attempt to regain his balance, the female's black skirts flapping like the wings of some predatory bird.

"No!" Pickett screamed, desperation lending speed to his feet as he closed the distance to the path.

Gavin Kirkbride bounced twice on the rocks in his precipitous plunge to the beach, but Pickett hardly noticed. His full attention was devoted to Lady Fieldhurst, whose descent had been miraculously halted less than six feet below the point from which she had fallen. Lungs on fire, he scrambled up the uneven trail until he reached the spot; from this angle, he could see that she clung to a gorse bush growing out of the side of the cliff. He flopped down on his belly along the edge and stretched down his arm.

"Take my hand!" he commanded. "I'll pull you up."

"Mr. Pickett!" she exclaimed, looking up at him. "It was Gavin. He—he—"

"Yes, I know. You can tell me about it later, but first take my hand and let me pull you up."

"I dare not let go!" she said, her knuckles white with the strain of supporting her weight.

"You must, my lady. I promise I will not let you fall. No, don't look down," he said as she glanced over her shoulder at Gavin lying on the beach below, the incoming tide licking at his broken body.

After some coaxing, she released her left hand and stretched it up toward his. A pitiful three inches separated their straining fingers, but it might as well have been three miles.

"I—can't—reach!"

Pickett inched closer to the edge, but he dared not go further;

he had to have sufficient leverage to haul her up the side of the cliff.

"You're going to have to lift yourself up," he told her. "Use the bush for leverage. Pull on it to raise yourself higher."

She tried, but without success. "I—can't—" she protested, breathless with exertion.

"I won't let you fall," he promised. "Try it again."

"The boys—will you see that they are returned to their mother? Tell George—"

"Don't talk like that! We're going to get you out of here, do you understand?"

He wasn't at all certain he believed it himself, but he had to be confident for her sake. Then he heard a ripping sound as the roots of the gorse bush began to give way, and he knew the time for coaxing was past.

"*Do it, Julia!*" he ordered in a tone he had never used with her before. "*Now!*"

She too had heard that ominous sound, and knew what it meant. Without further protest, she heaved herself upward. The gorse came free in her right hand just as Pickett's fingers closed about her left wrist. He rolled onto his back, dragging her with him until she collapsed onto his chest, still clutching the gorse. Trembling with delayed reaction, she pushed herself up on her elbow and looked at him, her face scant inches from his.

"You—you—"

"It's all right," he said soothingly. "You're safe now."

"You called me Julia," she said, and fainted dead away.

They lay there together for a long moment, Pickett allowing time for his labored breathing and pounding heart to return to normal while Lady Fieldhurst sought comfort in oblivion. At last, recalling the duty that awaited him at the foot of the cliff, he eased himself from beneath the viscountess. He removed the gorse bush from her unresisting hand and tossed it over the cliff, then scooped her up in his arms. It was an awkward business to rise to his feet thus encumbered, and Lady Fieldhurst began to struggle in his arms. "No—no—!"

"Shhh, hush, my lady," he said, softly as if comforting a child. "It's me—John Pickett. I've got you. You're safe now."

This information apparently calmed her, for she ceased struggling and instead clung like a barnacle. If Pickett found her stranglehold about his neck to any degree uncomfortable, he gave no outward sign.

Slowly, painstakingly, he made his way back down the path with the viscountess in his arms. As he reached the foot of the cliff, he was surprised to discover that Miss Kirkbride was not alone. In fact, she and Duncan Kirkbride were embracing with all the fervor of those who had each believed the other forever lost to them.

"—Heard the screams—" Duncan's voice came in snatches, carried by the sea breeze. "—Thought it was you—too late—never forgive myself—"

"—So angry with me—I wanted to tell you—" Elspeth's voice, too, came in fits and starts until it was finally swallowed up by Duncan's mouth on hers.

Pickett cleared his throat loudly, and the couple broke apart, regarding him rather sheepishly.

"We'll need some stout men to fetch the body back up to the house before the tide comes in. If you will wait here, I'll take her ladyship back to the inn and send some men from there." He glanced at the path hugging the side of the cliff. "That way might be quicker, but I believe her ladyship and I have had our fill of it for one day."

" 'Ladyship'?" Duncan murmured in an aside to Elspeth. "I thought she was Mrs. Pickett."

"I shall explain later." To Pickett, she said, "You are quite right. Shall I accompany you? She needs the peace and quiet of her own bed, and with the assistance of the innkeeper's wife, I shall see that she gets it. You may leave her ladyship in my hands."

In fact, Pickett was quite content with her ladyship in his own hands. He turned aside Miss Kirkbride's suggestion with thanks, and likewise declined the usually taciturn Duncan's offer to relieve him of his burden (which was, in truth, growing quite heavy for so slender a female) and, leaving the pair of them to keep watch over their cousin's body, set off down the beach.

He had not gone far when Lady Fieldhurst began to stir in his arms.

"Mr. Pickett? Am I—Gavin Kirkbride—is he—?"

"He's gone, my lady."

"Is he dead?"

He hesitated only a moment. "Yes."

"You saved my life—for the second time."

"Yours is a life worth saving, my lady."

She pushed away from him slightly, as if suddenly aware of the intimacy of their circumstances. "You may put me down now, Mr. Pickett. I am quite capable of walking, and it isn't much farther to the inn." She gave him a shaky smile. "I shan't faint on you again, I promise."

He lowered her to the ground with considerable reluctance, even as his arms welcomed the respite. He allowed himself the luxury of keeping an arm about her waist, however, and she made no objection; apparently she was not quite as steady on her feet as she claimed.

"It was Gavin who killed him, you know."

"Yes." Pickett nodded. "I know."

"He killed Neil, the stable hand, too. I was coming to tell you when Gavin found me. I knew I could not save myself, so I made sure he went over the edge with me." She raised her pale, worried face to his. "Will I have to stand trial, Mr. Pickett? Will it be like it was after Frederick?"

Pickett felt a sinking feeling in the pit of his stomach. That decision was entirely up to the Kirkbride family, or what was left of it. Even if they chose to prefer charges—and Pickett knew that it was often easier for families to unite in blaming an outsider than to admit to a fatal flaw in one of their own—there was every chance Lady Fieldhurst would be acquitted once it was proven that she had acted in self-defense. Still, he would do anything in his power to spare her the necessity of standing trial.

"I don't think so," he said, but honesty compelled him to add, "But if you do, you may depend on me to testify in your behalf."

She said nothing, but gave him a wan smile and leaned her head against his arm. In this manner they reached the inn, where their appearance created quite a stir. Pickett was dirty and disheveled, but Lady Fieldhurst was far worse. Her bonnet was gone—presumably blown out to sea—and her tangled hair spilled over her shoulders. Her once-elegant black gown was torn and filthy. More alarming than the state of her clothing, however, were the numerous scratches that scored her hands and arms; the gorse might have saved her, but not without exacting a price.

"I must look as if I've been dragged backward through a hedge," she murmured to Pickett, becoming uncomfortably aware of the dismayed looks being cast in their direction.

Privately, Pickett thought she was still the most beautiful woman he had ever seen, but he found it encouraging that she was sufficiently recovered to fret over her appearance. "You're alive, and at the moment that is all that matters."

Seeing the doctor wetting his whistle in the tap room, Pickett called to him. "Mr. Reid, you are just the person I hoped to see."

"Yes, Mr. Pickett?" The doctor set down his teacup. "How may I help you?"

"There is a body at the foot of the cliff adjacent to Ravenscroft Manor. The body is that of Gavin Kirkbride."

"Good God!"

"I am almost certain he is dead, but you will want to examine him. Take a couple of men with you, for the tide is coming in and we'll need to get the body back up to the house." The doctor was already out of his chair, but Pickett detained him. "Before you go, is there anything you can give La—Mrs. Pickett? She tried to take a shortcut off the cliff path."

The doctor bent his keen gaze onto the drooping Lady Fieldhurst, and Pickett silently blessed the man for both his perspicacity and his discretion. "A good dose of laudanum, ma'am," the doctor assured her, reaching into his bag, "and I guarantee you will sleep the clock 'round."

Having seen Lady Fieldhurst dosed with laudanum, Pickett was obliged to surrender her into the hands of the innkeeper's wife (who promised to bathe her and put her to bed, two tasks for which Pickett was eminently unsuited) and attend to unfinished business at Ravenscroft Manor. Upon his arrival there, he found Duncan Kirkbride eager to make explanations.

"I'm afraid I must beg your pardon, Mr. Pickett," he said. "I believe I may have made your task more difficult than it should have been. Elspeth has told me all about poor Uncle Angus's death. I daresay under the circumstances my absence last night must have appeared most suspicious."

"It did at the time, but since then I've realized you could not have known of your uncle's plan to cut you out of his will. You had already left the ballroom before he made his announcement, and no one had seen you from that time until this morning on the beach."

"Nonetheless, I'll feel better for giving an account of myself. After Uncle Angus announced Elspeth's betrothal to Gavin, I took myself off for a bout of drinking, the likes of which I haven't indulged in for fifteen years." He looked at Elspeth, and Pickett realized that Duncan's confession was for her ears as much as his own. "I couldn't bear the thought of losing you a second time, of your living here as his wife, of having to see you every day—"

Elspeth laid her fingers across his mouth. "You need say no more, Duncan."

He took her hand and gently withdrew it from his lips. "Let me finish, love. I finally passed out in the wine cellar, where I slept off the results of my overindulgence. When I awoke at dawn with a pounding head, I took a long walk on the beach to clear my thinking, still having no idea of what happened in the night until I heard the lady's screams and came running. God help me, Elspeth, I thought it was you."

"Oh, Duncan!"

Pickett, seeing that the conversation was about to devolve into an exchange of lovers' vows, interrupted before matters could progress further down paths best explored in private.

"I am afraid that, from an economic aspect at least, you are bound to be the loser in all this, Miss Kirkbride," he told her. "Your father had no opportunity to change his will in your favor, and with one of his two heirs dead, Duncan now stands to inherit the lot."

Elspeth and Duncan exchanged a look, apparently having already established (or re-established) the unique ability of lovers to communicate without speech. Then Elspeth gave Pickett a secretive smile. "I don't believe it will be an insurmountable problem, Mr. Pickett."

He nodded, returning her smile. "I thought as much. I am glad of it. I fear, though, that Duncan's gain will be Drury Lane's loss. May I be the first to wish you happy?"

She held out her hand to him. "You may. And I trust you will allow me to do likewise."

He glanced uncertainly at Miss Kirkbride. He was not quite certain what he was being offered felicitations for—not his brilliance in solving her father's murder, of that much he was certain—but at the moment he had another, more pressing concern to address.

"Miss Kirkbride, Mr. Kirkbride, I fear I must ask what are your thoughts regarding the manner of Gavin's death. Lady Fieldhurst is concerned that she will have to stand trial for her part in it. With your permission, I should like to be able to reassure her on this head."

They did not disappoint him. "I think my family has had enough of scandal and bloodshed, Mr. Pickett," Elspeth said. "Gavin has paid for his crimes with his life, just as the law would have demanded. Let it be said that Father died of an accidental overdose, and that Neil committed suicide, and that Gavin inadvertently fell from the cliff path in his haste to impart the terrible news to Duncan." She sighed. "Someday, if we repeat the tale often enough, we may eventually come to believe it ourselves."

Chapter 19

IN WHICH JOHN PICKETT RECEIVES SEVERAL SURPRISES

Lady Fieldhurst awoke the next morning to grey skies and the pounding of rain on the roof. Clearly, the unseasonably warm weather was past; the Scottish skies had finally recalled that the month was October, not June. She sat up, and every movement of her aching muscles brought back the terrifying events of the previous day. She bent her arms and legs in turn, as if to assure herself that each one worked properly, then pushed up the long sleeves of her linen night rail. Her hands and arms were scored with long scratches from the gorse bush that had broken her fall, and on her left wrist, she could trace one, two, three, four perfectly formed oval bruises marking the place where Mr. Pickett's fingers had bitten into the tender flesh as he'd dragged her to safety.

Her head was still a bit befuddled from the laudanum she'd been given, but on one point her mind was perfectly clear. Yesterday, with her life hanging precariously from a clump of gorse, she'd been aware of one overwhelming regret, one thing in her life left undone, one experience without which she could not bear the thought of dying. And, miraculously, she had *not* died. She had been granted a second chance, and she intended to make certain it did not go to waste. Mr. Colquhoun might not like it—in fact, she was quite sure he would hate it, should he ever learn of it—but Mr. Pickett was a grown man (albeit a young one) and at four-and-twenty was surely old enough to make his own decisions.

She threw back the sheets, then poured water from the pitcher on the stand beside the bed and scrubbed her face until it shone. She then snatched a fresh gown from the clothes-press, wishing she had something—anything!—less funereal than the unrelieved black deemed suitable for a widow of six months' standing. Having attired herself in this despised garment, she turned her attention to dressing her hair. Soon, after pinching her pale cheeks to lend them color, she regarded her image critically in the looking-glass and judged herself presentable.

She hurried down the corridor to the chamber occupied by Mr. Pickett and his magistrate, and drew up short on the threshold. The door was open and the room empty save for a collection of valises and fishing tackle piled beside the door, clearly waiting to be taken downstairs. Outside the window, the stable yard buzzed with activity as the Royal Mail Coach discharged its passengers and offloaded its sacks of mail prior to changing horses and speeding on its way with a new contingent of travellers. Mr. Pickett and his magistrate, it appeared, would be among them.

With a renewed sense of urgency, she spun away from the chaotic scene, clattered down the stairs, and burst into the private parlor. As she had hoped, Mr. Pickett sat alone there, addressing himself to a plate of kippers and buttered eggs.

"My lady!" he rose at her entrance, his breakfast forgotten. "I feared I would not—I had not expected to see you up and about so soon. How do you feel? I hope you are recovered from your ordeal?"

"Except for some soreness and a few scratches which I daresay will soon heal, I am quite well. Are you—are you leaving Scotland so soon? I thought you and Mr. Colquhoun were fixed here for a fortnight."

He nodded. "That was the original plan. But my work here is done, and Mr. Colquhoun is persuaded the fish have too much sense to be out and about in this weather," he added with a hint of a smile.

"I should have been sorry to have missed you. I have—I have wanted to speak to you ever since—ever since you rescued me on the cliff—"

"You need have no fear, my lady," he assured her. "You will not be forced to stand trial. In fact, Miss Kirkbride and Duncan will be far too busy planning their wedding to think of preferring charges."

"That is good news." She smiled fleetingly, but her manner seemed so distracted he could tell it was not the prospect of standing trial that burdened her mind. She clutched her hands tightly together at her waist and took a deep breath. "Mr. Pickett, my friend Lady Dunnington—you may remember her, you met her once in London—Lady Dunnington, it seems, has been telling me for some time now that I should take a lover—"

"Lord Rupert Latham," he said, trying to keep his voice devoid of the distaste he felt whenever Lord Rupert's name was mentioned. "I remember him."

She shook her head impatiently. "No, no, Lord Rupert and I are quite *passé*. In fact, we were finished before we even began. Actually, I had thought—it occurred to me that—well, you and I do seem to have a habit of ending up in each other's arms, so I thought perhaps that you—that you and I—that we should—"

She broke off, blushing crimson. Pickett, listening to this disjointed speech with dawning incredulity, was moved to ask, "Are you saying you want to—to—with *me*?"

"Not here, of course," she assured him hastily. "Not while I have the boys in my charge, but later—after we return to London—shall I—may I send for you, Mr. Pickett?"

Pickett hardly heard the question, so distracted was he by the images conjured up by the viscountess's proposition. At last he might end his self-imposed celibacy, and in the arms of the lady

he had always imagined to be as far beyond his reach as the
stars in the heavens. It was more than he had ever dared hope
for—no, it was all he had ever dreamed of, ever since the night
he had first seen her, pale and frightened, standing over her
husband's body.

And yet, even while he contemplated the delights inherent in
such an arrangement, he knew how it would end. Eventually
she would meet a man of her own class and think of marrying
again. When that time came her summonses would grow less
and less frequent, and the intervals between them longer and
longer, until at last they ceased altogether. Perhaps, he thought
bitterly, she would present him with a handsome parting gift,
like the gentlemen of her class were wont to give their cast-off
doxies; perhaps he would not know the reason for her loss of
interest until he read the wedding announcement in the *Morning Post.* Either way, it was unthinkable. Surely it was better to
avoid an alliance that could only end in heartache, better not to
know what one was missing than to be tormented with
memories of what must be forever lost.

"My lady," Pickett began, choosing his words with care, "I
am more honored than I can say by your, er, interest in me, but
I am afraid I must decline your very flattering offer."

"Oh." Lady Fieldhurst gave a shaky laugh that held nothing
of humor. "Oh dear, how very awkward! Pray forgive me. I
thought you—that is, I was under the impression that you—"

"You have nothing to apologize for, my lady," Pickett assured
her hastily. "It is not the inclination I lack, but the—"

"*There* you are!" The door to the breakfast parlor was flung
open, and none other than George Bertram, seventh Viscount
Fieldhurst, entered the room, his greatcoat dripping with rain
and his person dripping with righteous indignation. "I should
like to know what you are about, Cousin Julia! When I received
word that you had never arrived at Inverbrook, I naturally as-

sumed the worst. I never thought to find you gallivanting all over Scotland with my sons when you were supposed to have been settled at the family estate for the last fortnight!"

"George," she acknowledged him feebly. "This is not at all what you seem to think. The boys merely wished to see the ocean and, well, I meant to write the housekeeper and tell her not to expect us, but then we found Miss Kirkbride on the beach and—"

"And I suppose this fellow's presence here is the merest co-incidence!" The viscount gave Pickett a contemptuous glance.

"As a matter of fact, yes, it is," Pickett put in.

He might have spared his breath, for all the attention the new Lord Fieldhurst paid him.

"Go upstairs and gather your things at once, Cousin Julia," George commanded. "We will leave for England as soon as you and the boys have packed."

"Oh, are we to travel on the mail, then?"

She glanced uncertainly toward Pickett, and then at the mail coach outside the window. Pickett wondered if she were hoping for an answer in the affirmative, or wanting only to avoid him.

"I should say not! Do you think I want to announce your indiscretions to the world? I have hired a private conveyance—and a pretty penny it has cost me, let me tell you!" he added peevishly.

"I beg your pardon, George. I shall pack my things directly."

She left the room without looking back. George Bertram followed in her wake, no doubt to stand over her and harangue her as she accomplished the task he had assigned. It infuriated Pickett to see the way her late husband's family treated her. It sickened him to know that her willingness to comply so meekly with her husband's heir was due to his own apparent rejection of her. It was either the noblest or the stupidest thing he'd ever done—he was not quite sure which—and it was clear he would have no chance to offer her an explanation for his seeming indifference; Cousin George would see to it that she was bustled aboard his expensive private conveyance with no opportunity to see him again, even if she had shown any desire to do so. *It can't end like this,* he thought desperately. *It can't end like this.*

Upstairs, George Bertram soon made the unwelcome discovery that his cousin's errant widow was the least of his problems. In the room shared by his three sons, he found himself confronting three boys he scarcely recognized, boys with skin bronzed by the sun and cheeks ruddy from the stiff ocean breeze.

"Good God!" he exclaimed in dismay. "You look like gypsies!"

"Father! Father!" cried his two youngest sons, both talking at once and each trying to outdo the other in volume. "We found a dead lady on the beach—"

"Only she wasn't really dead, and then—"

"And Harold got to go out on the sea in a boat, only we didn't get to go, which I call the shabbiest thing ever—"

"Will you hire someone to take us out on a boat, Father? Harold says it is the jolliest thing!"

"Except that it made Uncle John sick, only he isn't really our uncle, but a Bow Street Runner, Father, if you can imagine that! He came to investigate the dead lady—"

"And since we didn't get to go out on the water with him and Harold, he bought us these little boats, and only look at all the things we found on the beach!"

Each taking an arm, the two boys all but dragged their father into the middle of the room, where they eagerly displayed for him the tiny cork boats, along with an assortment of seashells, pebbles, and gulls' feathers collected during their seaside ramblings.

"Yes, yes, I see," the new Lord Fieldhurst said, dismissing these valuable items with a shooing motion. "Nasty things!

217

Dispose of them at once!"

"I won't!" the usually quiescent Robert declared mulishly. "I intend to take them home and make a study of them. May I have a microscope, Father, so I might examine them more closely?"

"A microscope? No, you may certainly not! What possible use would you have for—"

"Or should I ask Mother for one? I'll bet she would buy me a microscope, if I told her you wouldn't let me have one—"

"What's that?" asked George in genuine alarm. "No need to be plaguing your mother over such a thing. Very well, I shall purchase a microscope for you once I return to London, and send it to you. Only pack your things so we may leave!"

At the mention of their mother, the Bertram boys were stunned to see their father's ill temper give way to shame-faced guilt. With dawning glee, they realized they might exploit this useful tool to gain almost anything their hearts desired.

"Father, I have been thinking about my return to Oxford," put in Harold, who up to this point had allowed his younger brothers to do all the talking. "The last term has been most uncomfortable, for reasons I am sure I need not explain to you. I believe I might do well in His Majesty's Navy. I have been meaning to ask if you will use your influence to help me obtain a berth as a midshipman."

"The navy?" echoed George in dismay. "Of all the queer starts—"

"It's *not* a queer start, Father! I find I like the ocean, and Mr. Boyd—he's the fisherman who took Mr. Pickett and me out in his boat—Mr. Boyd says he thinks I have a knack for it, for even when Mr. Pickett was hanging his head over the side, I never felt sick at all! So will you do it for me, Father?"

"No, Harold, you cannot have thought! What would your mother say?"

"Very well, then, I shall run away from school and enlist as a common seaman, and once everyone hears of it, there will be such a scandal that Cousin Julia's will be as nothing to it!"

"Oh, all right, I'll think about it," said George reluctantly, as Harold and Robert exchanged triumphant grins behind their father's back. "But I daresay there will be the devil to pay when your mother hears of it."

"What about me, Father?" young Edward piped up.

"You are rather young for the navy, Edward, unless you intend to go for a cabin boy—"

"No, Father! I want to be a Bow Street Runner!"

"*What?* Good God, no! No gentleman's son would ever—of course, I need not ask who put such an ill-conceived notion into your head, for I can see that Pickett fellow's hand at work—yes, Robert, I see your hermit crab, but I haven't the slightest desire to hold it! Now, will you all cease plaguing me and pack your things so we may *go*!"

Left alone in his misery, Pickett stood at the window of the breakfast parlor, staring unseeing at the confusion in the stable yard. As ostlers rushed forward with fresh horses for the mail coach, an elegant black equipage drew as near to the door as the commotion in the yard would allow. No coat of arms adorned its door panel, but Pickett had no difficulty in identifying George Bertram's expensive private conveyance.

A moment later, as if to confirm his assumption, the door to the inn was flung open and a man, heavily bundled against the inclement weather, hurried across the mud-spattered yard. He held an umbrella over a lady swathed in a black pelisse and bonnet, but in spite of this seemingly solicitous gesture, his grip on her arm resembled less a gentleman escorting a lady than a prison warden hauling an escaped convict back to the round-house. Behind the truant female were three boys whose descending heights made them resemble nothing so much as a set of stair steps. The five entered the conveyance with minimal ceremony, the female being thrust inside first, to be followed higgledy-piggledy by the three boys, with the gentleman bringing up the rear. For one brief moment, Pickett's eyes seemed to meet those of the lady, framed as she was in the carriage window, but a moment later the man's arm reached up and drew the blind closed, leaving Pickett to wonder if he had imagined the exchange.

He had not long to dwell on the matter in any case, for he was soon interrupted by his magistrate, who entered the breakfast parlor lugging a bulging valise in one hand and his fishing tackle in the other.

"Well, Mr. Pickett, if you've finished your meal, we'd best see our bags stowed and stake out a couple of seats on the mail coach. I don't know about you, but I've no intention of being obliged to sit on the roof in this weather." He gave a satisfied nod. "Still, one can't complain. At least the rain held off until the day of our departure. An excellent trip, all told."

"Yes, sir," Pickett said without conviction.

"What's this?" Mr. Colquhoun regarded his youngest Runner with an all too piercing gaze. "You're looking mighty long-faced for a fellow who's nabbed both a murderer and a wife, all within a matter of days."

"Hardly 'nabbed,' sir. Gavin Kirkbride will never stand trial for his crimes. As far as the Kirkbrides are concerned, his death was an accident, as was his uncle's, and that poor stable hand committed suicide over the fair Elspeth."

"Nevertheless, he paid with his life for his crimes, although they will never be publicly acknowledged."

"Miss Kirkbride said something to that effect," Pickett recalled.

"Aye, you'll find that justice is sometimes a messy thing, my boy. And, on a happier note, there's still the matter of the wife."

Pickett pushed his unfinished plate away, having long since lost his appetite. "I believe you know that any 'marriage' between Lady Fieldhurst and myself was no more than a ruse." He heaved a sigh. "I very much doubt that I will ever see the lady again, unless someone in her circle is so obliging as to get himself murdered."

Mr. Colquhoun scowled, his bushy eyebrows drawing together over his nose. "I believe you need to acquaint yourself with Scottish civil law! Tell me, John, are you familiar with the concept of marriage by declaration?"

"No, sir, I can't say that I am."

"I thought not. Simply stated, all it takes to make a valid marriage in Scotland is for the couple to declare before witnesses that they are man and wife."

"What?" Pickett rose from the table so abruptly that his chair fell over backwards.

"Aye, why do you think Gretna marriages are so popular? You'll want to consult a solicitor to be certain, but I believe there is a very good chance that you and her ladyship are in fact married." The magistrate bent a fierce glower on his young protégé. "I warned you to be circumspect in your dealings there, but did you listen to me? Of course not!"

"But—but surely there is the—the matter of consummation!" Pickett sputtered.

"There is actually quite a bit more to it than that, but even if there were not, recall that the pair of you have been at great pains to convince the innkeeper that you were sharing the room assigned to her ladyship. And at the Kirkbride ball you were observed to be behaving very, shall we say, affectionately toward one another. I wish you joy in finding anyone present at the ball or staying here at the inn who could be persuaded that the marriage has *not* been consummated. No, my boy, I'll admit I am more conversant with criminal law than civil, but I believe you may find yourself well and truly hitched." He took Pickett's unresisting hand and began pumping it vigorously. "Allow me to be the first to congratulate you on your recent nuptials."

Pickett hardly heard his congratulations, for his mind was reeling. There had to be a mistake. This was impossible. Viscountesses did not marry Bow Street Runners, not even by accident.

And yet . . . she had invited him to be her lover, so she must feel *something* for him. It occurred to him that if he had taken her up on the offer, he could have bound her to himself for the rest of her life. But it would not have done; she would have hated him for it, and who could blame her? No, when he reached London he would have to seek her out and tell her what had happened. He had no doubt the Fieldhursts would be willing to pay through the nose to ensure that any marriage between them, if such a marriage indeed existed, was set aside. And that it would have to be set aside somehow, he had no doubt. Viscountesses did not marry Bow Street Runners.

Except, he thought with rising elation, except that one *had*, however unintentionally. Was it too much to hope that lightning might strike twice, that a marriage begun in such a disastrous manner might somehow, impossibly, survive? Well, yes, it probably was. It would not do to fill his head with false hopes.

Still, it was with a much lighter heart that Pickett hefted his old valise and followed the magistrate outside to the coach that would take him back to London—to London, and his wife.

ABOUT THE AUTHOR

Sheri Cobb South is the award-winning author of sixteen novels, including the popular John Pickett series of Regency mysteries, the critically acclaimed Regency romance *The Weaver Takes a Wife,* and the hard-to-find Sweet Dreams title *Wrong-Way Romance.* A native and longtime resident of Alabama, she recently moved to Loveland, Colorado, with her husband, and now has a stunning view of Longs Peak from her office window. When she is not writing, she enjoys reading, doing needlework, and singing in her church choir. Sheri loves to hear from readers, and invites them to email her at Cobbsouth@aol.com, "Like" her on Facebook, and/or visit her website at www.sheri cobbsouth.com.